FIVE DOG
VOODOO

Previously published Worldwide Mystery title by
LIA FARRELL

TWO DOGS LIE SLEEPING
THREE DOG DAY

FIVE DOG VOODOO

LIA FARRELL

WORLDWIDE.

TORONTO • NEW YORK • LONDON
AMSTERDAM • PARIS • SYDNEY • HAMBURG
STOCKHOLM • ATHENS • TOKYO • MILAN
MADRID • WARSAW • BUDAPEST • AUCKLAND

Recycling programs
for this product may
not exist in your area.

Five Dog Voodoo

A Worldwide Mystery/May 2019

First published by Camel Press, an imprint of Epicenter Press, Inc.

ISBN-13: 978-1-335-45541-3

Copyright © 2016 by Lia Farrell

This book is dedicated to the wise and learned
Dr. Jualynne Dodson, Professor and Director of the
African Atlantic Research Team in the Department of
Sociology at Michigan State University. She helped us to
understand the religion and culture of Voodoo by giving
generously of her time and knowledge. If we correctly
depicted Voodoo ceremonies and got the details right,
it's to her credit. Any mistakes are entirely our own.

Lyn also wishes to remember Milly Roo, Fiona's
singleton puppy with one blue eye. She misses her little
corgi daily. One of Milly's particular joys was riding
the tractor on Lyn's lap. She steered the vehicle with
her teeth! The tooth marks on the steering wheel will
never be removed. In her entire short life, she brought
Lyn happiness every day.

ACKNOWLEDGMENTS

In addition to dedicating the book to Dr. Jualynne Dodson, we wish to thank her for all her *pro bono* hours of reading and correcting the manuscript. We also wish to acknowledge the following publications we consulted prior to writing *Five Dog Voodoo. The Serpent and the Rainbow* by Wade David, *Secrets of Voodoo* by Milo Rigaud and *The Way of Trance* by Dennis Wier.

Many thanks to the members of the MSU Creative Writing Group (MSUCC) who gave us so much helpful feedback. As always, we are grateful to our publication team: Dawn Dowdle, our literary agent (Blue Ridge Literary Agency), Catherine Treadgold, Publisher and Editor-in-Chief, and Jennifer McCord, Associate Publisher and Executive Editor as well as Sabrina Sun, graphic artist for Camel Press. Lastly, we continue to be grateful for the help of Will Schikorra, our webmaster.

ZOÉ CANJA CHECKED her reflection in the break-room mirror before starting her Thursday night shift at Randall's Tavern. Her smooth, black hair, falling without a ripple past her shoulders, showed her Creole ancestry. She braided it quickly and fastened it with the hair tie she wore on her wrist. The three tiny moles that dotted the caramel skin of her right cheekbone framed her eye like a miniature constellation. She centered her gold cross pendant in the hollow of her throat. *Enough staring at yourself. You know what you look like.* Zoé tugged on the bottom of her white shirt to straighten it before putting on her clean, black apron. It would be a mess by the end of the night, but at least she could start out looking presentable.

She walked out into the bar, which was as familiar to her as her own living room—she had worked here since the day after she turned eighteen. Other than some new flooring in the women's bathroom, nothing had changed in the last eight years. Zoé had worked her way up from kitchen helper to waitress and then to bartender. *If that fat, creepy Randall would only admit it, I run this place.* She shook her head to dislodge her uncharitable thoughts about the owner, then began slicing lemons, wiping down glassware, and preparing for the evening rush.

By seven thirty Randall's was in full swing. Classic Rock mixed with Halloween music blared from the speakers in the ceiling, and the crowd of locals—mostly men—lined the bar and filled the tables and booths. Jeanie and Caroline, the two cocktail waitresses, slid smoothly through the dim room with their trays, continually replenishing snacks and drinks for the thirsty patrons. Behind the bar, Zoé was in constant motion, satisfied with the rising height of bills and coins in her tip jar. It was going to be a good night.

A raised hand holding a ten-dollar bill caught her eye and she hustled to the other end of the bar.

"Jack and Coke please, sweetheart."

"Coming right up." She gave the man in the dirty Atlanta Braves hat a smile and he smiled back. He had nice teeth despite the dirty hat, and Zoé pegged him as a rich redneck.

"Keep 'em comin'," he said, pressing the bill into her hand. "There's plenty more where that came from." His hazel eyes flickered down to her chest and back to her face. "In fact, why don't you start me a tab? I have some business partners joining me in a few minutes."

She kept the man and his two companions well supplied with their drinks of choice for the rest of the evening. Their voices were quieter than the other patrons, and more than once, Zoé caught all three of them giving her sidelong looks. She was cleaning up a spilled glass of red wine with her back to the group when she heard one of the men mention the Voodoo Village before his voice dropped back to a murmur. Inching closer, she heard the man in the Braves hat reply. For a moment she stood still, the shock of his words rooting her to the floor.

"Where's that pitcher of Bud Lite?" Jeanie's voice was loud, and Zoé jumped, dropping the wine glass, which shattered at her feet.

"Zoé, are you okay?" Jeanie tilted her head with a little laugh. "I mean, honey, I break something almost every shift, but I've never seen you do that even once."

"I'm fine. Listen, can you clean up the broken glass and take over the bar for a little while? I need to make a phone call."

Without waiting for a reply, Zoé shucked her apron. Handing it to Jeanie, she hurried to the storeroom. It would be quieter there. She flipped the light on and leaned against the door. Her hands were shaking as she pulled out her cellphone and tapped the numbers in.

ONE

Mae December

MAE PUT DOWN her paintbrush and stepped back. She was working on a new series of paintings inspired by a joint project her parents had embarked on last month. Mae's mother Suzanne wrote a column for the local paper in Rosedale, Tennessee. When Suzanne heard about the Voodoo Village in the far reaches of Rose County, she had convinced her editor that it was a perfect subject for the Halloween edition. Don December, Mae's father, a professional photographer, was captivated by his wife's descriptions of the place. He had gone with her to the village and taken multiple photos to accompany Suzanne's column, which would run in Sunday's paper. Mae had appropriated and enlarged several of his best shots, which were pinned to the walls of her studio.

She was halfway through her second painting in the series—a young woman with long dark hair opening the door of a marigold-colored cottage. Mae squinted at the large oil painting. *This one's coming along well, but I probably need to stop for today and make sure everything is set for the debate.* At this point in her thirty-one years, Mae wore many hats. She ran a successful boarding kennel—Mae's Place—out of the barn that sat behind her historic farmhouse, and did some dog training as well as breeding. Her paintings, signed only with her middle name of Malone, were in high demand at the art gallery in Rosedale. Plus, she was an unofficial stepmom to adorable Matty, Ben's five-year-old son. Engaged to Rose County Sheriff Ben Bradley, Mae had agreed to act as his campaign manager. The election would be held on November 4th, the Tuesday after Halloween. Ben would debate his opponent, Ramsey Tremaine, at the Town Hall in Rosedale this coming Tuesday, October 28th.

The sharp smell of turpentine permeated the room as she cleaned her brushes. Covering her palette with plastic wrap, Mae put it aside and took off Ben's old dress shirt, which she wore as a painting smock, and hung it on the back of her easel. Her studio had a Dutch door. The top half was always open to let in more light, but Mae kept the bottom half closed when she was painting, to keep her four dogs from getting underfoot. Before opening it, she peeked over the door and smiled at the sight of Cupcake and Tatie curled up together.

"Wake up, you two." Cupcake the basset hound looked up at her, tail thumping on the wooden floor. At six months, she had almost grown into her ears. A sweet and mellow pup, she belonged to Ben's son, who spent three or four days out of every week with Mae and her fiancé. The original plan was that Cupcake would go back and forth with Matthew between their house and his mother's, but Katie's boyfriend was allergic to dogs and Cupcake now lived with them full-time.

Mae pulled the door slowly toward her, dislodging Tatie, her young corgi. She and Cupcake followed Mae down the hall. She called Titan and Tallulah from their beds in the laundry room and the two older dogs joined the procession. Opening the back door to let them all outside, Mae took an appreciative sniff of the fragrant autumn air. Allowing the screen door to bang behind her, she followed the dogs into her sunny backyard. Ben and Matthew had spent last Sunday raking leaves and burning them in the fire pit, but the ancient maple tree behind the house had already blanketed the ground once more. Her elderly black pug, Tallulah, scuffled back toward the door, red leaves up to her shoulders. Yawning, she leaned against Mae's ankle.

Mae stretched her arms overhead, pulling on one elbow and then the other to ease the tightness in her shoulders from hours of painting. She bent down to rub the wrinkled skin of Tallulah's forehead, and the little pug gave a contented groan. Mae's older male corgi ambled over to the steps and looked back at her inquiringly.

"You're right, Titan," Mae sighed. "It's time to go back in. Mama's got work to do."

After a quick lunch of tuna salad and iced tea, Mae called TV reporter Carrie Allen to confirm the debate coverage.

"Yes, I'll be there with my crew next Tuesday."

"And you'll get there early enough to set up and interview Ben beforehand, right?" Mae asked.

"Of course," Carrie snapped. "I *do* know how to cover a debate. And I'll interview Mr. Tremaine afterward."

It might be better for Ben to have the last word. "On second thought, could you interview Ramsey first?"

"Fine." Carrie gave a curt sigh. "I'm pretty busy right now, so if there's nothing else—"

"That's it. Thanks, Carrie. See you Tuesday night."

Mae called the caterer and ordered food for the election night gathering at the house. "I hope it's going to be a victory party," she said. "But either way, we need to plan on feeding forty hungry people."

After she ended the call, Mae pulled up her website and added some information to the 'purchase a puppy' link. She had become a breeder by accident years ago before when she and Noah West, her first fiancé, adopted Titan and Tallulah from New Orleans in the aftermath of Hurricane Katrina. When she realized Tallulah was pregnant, she had planned on giving the puppies away, but her best friend Tammy convinced her there was a market for "designer dogs." Titan and Tallulah had been proud parents of several litters of porgies—a pug/corgi cross—before Mae retired them.

She had initially planned to breed Tatie, her young corgi, to a friend's apricot male pug to get strawberry-blond porgies, but recently changed her mind. Interest in non-shedding breeds was at an all-time high, so 'December's Sweet Potato,' known as Tatie, would be bred to a non-shedding Maltese right after Christmas. If all went well, she should have a litter of cortese puppies ready to go to their new homes in mid-April. Mae added the information to her website with pictures of Tatie as well as Sammy, the male Maltese, then shut her computer down. It was almost two thirty.

I've got time to take care of some kennel chores, go for a run and shower before Ben gets home.

TWO

Evangeline Bon Temps

THE LEAVES FROM the locust trees lay in drifts along the sidewalks, thin and golden as ancient coins. Evangeline picked up a handful and let them trickle through her fingers, catching the light as they fell to the ground. She reached for the Sunday paper that the feckless paperboy had pitched on the ground by the mailbox. Walking up the driveway, she entered the house through the kitchen side door. The screen door banged shut behind her, bringing with it the warmth of a late autumn day in Rosedale.

She put the newspaper on her kitchen counter and leafed through to the Country Life section. Glancing at the front page photo she felt a tug at her heart. It was an image of a small village with brightly colored houses so close together they almost touched. Her grandmother was Haitian and had lived in an area of small crayon-colored houses much like the ones in the picture. Evangeline had visited her once as a child and still remembered the warmth and generosity of the people there. Sitting down at the kitchen counter, she quickly read the accompanying article, then pulled out her cellphone and called her friend Dory Clarkson.

Evangeline and Dory had met during the sheriff's office investigation into the Ferris murder case almost a year and a half earlier. It started when Sheriff Bradley

met with Evangeline, Tom Ferris' attorney, to obtain information about his Last Will and Testament, a document she had prepared just days before Tom's murder.
Ben wanted to know what was in the will for his investigation. Evangeline had refused to share the particulars,
insisting on having the document go through Probate
before she could release it. Sheriff Bradley had asked
Dory to take Evangeline to dinner, to elicit the information he needed. Although Evangeline only shared what
she legally could, she and Dory had begun a friendship
that night. Later on, when Dory failed the physical challenge to become a deputy, Evangeline advised her to become a sheriff's investigator instead. As she told Dory
then, an investigator wouldn't have to wear a uniform or
clunky shoes. A fashionable dresser, Dory immediately
saw the advantage.

The phone rang multiple times before the call was
picked up.

"It's about time you called me, girlfriend. What've you
been up to? Besides trying to keep that good-lookin' man
of yours in line, that is." Dory's laugh was infectious.

"My N'awlins roots are calling me." Evangeline had
been raised in New Orleans, where her mother still lived.
"Are you free this afternoon? I'm wanting to drive out to
the Voodoo Village."

"Never heard of it, but I don't have any plans. Oh, hang
on." Evangeline heard a man's voice in the background,
and her friend saying goodbye, presumably to her boyfriend, Al. "So what's the Voodoo Village?"

"Check out the Sunday paper—Suzanne December's
article." Evangeline ran her finger along the fold below
the photograph, smoothing it out. "Looks like her husband, Don, took the pictures. It's a tiny little place in the

far corner of the county. If you want to come over to my house, I'll drive us out there."

"I can be there by one. Sound good?"

"Perfect. I'll make us a bite to eat before we depart on this little field trip."

They said goodbye and Evangeline went upstairs to change her clothes. After taking off her sweatshirt and yoga pants, she got on the scale in her underwear. Regarding the number on the scale with dismay, she stepped off and gave it a kick. There was a knock on the bathroom door. "Can I come in?" It was her husband Jason. It had taken some serious persuading, but Evangeline had finally trained him not to barge in on her.

She opened the door and her tall, dark, and hunky husband came in. He put his hands up in the air.

"Just got back from the gym. I'm not going to get near you with my sweaty self. But give me a second to rinse off and you're welcome to join me in the shower." He gave her a wicked grin.

"Oh, Lord, do you ever quit?" Evangeline gestured at her hips. "Look at me, Jason. There's something wrong with my metabolism, I swear. I've gained five pounds in the last month and I've been really careful about what I eat."

Jason's eyes widened. "Five whole pounds, huh? You've always been the skinniest black woman I know. Gain about five more, right here," he swatted her rear end, "and you'll be perfect."

Evangeline shook her head. Jason was peeling off his clothes. She gave his nicely muscled torso an appreciative glance.

"Sure you don't need a shower?" he asked.

"Already took one this morning. Did you see the Voodoo Village article in the paper?"

"I saw the picture when I walked through the kitchen." He stepped into the shower and turned on the water.

"Dory and I are driving out there this afternoon," Evangeline raised her voice over the splashing water. "I figured you'd want to watch the football game anyway."

While her husband showered, Evangeline put on her jeans—she struggled a little to zip them up—and a long sleeved V-neck turquoise shirt. Jason was humming "Let's Get It On" by Marvin Gaye. He winked at her as she walked out of the room.

They say only women can multitask, but seeing as how men are always thinking about sex, maybe they can also think about two things at once. She grinned.

DORY TAPPED ON her side door at one o'clock.

"Come on in," Evangeline called out. "Do you think I look fat in these jeans?" she asked her friend as soon as she entered the kitchen.

"Excuse me, what did you just say?" Dory turned around, revealing her own generous bottom. "Until you have more than *this* in your jeans, I don't want to hear about it."

"Amen," Jason said with fervor from the adjoining den, and the two friends dissolved into laughter.

Evangeline took a plate of food and a beer into the den for her husband. She and Dory sat at the kitchen island to eat their turkey and avocado sandwiches and drink their iced tea. A county map was unfolded on the granite surface.

"Here's the location we're headed to this afternoon." Evangeline pointed to the bottom right-hand corner of the map. "I didn't know this place even existed until I saw Suzanne's article. Don December's photos remind me of the village in Haiti where my grandmother lived."

DORY AGREED TO navigate while Evangeline drove. They got in the car and she drove through the historic downtown of Rosedale, southeast toward Chattanooga. About an hour out of town, Dory told her to take the next exit and then turn at the first left, a little surface road heading east. It quickly changed from pavement to gravel and then to the washboard effect that rain creates on poorly maintained gravel roads.

"Would you tell me a little bit about Voodoo?" Dory asked. "All I know is the usual stuff about charms and curses and sticking pins into dolls."

"Unfortunately, that's what most people think of when they hear the word 'Voodoo.' Most of that was made up in Hollywood. In fact, it's more appropriately called Vodou, spelled V-O-D-O-U. Vodouists believe in a distant and unknowable supreme being called Bondye. Bondye does not intercede in the affairs of mankind. For help in navigating daily life, Voodoo people call upon spirits called the Loa. The Voodoo religion of today is closely related to the West African religion as practiced by the Fon and Ewe people."

"Voodoo people do use charms, though, right? To ward off evil and whatnot. Something similar to gris-gris, those little bags some black women wear on chains around their necks?"

"You're right. My mama's has little poems in hers, plus something she would never discuss with me that she apparently used for years as a method of birth control. I *am* an only child, you know." Evangeline winked.

Dory looked down at the map. "You need to turn right here."

Evangeline braked abruptly to turn down the tiny lane, really only two sandy ruts with tall yellow grasses on both sides. Chinkapin Oak and Pecan trees bordered the trail that turned and twisted, finally rising up a hill. When they reached the crest of the hill, the Voodoo Village lay below them. There were only about two dozen houses, all in a row, so close together an adult could hardly pass between them. The colors on the houses were paint-box rich—magenta, royal blue, purple, golden yellow, and emerald green. On the other side of the street there were more buildings, but these appeared to be stores and what looked like a primary school. None of the houses or stores had front yards; there was nothing but beaten earth, clean and swept.

They could see a woman sweeping her front yard as they drove over the hill and down into the village. The sweeper was wearing a brightly colored dress in a geometric kente pattern with a wrap around her hair. She stopped sweeping and stood holding her broom against her chest, looking toward them with an expressionless face.

Evangeline parked the car and she and Dory got out.

"Good afternoon, my sister," Evangeline said to the woman. "I see you are a proper Fon. *A do gangi a*?"

"Thank you for asking. Yes, I am well and you, my sister?" the woman asked.

"I am also well. I am Evangeline Bon Temps. This is my friend, Dory Clarkson. My mother is a Voodoo singer in New Orleans."

"I am Marie. Why have you come here?" she said with a slight frown.

"Only to see the beauty of your village for ourselves," Evangeline said.

"Come in. Come in." Marie led the way to her house. "Will you take tea with me?"

They nearly had to duck to get through the low front doorway, but once inside, they found the home comfortable. There were three couches in the tiny living room, draped with fabric made of interwoven cloth strips similar to the patterned dress Marie wore.

In one corner was a devotional sacred space. The top of a bureau featured a framed photograph of a young woman draped with beads and surrounded by lighted candles. Marie led them past the couch where a very old man was seated. He nodded at them.

"I greet you, my elder," Evangeline said and ducked her head. He gave her a toothless grin.

ONCE IN THE kitchen, they were invited to sit at a small table by an open window. A window box outside was filled with bright four o'clock flowers. Different colored blossoms were opening on the same plant. The fragrance was just beginning to be released; it was strong and sweet as it drifted through the open window.

Marie brought them hot tea in old cracked mugs. She served them with the air of a queen bestowing her favors on lesser beings.

"I use my own catalpa honey in this tea," she said. "Tell me, my sisters, do you come from Nashville or Memphis?"

"No, from Rosedale," Dory said. "It's a little town outside of Nashville. I'm an investigator for the sheriff's office there."

Evangeline gave her an irritated glance. She was get-

ting a little tired of Dory bragging about being an investigator, plus this was not the place to bring up the law.
Councils of Voodoo elders normally dealt with breaches
of community mores.

"And I am a *médiatrice*," Evangeline said. In point
of fact, she was an attorney, but chose to use a term she
hoped would be more acceptable to her hostess. Plus, she
wanted to change the subject. Dory narrowed her eyes
at Evangeline.

"We saw the article about your beautiful village that
our friend Suzanne December wrote for the local Rosedale paper," Evangeline said. "It's because of my respect
for Voodoo that we came here today. I miss my roots."
She smiled a bit sadly, feeling nostalgic.

"It is as I thought," Marie said, nodding. "You came
here to do good today. Perhaps you can help us. My sister Mira Canja is very worried about her granddaughter Zoé."

"Granddaughters are often worrying, I understand."
Dory spoke calmly. "Although I have no children myself, I have heard this from my friends. Is Zoé a child?"

"No, a young woman. Very beautiful."

"Perhaps it's an unsatisfactory boyfriend?"

"Oh, no. Such a thing would not worry my sister. She
has many ways to send such men packing. It is that Zoé
is missing. We have not seen her since Thursday evening.
Mira raised her after Zoé's mother Laure, abandoned the
true religion and left the community. Zoé would never be
gone so long without letting Mira know where she was."

"I'll inform the sheriff. A missing person is a job for
the sheriff's office," Dory said, sounding just a touch
officious.

Evangeline touched her finger to her lips, shushing her

friend. She gave Marie a long look. The woman seemed frightened. The shadows on her face had deepened when she said Zoé was missing.

"What do you fear has happened to Zoé?" Evangeline asked gently. It was quiet in the room. They could hear only the low murmur of a talk show on the television. Hanging in the window was a crystal amulet that caught the light and moved in the breeze.

"I fear...the worst," Marie said and she sagged back against the kitchen chair like a rag doll.

The women finished their tea. Marie roused herself sufficiently to say she had some beehives out back and that her catalpa honey was used in the cakes for their religious ceremonies. Both women complimented her honey-flavored tea. Evangeline was reluctant to pry further into the matter of the missing granddaughter, thinking it was about time to leave, but despite Marie's non-verbal hints, apparently Miss Dory Clarkson was not ready to go.

"Do you think your sister Mira would talk to me about Zoé?" Dory asked.

"*Peut-être*," Marie said.

Evangeline whispered to Dory that the word meant 'perhaps.'

"Actually, I think we need to get going soon, Dory." Evangeline looked pointedly at her friend.

At that moment, they heard the back door opening. Marie rose to greet a woman dressed in loose cotton pants and a long white shirt. Her shiny dark hair, braided in many tiny plaits, was wrapped around her head. She was dark-complexioned and looked much more African than her sister, whose skin was the color of tea with milk.

"This is my sister Mira," Marie said. She rose and put the kettle back on the stove.

"Peace, my sister," Evangeline said and Mira nodded. "I am Evangeline Bon Temps. I'm from New Orleans originally, but I live in Rosedale now. This is my friend, Dory Clarkson. We hear from your sister that your granddaughter, Zoé, has been absent from the community these last few days."

Mira seemed distracted, looking around the room everywhere but at the two women seated at the old kitchen table, although she kept taking quick peeks at their faces. Finally, she nodded.

Dory took out her steno notebook and pen, but Evangeline shook her head and Dory slid them back into her purse.

"When did you see Zoé last?" Dory asked.

"It was Wednesday afternoon. I didn't see her on Thursday, but I did talk to her on the phone. She tends bar at Randall's Tavern in Richfield and I know she was at work Thursday night. I've been worried about her working so late. She often closes up around three in the morning. I'm glad she has a job, but many bad men look at her. She is a lovely girl."

"Does she have a boyfriend?" Dory asked.

"Not now. She was with a boy—a good Creole boy named Georges Allard—but he could not find work here. He drifted away from the village. His Mama died last year and he has not been here since her funeral. Ah, that was a good day, *la Grande celebration*," Mira said, and despite her distress a small smile crossed her lips. "She dated someone else after that, a man she works with. I don't think it was serious because she never introduced him to me."

"I didn't see her this morning," Zoé's great Aunt Marie

said. "Usually she stops by on Sundays. I make beignets for her and chicory coffee before she leaves for church,"

"She attends church?" Evangeline asked.

"Yes, the Catholic Church, St. Francis in Richfield."

"When is the next Voodoo ceremony?" Evangeline asked. There was a pause as the two sisters looked at each other. Then Mira spoke.

"It will take place this week on Friday night. Are you a practitioner?" she asked, looking at Evangeline doubtfully.

"I believe in *le bon dieu* and *les bons anges*. Voodoo was the religion of my childhood and my mother, a famous singer, but I am Catholic now."

"Would Zoé normally attend this ceremony?" Dory asked.

"Of course. She always petitions the spirits for help in finding her mother. It is a quest she has undertaken since her mother, Laure, left us when Zoé was six. It has been twenty years now." Mira looked despondent.

"Perhaps she left the village of her own accord to try to find her mother," Dory said, "or to join the boyfriend and just didn't tell you."

"She would never do that to me," Mira said. Her voice was fierce with passion. "Never. I have raised her since she was *une petite fille*. She is a girl who is grateful, who honors the love I have for her."

"This is definitely a matter for the sheriff of the county," Dory said. "The sooner we look into this officially, the sooner we'll find out what's become of her."

"I will ask the Houngan, our priest, if I can do this," Mira said. Then, turning to her sister, she whispered, "But I have already done the string ceremony, tying the soul to the body."

"Did you feel the connection?" Marie asked her sister quietly.

Mira only shook her head, blinking away the tears in her eyes.

"We should tell them about the dogs," Marie said. Turning to Dory and Evangeline, she said, "Zoé owns a female Weimaraner who has four puppies. She was raising the pups to sell. She wanted the money to pay for a private detective to locate her mother."

"I've been going over to Zoé's house several times a day," Mira added. "I feed and water the mother dog and take her outside. She is very upset, though, pacing and digging at the back door. She knows something, I'm sure of it. She howls and howls when I leave."

"Best you go home now." Marie stared intently at Dory. She started to pick up the teacups.

DRIVING BACK HOME, Evangeline was deep in thought when Dory said, "I don't know why Mira seemed reluctant to inform the sheriff. A missing person is a matter for the law. Plus, she seems to need permission from this Houngan person to report her granddaughter's disappearance. Is this Houngan Zoé's father?"

"No, the Houngan is the priest or priestess for the village. In Voodoo, priests can be either male or female. They must approve all that happens in terms of contact with the outside world."

"Evangeline, you kind of cut me off every time I tried to get more information about Zoé. I wanted to ask for her address, her cellphone number, her social security number, whether she had credit cards—all the details I'd need to trace her. Plus, I really wanted a photograph."

"You don't understand the culture, Dory. If you'd

asked those questions, they would have completely shut us out. If I hadn't spoken in the Fon language to Marie when we first got there, we wouldn't have been allowed in the house. I was trying to gain their trust."

"I saw that, but I have to say I find the religion very confusing," Dory said. She paused and glanced out the car window at the passing scenery. "What's this *bon ange* thing you said you believe in?"

"In Voodoo, the human soul is seen as having two parts. The *ti-bon-ange*, or little guardian angel, is your individuality, your personality. It leaves the body when you are asleep so you can dream. It also leaves the body during rituals of possession so a Loa—Voodoo spirit—can take over your mind and provide guidance."

"I noticed neither of the women mentioned these Loa spirits," Dory pointed out.

"The Loa aren't usually spoken of to outsiders. Voodoo practitioners have been persecuted for centuries. Believers have learned to be secretive about their rituals and especially the Loa." Evangeline pulled onto the freeway, still deep in thought.

"How do you know when the Loa spirits have arrived at the ceremonies? Aren't they invisible?" Dory's face was a picture of doubt.

"That's the hard part for anyone unfamiliar with Voodoo. The Loa "mount" the celebrant. It creates a kind of spirit possession and the person who is "ridden" by the Loa enters a trance state. They will writhe or fall to the ground. It's similar to an epileptic seizure."

"Good Lord. Has that ever happened to you?"

"No, but it happened many times to my mother. I first witnessed the ceremony when I was a little girl visiting my grandmother in Haiti. It's terrifying because once in the trance, the person recognizes no one. To see that happening to my own mother was very troubling. In fact, it's one of the reasons I ultimately chose to join the Catholic Church."

"This Loa possession thing sounds crazy to me. Sorry, Evangeline, I don't mean to be insensitive." After a pause, Dory added, "But I need to tell the sheriff about Zoé Canja being missing."

"If you must, but I can practically guarantee you that if Sheriff Bradley or Detective Nichols or any of the other sheriff's staff go to the Voodoo Village, they won't learn anything. Even with my background, I had the feeling they weren't telling me all they knew."

"So, how do you find a missing woman if nobody from the community where the girl lives will talk to you? In the past, I've been successful finding things out because people will usually open up to me."

"I'm afraid this time the only way we will find Zoé Canja is if she returns or…if they find her body."

"You think she's dead then?"

"Sadly, I do, because of the tying the soul to the body ritual Mira performed. When her sister asked her if she felt the connection, she said she didn't. I've seen that ritual performed many times and when the believer can't feel a connection, well…it's a bad sign."

"In that case, I have no choice but to report it." Dory gave her friend a challenging look.

"You must do as you see fit," Evangeline said. "But I'm afraid Zoé's disappearance might remain a mystery."

They were both quiet then. Everything that transpired during their visit to the Voodoo Village had affected Evangeline deeply. In some ways, it was like a homecoming. She missed the warm acceptance of the Voodoo community. It was almost as if she could feel her grandmother's arms around her. But she could not give herself again to the charismatic religion of her youth. It was just too foreign to the rational and argumentative world of the law, her chosen profession. Deep in thought, Evangeline pulled into her subdivision and up her driveway. She turned off the engine and sat in silence. After some time, she heard Dory's voice.

"We've been sitting in your driveway for a good five minutes," Dory said. "What's going on with you?"

"Oh, dear, you're right. My mind's wandering. All the way back from the Voodoo Village I was thinking of the time when I was young and believed wholeheartedly in Voodoo. The entire natural world was alive to me then. Every rock or tree or cloud could contain a Loa who would come to guide me. When I lost my faith, the world seemed ordinary and flat."

"What made you lose your belief?" Dory asked.

"College, and then law school, I suppose. And falling in love with Jason. He's Catholic. All my ambivalence came back today, though. When I told the Canja sisters I was Catholic, I wondered whether I was lying to myself." Evangeline reached for a tissue and dabbed at her eyes, which stung with unshed tears. She picked up her keys and got out of the car.

Dory joined her and they walked into the house together in silence.

THREE

Chief Detective Wayne Nichols

THE STAFF MEETING was winding down when Dory whispered to Detective Nichols that she needed to talk with him. Together they walked down the corridor to Wayne's office.

"What's up, Dory?" Wayne closed his office door. He had been having a hard time focusing on the minor infractions in Rosedale during the meeting. He had learned from his cousin who was living in Michigan's Upper Peninsula that the old house where he had been raised was condemned and would soon be torn down. The news had given him an idea of how to solve a problem that had haunted him for nearly forty years. Wayne had lived in that house as the foster child of Joci and Aarne Outinen along with a much younger boy named Kurt—a kid Wayne thought of as a brother.

Aarne had abused his wife, and on a foggy late-summer morning when Wayne couldn't take the horrible sounds of the beatings any longer, he ran away, promising Kurt he would return for him. When he finally did come back three years later, he found Aarne dead at Joci's hand. Overcome by rage, she had killed him after she discovered that her husband had shot Kurt dead. Wayne had helped cover up Joci's crime and concealed the gun used in the murder. He did it to protect Joci, but his intervention backfired when she confessed to the crime—fearing the weapon would draw the law down on Wayne. Four decades later, he finally had a chance to make things right by pinning Kurt's murder on Aarne, the actual killer.

But the timing couldn't have been worse. His boss, young Sheriff Ben Bradley, was up for reelection, and Wayne hated to ask him for any favors right now. A few days' leave would be all it would take to get the murder weapon to Michigan's Upper Peninsula. Once there, he could hide it where it would be discovered and taken to Escanaba law enforcement. Another worry concerned his girlfriend, Lucy, an emergency room physician. They were living together and he knew it would hurt her if he went to Michigan without asking her to go along. But this time he had no choice.

"Wayne! Earth to Wayne," Dory said. "Could I have your attention please, Detective?" She waved both hands at him.

He turned his focus reluctantly back to her.

"I went out to the Voodoo Village yesterday with Evangeline. Did you read about it in the paper?"

"No. Don't know anything about the place." Wayne was looking out the window. Leaves were swirling in the air outside the office, caught by the rising wind. It was cloudy. He was thinking of the phrasing he should use to ask his cousin to put him up for a couple of nights.

"Evangeline and I went out there yesterday and talked to two women residents. One of them, Mira Canja, said her granddaughter, Zoé, was missing."

"Kid or adult?" Wayne asked.

"Young woman, mid-twenties I think. She's been missing for several days now."

"Well, adults are not exactly in our purview, you know.

They have the right to go where they want to go. Girl probably took off with her boyfriend."

"The grandmother was adamant that Zoé wouldn't go away without telling her first."

"Sorry, Dory, but I don't see the need to look into it. I'm sure she'll show up again in a week or two." Wayne turned away and looked at some papers on his desk, in particular one yellow sticky note with his cousin's phone number on it. He needed to call her today.

"But she left and made no arrangements to care for her dog," Dory insisted. "A female with four puppies. They're purebreds and apparently worth quite a bit of money. She planned on selling them. I doubt a young woman would've just walked out on a mother dog and four valuable *nursing* puppies."

"Unfortunately, people do it all the time," Wayne said, shaking his head.

"True, but not this girl. She was raised right. Plus, the grandmother said the dog has been howling and acting desperate. Miss Canja thinks it may know where the girl is."

"Okay." Wayne's attention was fully caught. "In that case, we better talk to the sheriff about this."

Dory and Wayne walked down the hall to Ben's office. He was on the phone, but motioned them to come in. "I'll see you tonight about seven, hon," he said. "Love you, too."

"Sheriff, something came up that our investigator here wants us to look into. Go ahead, Dory." Wayne shut the door behind him.

"Evangeline and I went out to the Voodoo Village yesterday."

"The place in Suzanne's article, right? Mae's working on some paintings from the photos her dad took out there. Got 'em pinned up all over the walls of her studio. Have a seat, you two." He smiled at Dory. "What's on your mind?"

"We talked to two women who live there. One of them, Mira Canja, has a missing granddaughter named Zoé. Detective Nichols already told me that since she's an adult, we have no interest or jurisdiction in the matter, but...." She looked at Wayne.

"Then I heard about the dog," the detective said.

Ben sighed. "I already have more than enough dog complications at home."

"I know, Sheriff, but the girl disappeared four days ago, leaving a valuable purebred mother dog and four puppies who're still nursing. The pups are worth several thousand dollars. Her grandmother said Zoé was planning on selling them."

There was a sudden, loud knock on Ben's door. He called out, "Come in."

Attorney Evangeline Bon Temps was standing out in the hall behind Sophie Coffin, who was trying to block her from entering. "It's all right, Mrs. Coffin, you can let her in," Ben said.

"Sheriff, Detective Nichols, Dory, something terrible...." Evangeline was out of breath. "You have to come see this. It's supposed to rain and it'll be washed away."

"Calm down, Evangeline." Wayne stood up and put his hand on her shoulder. "It's okay. Just take your time and tell us what you want to say."

The distraught woman took a deep, shaky breath. "You left your notebook in my car yesterday, Dory. I was going to put it in your mailbox on my way to the office this morning when I saw it—the symbol. It's on the sidewalk leading up to your front door." Her eyes were wide open, and she looked on the verge of panic.

"What did you see?" Dory demanded.

"A *veve*! It's been left on your sidewalk." She paused. "I hardly know how to say this." Evangeline was breathing hard. "It's the Maman Brigit veve. She's the mother of cemeteries, the Loa of money and death. She's very powerful. I have a horrible feeling, Dory, that…you've been marked for death."

"We better go check it out." Wayne looked out the window at the darkening sky. "Just a minute and I'll get Emma from the lab. She can take pictures of this symbol and get a sample. Do you want to come, Sheriff?"

"Yep. We'll follow you back there, Evangeline. Dory can ride with you."

Fifteen minutes later, Wayne, Evangeline, Emma Peters from the crime lab, Dory, Deputy George Phelps, and the sheriff were standing on the sidewalk in front of Dory's little house in the Flowerpot District. A dark red design had been drawn on Dory's sidewalk. The symbol was a heart shape placed on top of a triangle. The point of the heart touched the top point of the triangle. Horizontal lines were drawn through it, ending in crosses. A series of stars surrounded the image. Emma Peters put on the white paper suit and booties she wore for collecting evidence. She knelt down and started taking pictures from a variety of positions.

"Emma, try to get a flake of the paint so we can use it to identify where it came from," Wayne said. "It might've been purchased from a local hardware store. And George, take a look in the bushes. Maybe you can find the paintbrush or a can of paint. That ought to have fingerprints on it. And then start talking to the neighbors. See if anyone saw anything. It would be nice to know when this was painted."

"Veves are not painted, Detective," Evangeline said quietly, staring down at the symbol and clutching Dory's hand. "They're usually drawn by strewing a powder-like substance, commonly cornmeal, wheat flour, or red-brick powder. I suspect it was created last night around midnight. They usually are." Her voice was hushed.

Wayne looked around at the beautifully kept small houses, their tightly clipped lawns and window boxes filled with flowers. On the corner of the street there was a little playground occupied by two mothers with small children. He could hear the happy laughter of the kids. It seemed impossible to imagine a person bent over, creating a death threat at midnight. He shook his head, uncomfortable with the sense of mystery emanating from the dark red symbol. *This isn't the kind of crime I'm used to.*

"Boss," he said. "If Evangeline's right, Dory's going to need protection until this is settled."

Dory was standing next to her friend, looking smaller somehow. The color had drained from her café au lait complexion and Wayne could sense fear radiating from her body. The wind was dropping and there was a lull—the tiny slice of quietness before the rain began.

"I think I'm going to get my dog, True, and pack some things. I can go stay with Al for a few days." Dory's voice was shaky.

Wayne had forgotten about the dog. "Did you hear True barking last night or acting strangely at all?"

Dory looked at him with wide eyes. "Around midnight. She sleeps in my room and she was pacing and growling."

"You didn't notice the symbol on the sidewalk when you left for work this morning?" he asked.

"I park my car around the back, so no." She pulled on her friend's hand. "Come with me, please. I need to pack and I'm not going in there alone." Evangeline was rooted to the spot, watching the lab tech kneeling on the sidewalk.

"Emma, have you got that scraping?" Ben asked.

"Sorry, but I can't get an actual flake of the substance. It's just mixing with the dirt from the sidewalk on my collecting knife. I think it's something organic." She frowned, looking up at the sheriff.

The rain started then, suddenly. "Get something, Emma, now," the sheriff ordered. Emma knelt down with a Q-tip, rubbing it furiously on the symbol. Only minutes later, the intricate red design was sluicing away in the rain. Dashing to his car, Wayne thought about the threat to Dory. They would need to keep her safe until they had the perp identified and put away.

FOUR

Sheriff Ben Bradley

AFTER THE DISTURBING events of yesterday, Ben hadn't slept well. Knowing that Dory and Mae's mother Suzanne were close friends, he hadn't mentioned the threatening symbol on Dory's sidewalk to Mae. Plus, a mother dog and puppies were involved. He figured Mae would hear about it soon enough. He'd woken up with the beginning of a headache, and the minute he entered the kitchen, Mae had once again mentioned the disagreement she and Matthew's mother were having about his son's Halloween costume.

"I wish you'd talk to Katie about it." His fiancée's blonde curls were more exuberant than ever. She was standing at the stove, braless and wearing navy athletic shorts and a thin white tank top.

"Is that bacon I smell?"

"And eggs; there's a frittata in the oven." Mae tilted her head to one side, dark eyes pleading. "Please, Ben. I *really* want Matty to be a fireman. I got a Dalmatian costume for Cupcake and they'll be so cute together."

She's really working it. Not that I don't appreciate bacon and skimpy attire as much as the next man…. He suppressed a grin.

"So let me get this straight. You bought a Dalmatian costume for a basset hound?"

She nodded, pulling the bacon out of the skillet with tongs and placing it on a paper towel to drain the grease. "Uh-huh, and Cupcake looks adorable in it. Perfect sidekick for a fireman, but Katie wants him to be Batman. It's a disaster."

"I don't want to get in the middle of it, babe. I've got to debate Ramsey tonight, so tangling with Katie isn't on the top of my list. I'm sure you two can work this out without me." His fiancé gave him an irritated glance that he resolutely ignored.

AFTER A DELICIOUS BREAKFAST, Ben got to the office at eight twenty, much later than usual.

"Good morning, Sheriff."

"Good morning, Sophie." His office manager was alone at her desk, or he would have addressed her as "Mrs. Coffin." They had bonded over a mutual loathing of his opponent for reelection, Ramsey Tremaine, and she'd asked him to call her Sophie—as long as the rest of the staff weren't around.

"There's quite the welcoming committee in your office." She shook her head, but her permed gray hair never moved. "Miss Clarkson and her friend Evangeline are in there with both your detectives. They may be plotting something." It was hard to tell behind her glasses, but she might have winked at him.

Ben sighed. "Thanks for the warning. Guess I'll get coffee later."

When Ben opened his office door, Wayne was leaning against his desk Dory and Evangeline were sitting in his visitor chairs and Detective Rob Fuller was actually in Ben's seat when he walked in. Rob jumped to his feet and hurried around the desk with a mumbled apology.

"Something wrong with the conference room?" Ben asked in a pleasant tone—sort of. He sat down and Sophie came in and handed him his coffee. "Thank you, Mrs. Coffin." She left with a nod.

"Sorry, we expected you a while ago," Wayne said.

"That's all right." Ben turned his attention to Dory. "Any problems at Al's house last night?"

She shook her head. "No. I didn't sleep much, though."

"Me neither." Evangeline gave him a direct look. "And now Detective Nichols is insisting that I can't go back with him to the Voodoo Village today."

"Rob and I are ready to run out there now, Sheriff. Do you want to come along?" Wayne edged toward the door, obviously ready to take action.

Ben gripped the edge of his desk and leaned forward to get his chief detective's attention. "I'm still the sheriff in this county," he said on a rising tide of indignation. "At least until the election. I give the orders around here!"

"Sheriff, please don't let them go without me," Evangeline said to Ben. "If your men go out there with sirens on and guns blazing, you won't find anybody who'll talk to you. I'm here because I wanted to ask you to let me go along. This is a persecuted people practicing a religion the authorities have tried to eliminate for centuries. Plus, a lot of them only speak a French dialect. I know the language and the culture. I've cleared my schedule already."

"Too dangerous," Wayne said, shaking his graying head. In Ben's view he was really pushing it. "We aren't taking civilians with us."

"Yes, you are, Wayne." Ben frowned. "I have some administrative details and debate prep to take care of today so I can't go, but I'm sure Ms. Bon Temps will be perfectly safe with you and Rob. You three can head out there. Besides the threat to Dory, there's a missing girl we need to find. Be careful not to alienate her family." Rob and Wayne were both frozen in place, staring at him in surprise. "You're dismissed. Go on."

"Thank you, Sheriff Bradley." Evangeline rose gracefully to her feet and followed the two detectives out the door. Dory stood up and started to follow her friend.

"Not so fast, Clarkson."

She looked over her shoulder at him. "What? I'm the investigator in this office. I need to go with them."

"I said *Evangeline* would be safe. No one's threatened her. You're not going near that place until we get a handle on this. Sit back down, please."

Dory stopped and turned around, a mulish look on her face. "What am I supposed to do today?"

"You and Cam are going to help me practice for the debate tonight. Do you want to be my opponent or the moderator?"

"Who's moderating?"

"Bubba Oustelet."

Dory gave a catlike grin. "The mayor? Okay then. I'll be Ramsey Tremaine. Watching Cam try to act like Bubba will perk me up for sure."

Good, then I can keep an eye on you. "I have a fair amount of paperwork to get through this morning; then we can grab lunch with Cam and do our debate practice this afternoon. Can I trust you to stick around until then?" he asked with a mock-stern look. Dory was one of his favorite people. "You're important to me, you know. Plus, Mae and my future mother-in-law would be all over my butt if I let anything happen to you."

She nodded and stood up. "I know, Ben. I'll behave.

Maybe I'll go see if George needs bossing around. And you're...important to me too."

As she walked down the hall Ben could hear her complaining aloud, muttering something about being kept under armed guard. He smiled.

FIVE

Chief Detective Wayne Nichols

WAYNE, ROB FULLER, and Evangeline Bon Temps were in the parking lot preparing to leave for the Voodoo Village. Wayne mentioned that he planned to stop in the nearby town of Richfield as well, since Dory had told him that was where the missing girl worked and attended church. At the last minute the sheriff came out with a bullet-proof vest, insisting that Evangeline wear it. Dory again pleaded to go with them and Wayne was relieved when Ben held his ground.

Then, just as the three of them were getting into the unmarked patrol car, Mae arrived unexpectedly at the sheriff's office. Dory had told Mae's mother about the abandoned Weimaraner and her puppies and now Mae wanted to go with them. She texted Ben, and when he came out to the parking lot, she reminded him that she had fostered the pit bull puppies after the ASPCA raid last winter and could do the same for the mother Weimaraner dog and her pups. The sheriff was unwavering. He wasn't putting her at risk and insisted that she could not accompany them. Although Mae had reluctantly agreed, Wayne knew that when it came to canine welfare, Mae December would do what she thought was right—no matter what Ben Bradley said.

"Why did you say the vest was unnecessary?" Wayne asked Evangeline as he finally pulled away from the office.

"If someone from that village wanted to hurt me or Dory, they have a hundred ways of doing so using poisons or other means. I keep telling you people that it's a religion of peace. They don't use guns."

"You're probably right about them not using guns," Wayne glanced in the rearview mirror to see Evangeline wriggle out of her vest, "but that doesn't mean they aren't dangerous. Stay alert out there."

THEY REACHED RICHFIELD shortly before noon. It was a small four-corner town with a grocery store, a line of small shops, a First Federal bank, a large stone church, and Randall's Tavern. Wayne pulled off the road and parked the car in front of a small restaurant with a sign that said "Betsy's Home Cooked Eats."

"Why are we stopping here, Detective Nichols?" Rob asked. Wayne had told the younger detective many times that he could call him by his first name, except in front of suspects, but Rob continued to use his title unless the two of them were alone.

"I'm going to order us a bite to eat," Wayne said. "Rob, I need you to go over to the church. Dory said the missing girl, Zoé, attended mass in this town. See if you can dig up the priest. I want to find out if he knows Miss Canja and if she showed for church on Sunday. It's the stone church across the street. You're Catholic, right?"

"I am. Lapsed, though," Rob said with a rueful look. "Can you get me a hamburger?" When Wayne nodded, he headed across the street to St. Francis' Church. Wayne turned to Evangeline, who was sitting in the backseat of the patrol car.

"I got the feeling you knew more than you said about that red sign on Dory's sidewalk." She nodded, turning her head to look out the window. "Let's go get some lunch and you can tell me."

The two of them walked inside the small restaurant and were greeted by the scent of bacon-flavored corn chowder. They took seats in a booth at the rear, Wayne with his back to the wall so he could see the front door and across the street to the church. He hated to have his back toward a doorway. Decades working in law enforcement had taught him to be vigilant, even in rural small towns.

"Tell me about the symbol," Wayne said. Evangeline looked at him, eyes wide like a little girl who got caught eating dessert before dinner.

"Okay. As I said, it's the Loa or spirit for Maman Brigitte. The symbol or veve is a beacon calling her to come down to the petitioner. This particular Loa is often seen as the ancient primal feminine power, but she also leads the dead into the afterlife. In this case, I assume it's a warning for Dory to stay away from the Voodoo Village. If she were a believer, she'd be required to go before the Council of Elders and confess her crimes."

"Go on." Wayne sensed she was still holding something back. "What crime would Dory have committed?"

"She took the matter of Zoé being missing to the white man's law without first clearing it with the high priest. In fact, despite my efforts to get her to change the subject, she was quite insistent."

"And that's a crime?" Wayne asked dubiously.

"Yes, you see there's a Voodoo Court. It's like the religious courts in Judaism and indeed in other religions, although much less accepted by the regular culture. The case of the person who's committed the crime is taken before the court and sentence is pronounced."

"I'm still not understanding this," Wayne said. "Dory could be tried and sentenced without ever appearing before this court?"

"Yes, she could. I called my mother last night and spoke to her. She reminded me that every Voodoo community has its own rules, but she thought if Dory never tried to find Zoé or didn't go back to the village, she would be all right."

"Hmm," Wayne said, "but being an investigator is her job...."

A waitress came over, and after a few minutes of menu discussion, took their orders. Wayne looked across the street and spotted Rob coming out of the church. He crossed the street quickly and practically blew in to the restaurant. The wind slammed the door shut behind him. Evangeline waved him over.

"What'd you learn?" Wayne asked after Rob sat down.

"I found the priest, Father Thomas. He knows Zoé and hoped she would eventually join his church. She wasn't in church on Sunday morning, but he said she'd come in recently to request spiritual guidance and absolution."

Evangeline took in a sharp breath. "Until a person is baptized Catholic, they can't ask for absolution. She must have been in some deep trouble to do that."

Damn the priest-penitent privilege. Wayne knew that they would never know exactly what the priest and Zoé Canja discussed. Not even a court order could change that. He grimaced.

"Did he say anything else?" Wayne pressed Rob.

"Only that he was worried about her. She didn't attend mass regularly but had been coming into the church to pray at odd times. He would see her alone on her knees in the sanctuary. Once she told him she was praying for her mother."

Evangeline shivered. Outside the wind stopped abruptly, as it often did before a rain. The restaurant became completely still. "*Un ange passe*," Evangeline murmured.

"What did you say, Ms. Bon Temps?" Rob asked.

"My grandfather used to tell me when a sudden quietness descended on a conversation, it meant an angel was passing overhead. Like the soul of Zoé Canja," Evangeline said sadly.

THEY ATE THEIR food in silence. Wayne guessed that Rob was thinking about how to approach this alien culture. He had experienced the excluding of outsiders in the Native American culture and wondered if anything he had learned in his youth would help him here. He cast an oblique glance at Evangeline, who held the key to unlocking the closed world of the Voodoo Village. He wondered how much help she would really be.

"So what's our plan, Detective Nichols?" Rob's burger was gone. He wiped his hands with a paper napkin and pushed his glasses up on the bridge of his nose.

"When we get to the village, Evangeline, I want you to go visit Mira Canja again and see if you can at least get a photograph of Zoé. If she had a car, try to get a description and a license plate number. And find out if she had a bank account and a cell phone. See if anyone has heard from the girl since her Thursday shift at Randall's bar."

Evangeline didn't meet his eyes. She was looking out the window and her expression was fixed.

"I already hate this case," Wayne said in a gloomy

tone. "Too many priests, too few clues, and a closed community. I'm getting a bad feeling about it."

"We just got started," Rob said, optimistically. "I'm sure we'll get a lot more information today."

Wayne locked eyes with Evangeline. He could tell she had a bad feeling about it too. He doubted even now that she'd told him everything.

"Before we go to the village, though, I'm going over to the bar where Zoé worked to see what I can learn from the other employees. You two stay here until I'm done. It won't take long."

"Will do, Detective," Rob said. "We can have another cup of coffee while we wait." He signaled to the waitress.

WAYNE WALKED OUT of the restaurant and got into the car, watching to see if anyone went into the bar. He wondered if they served food. If so, someone would be along soon. Ten minutes later he saw an older black man walk into Randall's Tavern, wearing a gray jacket and galoshes. Wayne jogged across the street and followed the man into the dark space. It was obvious they had just opened, but the old guy took what was probably his usual seat at the bar. Behind the long polished wooden surface was a younger man, in his mid-thirties, washing some glassware. He was a good-looking African American guy, tall with prison tats on his neck. He turned, acknowledged Wayne with a look, pulled the tap and filled a beer glass. He held it in the air for a moment.

"Have you got money today?" he asked the old man, continuing to hold the beer aloft while the patron fumbled in his pockets. Wayne pushed a ten down the bar toward the old guy.

"What'll you have?" the bartender asked Wayne, taking the money and setting the beer down.

"A coke, thanks." He smiled at the patron at the bar.

"You a cop?" the bartender asked, handing him four dollars in change.

"Just passing through," Wayne said, not denying it to the bartender. Ex-cons could always tell. "Got thirsty. What's your name?"

"Darnell."

"I'm looking for someone, Darnell. Maybe you can help me. Anyone named Canja in the area?"

The man froze for a second, then continued polishing the bar with a rag. "Our head bartender's a girl named Zoé Canja," he finally said.

"Is she working today?" Wayne asked.

"Nope. Haven't seen her in a few days. I wasn't here, but I heard she left early last Thursday without telling the owner. Randall was pissed off."

"Did she work the following night, Friday?"

"No. I got called in to cover her shift." Darnell's face gave nothing away, but Wayne wondered if he was Zoé's boyfriend. If so, he was a suspect. He pulled a fat roll of bills from his coat pocket. They were mostly ones, but it often impressed those trying to make a few bucks. "I'm trying to find Zoé. I'll give you ten for her cellphone number."

"Twenty," the barkeep said, his deep voice calm, giving nothing away.

Wayne smiled at the two men. He'd done this dance before. It was the first step in acquiring a CI, a confidential informant. He placed his card upside down on the bar with a twenty under it and told the bartender to write Zoé's number on the card. The man wrote down the number. Clearly, he knew it by heart.

Wayne then turned to the older man, who'd already finished his beer. "I'm Wayne, by the way. Wayne Nichols."

"Jean Paul," the old guy said and reached out his hand to shake. It trembled and Wayne could see that he was in the first stages of the DTs.

"Are you familiar with the Voodoo Village?"

Jean Paul nodded, then looked at his empty glass. Wayne sighed. "Give him another one, Darnell." He handed the bartender another five and took a swig of his coke. When Jean Paul's second beer was half gone, Wayne put a hand on the old man's arm. "What can you tell me about the people who live in the village or the girl?"

Jean Paul drained the rest of his beer, set the empty glass down with a clunk and sat up straight. "If you give me twenty dollars, I'll tell you what I know."

Wayne doubted that Jean Paul was involved in the girl's disappearance—he was too old and shaky—but he might know something. He took two tens off the money roll and laid them on the wooden bar. Jean Paul pocketed them.

"Zoé was pretty girl...nice too. Her house is the only yellow one in the village. Got to see the Hounfour once," he said, gesturing with his thumb in the general direction of the village. "It's the temple for their ceremonies."

Hounfour. Wayne fixed the sound of the word in his mind. "I'd be interested in attending a service sometime," he said.

"Never happen." Jean Paul shook his head. "No cops allowed. I was here Thursday night and heard a couple of men talking about the village. They said something about there being a lot of money involved if some deal went through. The girl, Zoé, heard them too. She looked worried."

"Thanks. If you think of anything else concerning Zoé or the village, call me." Wayne handed the old man his card. He cast another suspicious look at Darnell, wanting him unsettled and nervous, and left.

BY THE TIME WAYNE, Rob, and Evangeline arrived at the top of the hill and looked down into the Voodoo Village, the sun had emerged, and the late afternoon light shone on the buildings. For a moment it looked as insubstantial and bright as a soap bubble. There was only one person Wayne could see, a boy riding away on a bike.

"Evangeline, please enter my cell number on your phone. Set it so all you have to do is touch the call button. If you get into any trouble, call me immediately. Otherwise text me when you're ready to go back to town." She nodded, exited the car and walked across the puddled street to the home of the Canja sisters.

Rob opened the car window and stuck his head out. "Look at this place. It's practically deserted."

"Yeah, they always know," Wayne said grimly. "I wouldn't be surprised if one of the guys from Randall's Tavern tipped 'em off that we were coming."

The two men got out of the car and walked down the sidewalk toward the end of the street. The kid continued to ride his bike through the puddles and an old man came out of what looked like a market. He was talking to himself as he walked down the wooden pallets that comprised the sidewalks of the town. He seemed to be in his own

world, humming and mumbling, but his wary eyes put
Wayne on the alert. *He looks like he knows something.*

"*Bonjour*," Rob said. Wayne looked at the young detective, whose accent had fractured the greeting. "Can
we ask you some questions?"

The old man didn't even look up, just continued past
them, singing quietly to himself.

"Let's talk to the kid," Wayne said. They walked toward the boy, age ten or eleven. He turned his bike around
quickly as he saw them approach and raced away down
the muddy street, brown water spraying from his wheels.
Then he vanished in between the houses.

"Take the far end," Wayne shouted and Rob ran to the
last house. Wayne headed for the first house in the row,
but when the men met up in an alley behind the houses,
they'd seen no sign of the boy.

"If they run they usually know something," Rob said,
stating a given in law enforcement. "Wish we'd caught
him. Do you know which house is Zoé's?"

"That one." Wayne said.

He pointed to a marigold-yellow house barely visible
through the heavy screen of foundation plantings. They
walked up the steps and onto the front porch. The drapes
were drawn. He knocked on the purple front door and
was answered by howling.

"Poor dog." Wayne looked at Rob. "She sounds miserable."

They walked around to the back of the house with its
weedy neglected yard that terminated in a forested area.
Peering into the back windows of the house, they could
see nothing through the tightly closed curtains. Wayne
wondered how far he could push in this situation. He
wanted to search the place—he'd brought his lock pick

set with him—but they didn't have probable cause that a crime had occurred.

"She's clearly not home. We'd need a warrant," Rob pointed out.

Wayne nodded. Sometimes he wished Rob were a little more flexible, but the young detective was right.

They'd started walking back to the car when Evangeline came out of the Canja sisters' house, followed by a black woman with a worried expression.

"This is Mira, Zoé's grandmother. She's going to let you into Zoé's place." Evangeline gestured toward the yellow house. "She's been inside every day since Zoé disappeared and said the girl isn't there, but if you want to have a look around, you can."

"We'd need Zoé's permission." Rob was still being a stickler.

"I checked. Ms. Canja owns the house, actually, just rents it to her granddaughter."

"Thank you, Miss Evangeline." The young detective smiled.

"Good work." Wayne patted her shoulder.

SIX

MIRA CANJA INSERTED the key into the lock of the yellow house. It turned with a click and Evangeline heard loud barking and howling coming from inside.

"Wait here. I need to go in first," Mira said. "The dog is jumpy, protective of her babies."

In just a few minutes, she came back out and opened the door to let the threesome inside.

"What's the dog's name?" Evangeline asked.

"Erzulie," Mira said.

"The Voodoo goddess of fertility…very appropriate." Evangeline smiled at her.

The house lacked a proper entryway. The front door led directly into a kitchen open to the living room. The kitchen walls had been painted a gray blue that contrasted nicely with the sunflower-yellow cabinets. The upper cabinets had glass fronts and Evangeline could see dark-blue dishes inside. Although Evangeline lacked the detectives' experience, she seriously doubted this was a crime scene. The house smelled clean.

Wayne and Rob walked through the kitchen and into the living room, skirting the mother dog in her bed. Erzulie rose up, growling, and Mira called her into the kitchen.

"She's beautiful." Evangeline admired the silvery fur and pale yellow eyes of the mother dog. The dog whined and pushed against Mira Canja's hand. "I think she wants to go outside."

"I know. I've been taking her out several times a day, but always on a leash. The way she pulls, I'm afraid if I let her off she will bolt. She knows where Zoé is—I'm sure of it. I had a dream the other night that Zoé was here in the village, held captive against her will." The woman took a shaky breath.

Evangeline shivered. She could hear Wayne and Rob's footsteps as they ascended the staircase to check the upstairs rooms. "Clear," she heard Rob say. There was no one else in the house.

"I'll take the dog outside if you like," Evangeline offered.

"If she will go with you, that's fine, but don't let go of the leash. She's stronger than she looks."

"Come on, Miss Erzulie, let's go out." Mira handed her a red leather leash and Evangeline clipped it to the dog's collar. They walked across the bare wood floors, through the sparsely furnished living room. Looking through the windows at the back of the house, Evangeline saw a screened-in porch, a wild backyard, and the shadowed woods. The sun was low, and even though it was only early afternoon, the shadows had turned the pine trees a deep forest green, nearly black.

She opened the door to the porch, which ran across the whole back of the house. The dog was pulling now, hard. "Erzulie, stop that," she said just as she tripped over a flower pot and fell down on the floor. In that instant, the dog pushed through the door, tearing the corner of the screen. Like a ghost, she vanished.

"Are you all right?" Mira asked as she helped Evangeline to her feet.

"I am," Evangeline said, brushing off her pants. "I'm sorry, the dog got away." Wayne and Rob clattered down the stairs.

"What happened?" Rob asked.

"Nothing. I just tripped, but the dog got outside. Ms. Canja is afraid she'll run away in search of Zoé." They could hear the dog barking and then a long horrible howl, a wail of near human pain. Evangeline could hardly breathe.

"We'll go after her," Wayne said brusquely. The two men moved toward the sound of the crying dog.

"I'm coming with you," Evangeline said. Following the men, she glanced back once at Mira Canja, who stood frozen in place. The wind rose and a sudden patter of rain hit the tin roof of the yellow house. The dog continued to moan and cry. They crossed the coarse grass and had reached the edge of the forest when Rob flicked on his flashlight. The beam hit Erzulie's yellow eyes. The dog's front legs were bent down in a crouching position but her head was held high as she gave vent to her anguish.

"Stay back," Wayne said, holding out an arm to stop Evangeline. "You probably don't want to see this."

Evangeline came to a halt, staring at the grieving dog. Wayne pulled a pair of gloves from his pocket and knelt down. Unable to keep still another moment, Evangeline moved forward to grab for the red leather leash that was still attached to Erzulie's collar.

"Erzulie, come away from there," Evangeline said and tugged on the leash. She didn't want the dog interfering with the work the detectives were doing. She was breathing raggedly, terribly afraid of what they would see. The men were both bending down now, moving dried leaves and some dirt aside.

"It's the girl," Wayne said. Rob walked unsteadily away toward the left side of the property. Evangeline could hear him retching into the weeds.

"Ms. Canja, can you come out here a moment?" Wayne called. She didn't appear to have heard Wayne's request. The detective stood up and walked toward the woman, murmuring something Evangeline couldn't hear.

Before Wayne and Mira returned, Evangeline moved closer to the spot the men had been excavating. Just before she glanced down, Rob returned and grabbed her arm.

"You don't want to see her like this, Miss Bon Temps," he said quietly. Looking away, Evangeline glimpsed something red caught in the brush.

"Hold your light still," Evangeline said. "I saw something over there." Rob pointed his flashlight in the direction she indicated. In the rising breeze, they saw a red scarf caught on the thorns of wild blackberry canes at the back edge of the wooded property.

Wayne returned with Zoé's grandmother.

"I'm sorry to ask you to do this, Ms. Canja, but is this your granddaughter?" Wayne asked Mira in a gentle voice. "It's probably best to just look at the clothing and her necklace." The woman glanced down and then back up again, bursting into anguished, racking sobs. She managed to nod and then turned to run back toward the house. Evangeline dropped the leash at a sudden tug, and the big gray dog loped after Mira.

"Even now you can tell that the girl's eyes were closed," Rob said.

"I noticed that," Wayne replied. "Probably means someone closed them after her death. It's possible there are fingerprints on her eyelids."

"Can the lab get fingerprints off skin now?"

"Decomp is pretty well advanced, but it's possible."
Wayne stood up and looked all around them at the shadowy, secretive Voodoo Village, now a murder scene. "See if you can get Ben on the phone, will you?" he asked and Rob punched the numbers into his phone.

"No answer on his private line," he said after a moment.

"Then call Dory, get her to go over to the debate. I think it was going to be held at the town hall. If Ben's already up at the podium, Dory can tell Mae we found Zoé Canja's body. And get Rosedale General to send an ambulance out here. Dr. Estes needs to come with them so he can get her body back to the morgue to determine cause of death. Call the lab, too. We need both Emma and Hadley here as soon as possible. You can go back and wait in the house, Evangeline." He turned to her. "It's going to be several hours. When the crime scene techs get here, can you direct them back to the body?"

Evangeline nodded and walked slowly back across the yard to the little yellow dwelling that seemed abandoned now. She caught a scent just as she walked up the three steps to the back porch. At first she thought that someone was making chicory coffee, but the scent was more floral. New Orleans came to her sharply—the swirl of colors and the sound of jazz. The sweetness recalled the French Quarter with its bustle, the tolling of bells from the cathedrals, the dusting of white powdered sugar on the beignets and the sounds of the riverboat horns on the Mississippi. Then she remembered. The scent was a perfume called Voodoo Love, supposedly made by the famous old Voodoo priestess Marie Laveau to draw a man to a woman. Evangeline had even worn the perfume herself when she was younger and still lived in New Orleans.

The house was empty. Mira had left, presumably to return to the home she shared with her sister—unable to stay another moment at the place where her murdered granddaughter had been found. Evangeline located a coffee pot and made coffee, strong and black. She found three pottery mugs and a thermos. Walking back through the living room, she saw that Erzulie was back in the house, quiet now, nursing her puppies. She had done her duty, drawing the men to the place where Zoé Canja's killer had hidden her body. For a few moments, Evangeline stood watching the mother and her four puppies. Their gray coats made them shimmer like wraiths in the dark room. She spotted a framed photograph of Zoé on a side table. In the picture she was lying back smiling in a pile of autumn leaves. A little gold chain with a cross was around her neck. She reminded Evangeline of a beautiful exotic bird.

She found the light switch beside the back door on the screened-in porch and turned on the exterior lights. When she called him from the steps, Rob came up to the house to take the thermos of coffee and two cups out to Wayne. The scent of Voodoo Love was strong here. She had a deep suspicion that Zoé Canja died on this porch. She looked around, noticing an overturned table and some potting soil that had spilled when she tripped over the clay pot.

In the back corner of the yard, she could still see the red scarf held by the thorns of the blackberry canes fluttering in the wind. Rob started stringing yellow crime scene tape around Zoé's body lying in her leafy, shallow grave. Then he walked to the back corner of the property and pocketed the red scarf.

On the back of the property nearly hidden by trees was a little building that Evangeline hadn't noticed earlier. Rob walked over to it, entered from the side door, and flipped on a light inside. It was a garage, and Evangeline saw a small red vehicle, probably the dead girl's car. *Either she didn't drive to work on Thursday night, or she made it home safely.* Rob reached into the car from an open window and picked something up from the seat.

As the moon rose, Evangeline watched the men standing guard over Zoé Canja. She sat down in a wicker chair on the back porch and pulled a crocheted afghan over her shoulders. She remembered the years when she and Jason had tried to get pregnant—the three IVF procedures, all the hormones she had to take, the injections that made her feel so horrible. *If I'd had a little girl, she'd be about Zoé's age now.* It was probably the reason Zoé's death was hitting her so hard. She texted Jason, saying she wouldn't be home for quite a while. Then she took a deep shaky breath. It was going to be a long sad night.

SEVEN

Mae December

TOWN HALL WAS hushed and the debate was about to begin. Mae was seated in the front row, flanked on her left by her parents, her sister July, and brother-in-law, Fred Powell. Her best friend, Tammy West, and her husband, Patrick, sat on her right. Dory and her boyfriend, Al Peckham, were directly behind her, sitting with Ben's parents. Everyone had gathered around Ben earlier, telling him not to worry, that he was certain to win. Joyce, Ben's mother, had been especially adamant. So much so that Ben had changed the subject, wondering aloud where his brother was.

Mae looked over her shoulder, glad to see David Bradley taking a seat in the back row. When Ben's older brother gave her a thumbs up and a reassuring wink, Mae took a deep breath and lowered her shoulders. Although she had tried to maintain a confident exterior in front of her fiancé, she was nervous about tonight. Ramsey had been so smooth in his pre-debate interview. Relaxed and smiling for the camera, he'd flirted with that snippy little Carrie Allen until she practically fell into his lap. And he'd been quick to blame Ben for every crime that had *ever* been committed in Rose County.

The microphone squealed and Mae's head snapped

back. "It's going to be fine," Tammy whispered. "Ben's going to make Ramsey look like a fool. Don't worry."

"Good evening," Mayor Oustelet said in his booming voice. "Welcome, ladies and gentleman. Let me tell y'all how tonight's going to work." As you might expect of someone who insisted that everyone call him Bubba—no one other than his wife seemed to know his real name, and she wasn't telling—the mayor was a large man with an even larger belly. His blue, button-collared shirt was tucked in to gray slacks held up by yellow suspenders. His face was red and sweaty in the lights that bathed the stage. Bubba Oustelet beamed at the assembled citizenry, who mostly smiled back at their popular mayor.

"I'm going to ask each of our fine candidates a series of questions and give them time to answer." He turned his massive head to fix Ramsey Tremaine with a sharp glance. "Two minutes is what you'll get, and not one second more, got it?"

Ramsey wore a navy suit, a crisp white shirt and a patterned silk tie in navy, burgundy, and gray. His silver hair was perfectly coiffed. Leaning on his podium, he gave the mayor the benefit of his excellent teeth in a smile that reminded Mae of a shark's. Looking at the audience, he said, "Of course, Mayor Oustelet. Have you ever known me to talk too long?"

Ben, who stood behind the podium to the left of the mayor, suppressed a laugh. His curly brown hair shone under the lights and his uniform was freshly pressed and immaculate. "The time limit's not a problem for me, Mr. Mayor. How long will we have for a rebuttal?"

"One minute. My assistant will run the timer, and there will be no interrupting during your opponent's turn. We clear?"

Ramsey and Ben both gave their assent. Bubba walked down the steps to the left of the stage and took his seat beside his assistant Renata at a table, his back to the audience. He cleared his throat and read from the paper in front of him. "These questions were selected from suggestions we got from community leaders and civic organizations. Sheriff Bradley, do you think Rose County is a safer place to live now than when you first took office?"

Mae's heart sank. Although overall crime was down, there had been several murders during Ben's tenure, and the smug expression on Ramsey's face indicated he was eager to exploit that fact.

Ben looked straight at her, blue eyes steady in his handsome face. "I don't just *think* so. I *know* it's safer here since I became sheriff. Theft and drunk driving are way down, we've made a dent in the drug problem, and domestic assault is also reduced. I've done my best to assemble a great team and to let them do their jobs without micro-management. We've teamed up with other law enforcement entities and shared resources, and I've encouraged community involvement as well."

Mae heard rustling and whispers from behind her and turned to see what was causing the commotion. Dory passed her cellphone to Mae. "From Rob—read it," she said in a voice just above a whisper.

Mae read the text on the screen and closed her eyes for just a second. She stood up and walked to the mayor's side. He smelled like aftershave and a hint of cigar smoke when she leaned down and spoke quietly into his ear. "Excuse me, Mayor Oustelet. I'm so sorry to interrupt, but a body's been found out at the Voodoo Village. We need to let the sheriff know."

Everything happened quickly after that. The mayor

beckoned Ben down from the stage and they conferred briefly in low voices before he announced that Sheriff Bradley had been called away on an urgent matter. "Y'all are welcome to stay and listen to Mr. Tremaine. He will be allowed to make his rebuttal and answer one question, but then we're cutting this short. In fairness to our sheriff, who has just been informed that a serious crime has taken place in Rose County, we can't do any more than that. I apologize to everyone who took the time out of their busy schedules and paid babysitters so they could be here, but it can't be helped."

Ben came over to Mae, who showed him the text. "He just sent this to Dory. Sounds like they found Zoé. Can I please go with you?" she asked.

He put his arm around her shoulder. "I'm sorry, Mae. Professionals only for this part." Ben handed the phone back to Dory and gave her a stern look before turning to the unflappable Al Peckham. "She's not to be out of your sight, okay?"

"Got it," he rumbled. "You go ahead, Sheriff."

"Thanks. I'll see you at the house, Mae. Probably be morning before I'm back." He squeezed her hand and walked away, neatly sidestepping Carrie Allen's outstretched microphone. "No comment at this time. We'll have something for you tomorrow." With a quick smile in the direction of his fiancée, Ben was gone.

Mae watched him go with a mixture of sadness and admiration. Always true to what mattered, Ben would do his job, even if it cost him the election. Looking at the smirk on Ramsey Tremaine's face, she knew that he would take full advantage of the situation. *And I'll be damned if I'm going to sit here and watch him do it.* She went back to her seat and picked up her purse. When Mae walked out, all of Ben's staff and supporters as well as her family and friends followed.

EIGHT

Sheriff Ben Bradley

IT TOOK BEN over an hour to reach the Voodoo Village, and it was after midnight when he took a break, gratefully accepting a fresh cup of coffee from Evangeline. She had made a second pot in Zoé's kitchen.

"I can have Detective Fuller run you home now, Ms. Bon Temps. There's no need for you to stay any longer."

Her graceful hands tensed around her mug as she sipped. "I want to stay. If Mira will talk to anyone, it would be me. And please call me Evangeline, Sheriff."

Cut close to her head, her dark hair accentuated the striking bone structure of her face. In the dim light of Zoé Canja's living room, she could have been any age. But there was no hiding the weariness in her eyes.

"That's a deal, Evangeline. As long as you call me Ben." He smiled at her. "I appreciate the coffee, but you've had a long day. You look almost as tired as I feel. And Mira Canja isn't up to talking to anyone tonight. I stopped at their home briefly, but her sister Marie said Mira had gone to bed and wouldn't speak to me." He gestured toward the woods, where the lights that the crime scene techs had set up were blazing. "They're taking her body away soon, and there won't be anything more for Rob to do until tomorrow. He can run you back to town.

I'll drop Wayne off on my way home. He and I will stay a while longer, but it's mostly up to the techs now."

She set her mug down with a sigh. "There's just something about that girl in the picture lying there in the leaves. She was…lovely. And the sound Erzulie made when she found her just broke my heart." To his great surprise, Evangeline began to cry.

"Erzulie?"

She gestured toward the corner, where the female Weimaraner lay sleeping, curled around her pups. "Zoé's dog. I feel better sitting here watching her with her babies. It's comforting somehow."

Faced with a crying woman, Ben did the only thing he could think to do. "If you'll let Rob take you home now, Evangeline, you can come back tomorrow with Mae. Someone from the office can escort you. She's going to be even more determined to foster the dog and her pups now that Zoé's dead. Maybe you can help her talk to Ms. Canja about that. You two might learn something helpful while you're there."

Evangeline sniffled and rubbed her cheeks with the heels of her hands. "Okay, Ben. That's a good idea. Thank you."

"All right, wait here. I'll send Rob to get you in a few minutes. And don't worry, we'll make sure Erzulie is taken care of before we leave. I'd be in big trouble with my fiancée if we didn't."

Ben took the back porch exit, found Rob, and sent his young detective back to the office. "You can drop Evangeline off there. She left her car in the parking lot. Make sure she's in her car and on her way home before you leave, though."

Rob Fuller too was looking tired. "Yes, sir. Do you

want me to follow her home and see her to the door?" He glanced back at the woods. "I'd hate for something to happen to Ms. Bon Temps."

Ben clapped him on the shoulder. "Good idea. See you tomorrow."

He walked over to stand beside Wayne. They watched in silence as Zoé Canja's body was loaded on a gurney and placed in the coroner's van under the gimlet eye of the pathologist. Dr. Estes slammed the double doors, raised a hand in farewell, and climbed into the passenger side. The van pulled away, following Rob and Evangeline in the patrol car. The quiet night got even quieter. Only Hadley Johns and Emma Peters, their CSI techs from the lab, continued to move silently in the brightly lit woods, taking pictures and collecting samples in their white paper suits.

"Did the grandmother have anything to say to you, Ben?" Wayne asked.

"No. Her sister told me that Mira turned her face to the wall and wouldn't speak. Marie, Zoé's great aunt, said she wasn't up to talking tonight either. They're both devastated, of course, and I don't think they really want our help."

Wayne frowned, the wrinkles on his forehead standing out in sharp relief from the crime scene lights. "Maybe they know who did it and they're going to take care of it within the community."

"Would you be okay with that?" Ben asked, startled.

"Hell, no. I'm familiar with a closed society, though. If it's anything like the Native American tribal system, the Elders will decide and their word is final. From what Evangeline said, that's what'll happen here if we don't intervene."

"It's too late for that." Ben gestured at Hadley and Emma, still collecting evidence. "Zoé's murder is in our jurisdiction now. I'll probably need to hire Evangeline as a consultant. She's our best hope of getting through to the family and the community here."

"That could work." Wayne nodded. "Let's go have some more coffee. It'll be a while until we can leave."

Ben followed Wayne up the wooden steps of Zoé's back porch. The big detective stopped suddenly at the screen door and Ben almost ran into him.

"Do you smell that?" Wayne demanded.

"I can't smell anything," Ben told him. "My allergies are bad this fall. What is it?"

"Perfume. It's strong. Whoever was wearing it was just here."

Wayne opened the door and the two men went to the kitchen.

"Probably Evangeline's perfume then. She just left," Ben said.

"I was with her all day. That's definitely not hers."

Ben poured what was left of the coffee, dividing it between his mug and Wayne's. Zoé's ghostly gray dog materialized at his side, and he sat down in a kitchen chair, patting Erzulie absentmindedly on her smooth head.

Wayne set his mug down with a clink. "Rob and I went through the house earlier today when we were looking for Zoé, but it was a quick look. Maybe you and I should search it again now that we know she's dead."

"I'll take the upstairs rooms," Ben said. He walked back toward the front door and turned to walk up the narrow stairs. Directly ahead was a small bathroom. He checked the cupboard drawers and looked in the medicine cabinet. Zoé had apparently been a natural beauty.

Her makeup bag held only lip gloss and mascara, along with tweezers and something he thought was an eyelash curler. The medicine cabinet was similarly bare—deodorant, Ibuprofen, and a bottle of allergy medication. Some lotions, a toothbrush and toothpaste, soap, and hair products completed the picture of a healthy, low-maintenance young woman.

Ben went through the smaller of the two bedrooms first. It seemed to be a guest room, very cozy with slanting walls and one small window. The double bed was covered with a worn quilt in pinks and lavenders. He switched on the bedside lamp. On the table beside it were several framed photos of a woman holding a baby with huge dark eyes. An old armoire held women's clothing that looked worn and dated, probably not Zoé's. A box under the bed contained photo albums with more pictures of the same woman and her big-eyed infant, who morphed into a toddler and then a little girl as Ben leafed through them. He pulled on his gloves and scanned a stack of postcards, all addressed to Zoé and signed *Maman*. The postmarks were from many different towns all over the south. The last had been sent over ten years ago.

The other bedroom was bigger, with two windows and a queen-sized bed. Ben went through the closet and checked the dresser drawers and under the bed. Nothing was out of the ordinary. Pulling on latex gloves, Ben took the bottle of perfume from the dresser top down the stairs and showed it to Wayne, who looked at the label.

"Voodoo Love, huh?" He sprayed it in the air and his nostrils flared. "That's the same fragrance I smelled on the porch. Someone else was wearing Zoé's perfume recently. It's definitely the same scent."

"I'll go put it back," Ben said. The screen door banged open behind them and he jumped.

"Sorry to startle you," Emma Peters said. "We've got what we need from the site. Hadley and I are heading back to Rosedale."

"Thanks, Emma. See you tomorrow." After returning the perfume to Zoé's dresser, Ben found Erzulie's leash and took her outside long enough to do her business; then he filled her water dish and she went back to her pups. "Did you find anything interesting?" he asked Wayne, who was sitting at the kitchen table.

"Not really." He yawned and stretched his big shoulders until Ben heard them crack. "I'm ready to go if you are."

They turned off the lights and left the small house, dark and empty except for the dogs. Ben looked back before he closed the door. Erzulie stood there watching them, her gray silhouette almost blending with the shadows of the room.

NINE

Evangeline Bon Temps

IT WAS A COOL, misty morning when Evangeline left her house to pick up Mae and take her to the Voodoo Village. Right after she woke up, she had gotten a call from Detective Rob Fuller, who said he and Deputy Cam would be following them. The sheriff had asked them to keep an eye on both women and also do a house-to-house in the village.

Mae was wearing blue jeans and a red corduroy jacket. She walked out her front door just as Rob and Cam pulled in behind Evangeline's car.

"I'm wondering…should we take my Explorer, rather than your car?" Mae asked Evangeline. "If we can talk Ms. Canja into letting me bring Erzulie and the puppies to my place, they would fit better in my car than yours."

"Good point." Evangeline transferred her purse and a leather satchel from her car to Mae's.

Mae walked back down the driveway and spoke briefly to Rob. He backed out of the driveway to make room for them.

"Will this be the first time you've been out to the Voodoo Village?" Evangeline asked when Mae got into the driver's seat.

"Yes. Both my parents have been there, of course, but although I've seen pictures and read Mama's article,

I'm anxious to see it for myself. I'm working on a series of paintings from Daddy's photos, but it's always good to see things in person. And of course I'm concerned about the dogs. What do you think my chances are of getting them?"

"Well, before we found out Zoé was murdered, I would have said your chances were slim to none. But after last night, I think both Zoé's grandmother and her great aunt will be more amenable to parting with them. They're grieving and probably don't feel up to exercising the mother dog. Marie told me Zoé was raising the puppies to earn enough money to pay a private detective to search for her mother, who's been missing for twenty years by now."

"How sad for Zoé. I was going to offer to foster the pups, but I could sell them and give the money to her family. I can put their pictures on my website. There are always people looking to buy my puppies, and I haven't had any to sell in a while. Maybe some people who wanted porgies would be happy with a Weimaraner pup."

Evangeline looked at Mae, vibrant and pretty in her red coat. *She's just a little older than Zoé, with her whole life ahead of her. It's so unfair that Zoé's is over.* She cleared her throat. "What about Erzulie? If Mira doesn't want to keep her, I mean."

Mae glanced over, brown eyes sad and full of compassion. "I was thinking about that too. If they want me to take the puppies, I'd need to take her as well, at least until the puppies are weaned." She shook her head. "The human tragedy is worse, but it's not like we can explain this to the poor dog."

"I don't think we'd need to explain anything to Erzulie, even if we could." Evangeline blinked back tears.

"After I saw her lead the detectives directly to Zoé's body, I knew that she understood all too well. And she's a beautiful dog. If Mira doesn't want her, someone surely will."

The women rode in silence for a while. Evangeline looked out the rear window and saw Rob behind them. A soft rain started, and as they reached the turnoff for the village, the air was filled with wisps of fog in the low places. Mae slowed the car down and turned on her headlights. The lights only penetrated the fog about a car's length ahead of them. By the time they reached the top of the hill and looked down into the village, the entire valley lay in a bowl of mist. Rob pulled up beside them and parked the unmarked car on the side of the road. Mae put her window down when he and Cam climbed out.

"We're going to hike down and scope things out before we do the house-to-house, so we'll be close by," Rob said. "Mae, if you or Ms. Bon Temps senses trouble, call me or Cam. Both of us are strapped."

"Oh, for heaven's sake! Nobody needs to shoot anyone here. These are peaceful people," Evangeline snapped.

"Be that as it may, Evangeline…" Rob said, eyebrows raised. To Evangeline, he looked like an earnest fourteen-year-old. "Someone from this town probably killed Zoé Canja. If I put you two in danger, the sheriff would never forgive me. And I would never forgive myself."

"We'll be careful," Mae reassured him. Rob and Cam disappeared into the mist, walking down the hill toward the Voodoo Village.

ONLY ONE HOUSE on the street had its lights on—the yellow one at the end of the row.

"Whose house is that? The yellow, with the lights on?" Mae asked. "I put it in my second painting, with a young woman with dark hair going through the door. In Daddy's photo she looked fluid and graceful, somehow, even though she wasn't moving."

"That's Zoé's house." Evangeline paused. "The woman in your painting must be her." *My God, she could already have been dead when Mae painted that portrait.* "How did you feel when you were working on that painting?"

"Peaceful," Mae said. "It's hard to tell a lot from someone's back, but she looked very *right* in that setting. No bad energy there. Of course my dad took that shot well before the tragedy."

"Probably the lights are on now because her grandmother or aunt is tending to Erzulie. They named her after the Voodoo spirit of fertility. I've been told the Loa spirit called Erzulie wears three wedding rings, one for each of her husbands."

"Good Lord. I think one husband's going to be plenty for me." Mae gave a little laugh.

"You got that right, girl," Evangeline said. "Sometimes even the best husband is one too many."

Mae drove very slowly down the steep hill and past the unlit multi-colored houses to the end of the row. She parked the car in front of the house just as Mira Canja walked out on the front porch. She looked exhausted, drained of every vestige of *joie de vivre.*

"It's a sad morning, my sister," Evangeline said, opening the car door. Stepping out, she enfolded Mira in her arms. The two women wept together for a short time. When Mira had regained her composure, Evangeline made her introduction. "This is my friend, Mae, who breeds and boards dogs in Rosedale. She would like to help you with Zoé's dog."

"I am so terribly sorry for your loss," Mae said.

"Come in, then," Mira said in a monotone. She didn't make eye contact with Mae, but took Evangeline by the hand and led her into the kitchen. Mae followed.

"Oh, how beautiful they are!" Mae said as she spotted Erzulie and the puppies. "They are just perfect."

She walked quickly into the living room and started to go down on her knees by the mother dog.

"Hold on a minute," Mira said. "She can be very protective." But just then Erzulie licked Mae's face. "Evangeline, your friend has an animal spirit."

"She does at that."

Mae continued kneeling beside Erzulie and the puppies, crooning, as the two older women put the kettle on in the kitchen. Evangeline watched as the young woman bonded with the puppies. One by one, she turned them on their backs and rubbed their small round tummies. When Mae picked up the fattest puppy, she held him to her nose, inhaling his baby self. The kettle whistled. Mira took mugs out of Zoé's yellow cupboards and added tea.

"Come and have tea, Mae," Mira said, and Mae stood up and joined them at the kitchen table. Erzulie padded behind her and sat down by her chair.

"Ms. Canja, would you consider letting me take Erzulie and the puppies home with me? I breed and board dogs."

"Erzulie has never been in a kennel," Mira said, pursing her lips.

"I wouldn't keep a mother dog and her pups in a kennel, not while she's nursing. I would keep them inside at my house," Mae said. "Evangeline told me that Zoé wanted to sell the pups to fund her efforts to find her mother. I could sell the males for eight hundred each and the females for twelve hundred if you have Erzulie's papers and the male's papers."

"What would you charge for this?" Mira asked, looking intently at Mae.

"Nothing. I would be happy to help you and find good homes for the puppies. That would be reward enough for me." She leaned down and petted Erzulie.

Just then Evangeline's attention was caught by a shadow passing by the front windows of the house. It was Rob. He and Cam were right outside.

"How do I know you won't just sell the puppies and keep the money for yourself?" Ms. Canja's eyes narrowed.

"Mira, I'm an attorney, a type of *médiatrice*," Evangeline broke in. "If my friend tried to keep the money, I would see that she was charged with grand theft, although I know she would never do such a thing." She paused. "Thinking about coming out here this morning, I made up a contract. It's in my purse." Evangeline walked to the area of the kitchen where she had hung her purse on a hook and pulled out a folded set of papers. "Here it is. It says that you have given Mae December your Weimaraner female and four puppies for the purpose of fostering and sale. It further says that Mae will return all monies from the sale to you. You both need to sign."

Mira Canja took the papers and read them carefully. "Don and Suzanne are your parents?" She glanced at Mae, who nodded. "All right. I will sign this. I am trusting you not to let anything happen to my grandbaby's dogs." She gave Mae a piercing glance.

"I will be worthy of your trust, Ms. Canja," Mae said with such obvious sincerity that the woman signed the document. When Mira was done, she handed the pen to Mae, who signed it as well.

After they had finished their tea, Mae took Erzulie's bed, dishes, and food out to her car. While Mae was gone, Evangeline asked Mira for some items to help find Zoé's mother, Laure.

"I can get started on a preliminary search. I have an investigator who works for my office who can start looking. In the case of a missing person, I can ask him to do some work in advance of payment. I'll be in touch with what he learns." Evangeline stood up and carried her teacup to the sink.

"I'll go get the dog's papers from my house," Mira said. "And the most recent picture of Laure. But it will be twenty years old or more." Shaking her head, she went to the door as Mae was coming back in.

"Thank you for trusting me with Erzulie and her babies, Ms. Canja." Mae stepped aside to let Mira pass. "I have a question before we go. Do you have any idea who would want to hurt Zoé?"

"That man, Randall. The one who owns the tavern where Zoé works.... I mean, where she *worked*." She swallowed, clearly trying to stop herself from crying. "He was trying to get her to go out with him. She said he told her he wasn't taking no for an answer."

TEN

Chief Detective Wayne Nichols

WAYNE WAS DRIVING to the morgue at Rosedale General Hospital. Dr. Estes, the pathologist for Rose County, had sent his preliminary findings on Zoé Canja's autopsy to the sheriff's office, but Wayne still had some questions. Finding the morgue's steel door ajar, he hesitated. He could hear Dr. Estes speaking to someone. He rapped and stuck his head around the corner of the door. When Dr. Estes saw him, he motioned for him to come in. He was on the phone.

"He's here now, Sheriff," he said. "I'll talk with him about the case. No problem. Goodbye." He set the phone back on its hook. Nichols had often wondered why it was hung on the wall, assuming it had something to do with keeping the phone clean. "Hang on a second, Detective. Need to get my gloves on."

Dr. Estes pulled on his latex gloves, walked over to a bank of silver drawers, and pulled one out. Inside lay the cold remains of Zoé Canja. "I presume you've already read my report?" Dr. Estes raised his eyebrows. Wayne knew he hated to waste time with anyone who hadn't done their homework.

"I have," Wayne said. "Just had some questions."

"Fine," Estes snapped. "You can stand over there by my desk." Glancing toward the right side of the room,

Wayne spotted a desk-height surface made of polished concrete supported by brackets between two banks of file cabinets. A laptop computer sat on the surface and a small desk lamp was turned on. Dr. Estes gestured for Wayne to stand by the four-drawer files. The senior pathologist took his seat and opened his computer to the file on Zoé Canja.

"What did you want to ask me?" Dr. Estes' face was heavily lined. His eyebrows, coarse and pure white, beetled above eyes that were dark and snapped when he was irritated, which he seemed to be at the moment, and indeed most of the time. He pushed his bifocals up on his nose.

"Among the contents of Miss Canja's stomach, you listed scopolamine. Do you have any idea how that was administered?"

"Ah yes, the so-called Devil's Breath or Zombie Poison." He paused. "She ingested the poison perimortem, in a liquid form. She probably drank it."

"Wouldn't she have noticed a bitter or harsh taste?"

"No. When scopolamine is processed and in a powdered form, it is devoid of taste and smell. It's one of the secondary metabolites of the deadly nightshade plant. When administered in too high a dosage, it is invariably fatal. In lighter dosages it produces absolute mind control and eliminates any memory of what the person did while under the influence of the drug."

"Wait a moment. Are you saying that Zoé Canja was poisoned?" Wayne frowned. He had read the autopsy report, and poison was not listed as the cause of death.

"No, not at all, Detective. I listed the cause of death as strangulation, which you would know if you had actually *read* my report." He frowned. Wayne raised his hands in the air. He had indeed read the report but chose not to defend himself. "Miss Canja's hyoid bone was broken and she had signs of petechial hemorrhaging in her eyes. Strangulation...no question."

"Then are you suggesting that there were two attempts on her life? One with the Zombie Drug and one by strangulation?"

"That, Detective, would be your job. Not mine. But if you are interested in my conjectures..." he trailed off, raised his caterpillar-like eyebrows, and looked at Wayne.

"Any help you can give me would be much appreciated," Wayne said, swallowing his pride and annoyance with the pathologist. "This is a very complicated case. The Voodoo people are secretive. They're outside our world, believe themselves outside our laws. We're working in the dark here."

Wayne took a deep breath and glanced away from Dr. Estes, across the sterile white room with its stainless steel tables and drawers containing the dead, toward the one small bank of clerestory windows in the lab looking out on a blue sky. Their world, the ordered scientific world, seemed entirely remote from the Voodoo Village and its people. It wasn't easy for him to admit, but he needed all the help he could get.

"My assumption, Detective, is that someone gave Miss Canja the scopolamine and subsequently strangled her. Or one person gave her the drug and a second person strangled her. In either case, the drug would render her incapable of resisting and make it far easier for the perpetrator to choke her to death. Plus, having the victim in a trance would make it less likely that the perp would leave trace evidence on the victim, since there would be no struggle.

There are some articles in the literature that maintain scopolamine gives a person retrograde amnesia."

"What does that mean?" Wayne asked.

"It means the person can't remember events that occurred several hours *before* they took the drug." Dr. Estes stood and walked over to the drawer in which the body of Zoé Canja lay. Sighing quietly, he added, "Mankind's inhumanity to man never ceases to depress me. And she was so young."

Turning on his heel, Wayne left the morgue. He carried Zoé Canja's face in his mind like a beacon, as he had since the night he'd found her body and seen her laughing face in the photo in her house. He didn't need Dr. Estes to remind him how young she was. He was all too aware that her life had been cut short. He had to find the perpetrator no matter what it cost or how long it took.

Once in his truck, Wayne dialed the sheriff's office and asked Mrs. Coffin if he could speak with Ben.

"Just a moment, Detective," she said.

"Wayne, what'd you find out?" Ben's voice was tense. Wayne knew that the election and the need to pin the Canja murder on someone were getting to him.

"Meet me at the usual two-top at the Donut Den in twenty minutes?"

"See you there." His boss was gone.

HAVING SNAGGED A coffee from the server, Wayne joined Ben at their usual table. The sheriff looked haggard and was drumming his fingers on the marred surface of the old table.

"What've you got, Wayne?" Ben asked.

"How about I summarize and you chime in if I forgot anything, okay?"

Ben nodded.

"The timeline goes like this. Zoé Canja worked her regularly scheduled shift at Randall's Tavern on Thursday night. Sometime around eleven she asked Jeanie to take over behind the bar—saying she needed to make a call. We found her cell phone on the seat of her car, but it's an iPhone, so its passcode protected. Unless we figure out her code, we won't be able to learn who she was calling."

"So what happened next?" Ben asked.

"Zoé left the bar without telling anyone, drove to the Voodoo Village, and parked her car in the little garage at the back of her property. It would have taken her about half an hour to reach home. We know she made it home, but after that the trail goes cold. No one will admit to seeing her after she left work. Sometime between eleven thirty and when she died of manual strangulation, she was administered scopolamine, the so called Zombie Poison. Dr. Estes lists the time of her death as between twelve thirty and three in the morning."

"So," Ben said, "unless somebody followed her from the bar out to the Voodoo Village and killed her for something she heard or saw that night, a person close to home is responsible for her death." Ben rubbed his forehead, his expression grim. "What are you thinking are our next steps?"

"We need to talk to the two cocktail waitresses at Randall's, the other bartender, Darnell Williams, and Randall himself. If you have time, it might be good for you to personally talk with the cocktail waitresses. Even if they weren't friends with Zoé, one of them might have overheard something about that phone call. Maybe one of them wears Voodoo Love perfume."

"What about the fingerprints on Zoé's eyelids? Did the lab get those?"

"They got one good print and Rob put it through every database imaginable. The person isn't in the system."

"Dammit. Did Dr. Estes think the perp could have been a woman?"

"Didn't ask him. What made you think that?"

"It seems like a woman's crime to me," Ben said.

"Because?"

"Because in Dr. Estes report there was no sign of sexual assault. We both smelled perfume at Zoé's house, and poison is almost always a woman's crime. Plus, the fingerprints on her eyelids. Seemed like something a woman would do, as if she regretted her actions."

"Interesting. Since Zoe was drugged, I'm sure a woman would have the strength to strangle her."

"Other than speculation, though, we have no leads," Ben said, shaking his head.

"Our only solid lead is from Mira Canja, who told Mae and Evangeline she suspected Randall, the owner of Randall's Tavern. He was trying to get Zoé to go out with him and she kept turning him down. I'm thinking that we could have Rob do one of the preliminary interviews with either Darnell or Randall."

"Okay," Ben said, but a worried frown crossed his brow. "I guess he needs to do a critical interview one of these days. But both those men should be interviewed in the office. I want to be in there with him."

"Sounds good."

"What're you going to do, Wayne?"

"I'm going to talk to my new confidential informant, Jean Paul, again. He said he had attended one of the Voodoo ceremonies. I'd like to hear more about that. And if possible, I'm going to visit the place where the ceremonies take place and the kitchen that adjoins it. That scopolamine came from somewhere and I believe practitioners of Voodoo would probably have had access to the Zombie Poison. But once I see what I can find out, if you want me in the room when Rob interviews our two suspects, I can be there."

"What about this Houngan?" Ben asked. "Both the Canja women seem to be in awe of him."

"If neither Randall nor Darnell pans out, he's next on my list," Wayne said. "But according to Evangeline, a Houngan can be either male or female. That could support your thinking that this was a crime committed by a woman."

"Interesting. Making an arrest would sure help me a lot in the election," Ben said, again drumming his fingers on the table.

"When Rob brings Randall and Darnell in for their interviews, he can check whether or not they have alibis for time of death. If they don't, or you can't confirm alibis right away, why not make an arrest, even if we have to release them later?"

"Right," Ben said, sounding more upbeat. "Lot going on tomorrow, so I'll have Rob bring them in on Saturday." He gave Wayne a satisfied grin. "Let's just hope this one is going to be that easy."

"Ben," Wayne said, avoiding his gaze, "I have something we need to talk about."

"Okay. Do you want to talk about it now?"

"No, it's personal. I'd rather do in a less public place. I'll catch up with you later."

Over the years of working together, Wayne had developed a deep respect for his young boss. He hated having to ask him for favors—especially on the eve of the election and with Zoé's murder unsolved.

ELEVEN

Mae December

ERZULIE'S LIFELESS BODY was sprawled on the floor. Blood poured from her throat as her puppies continued to nurse. Mae tried to run, horrified by the awful scene, but her legs seemed to be tied together and someone held her arm behind her back. "Let me go!" she screamed.

"Mae, it's all right. Ouch!" Ben said.

She opened her eyes to the worried faces of Ben and Matthew Bradley.

"What happened to you?" she asked her fiancé, who had a bleeding scratch on the back of his left hand.

"Daddy tried to wake you up from your bad dream and you scratched him," Matthew told her, sidling closer to the bed. "Want to get up now? It's Halloween morning."

Mae untangled herself from the bed sheet wrapped around her legs and gave Ben a rueful look. "I'm sorry I scratched you, but the dream was awful. I was trying to get to Erzulie and she was...." Realizing just in time how frightening a description of the nightmare would be to a five-year-old, Mae stopped. "Well, never mind. It was just a dream."

Ben nodded, rubbing absently at his injured hand. "It's okay. I need to shower and get going. Busy day today. Matty's had breakfast, our dogs have been out, and they've got food and water." He handed her a robe.

Mae wrapped it around her, climbed out of bed, and gave him a kiss. "Thanks for doing all that. Let me throw on my clothes and I'll be downstairs in a second. Is Erzulie eating?"

"Not yet. Can you run Matty to school today?" Ben asked.

Mae looked at her bedside clock. It was six forty-five. "Definitely. You need to get dressed too, Matty. I'll see you downstairs."

BEN WAS OUT the door shortly after seven a.m. By seven thirty, Mae had taken care of her three kennel guests and scrambled some eggs. The big silver dog's eyes stayed focused on Mae's breakfast. Her hunger strike appeared to be over. *Good thing, too. Those puppies need a lot of milk and Erzulie can barely keep up. I'm starting to see her ribs.* She scrambled four more eggs, let them cool, and put them in Erzulie's dish.

Matthew was lying on the living room sofa with Cupcake, his little basset hound, on his stomach. "Where's your backpack?" Mae asked. "I need to put your lunchbox in it and then we've got to go."

"Cupcake needs to come with us today, for the costume parade." Matty squeezed Cupcake around her chest, sat up, and attempted to hoist her in his arms as he stood. "Oof, she's getting heavy."

Mae smiled down at the cute pair. "Might be all the treats you give her. Cupcake can't go for the whole day, Matty. I'll bring her in her costume right after lunch. Your teacher said she can only be there for the parade."

The little guy flopped back on the sofa, arms folded across his chest. "If Cupcake can't go with us until after lunch then that's when I'm going to school." He stuck his lower lip out and gave Mae a defiant stare.

"I know you've been looking forward to taking Cupcake to school, but you don't want to miss the morning. Remember, all your school friends will be wearing their costumes. You'll want to see everyone dressed up. Plus, the teachers will be having you practice for the parade. So get your backpack right now, honey, and bring it to the kitchen."

Matthew narrowed his eyes and opened his mouth to speak.

Mae held up her index finger. "If you're not off this couch by the count of three…. One, two…."

Giving her one more glare, he ran for the stairs with Cupcake right behind him.

MAE DROVE BACK to Elm Hill Elementary at one fifteen that afternoon with Cupcake riding shotgun. The dog was wearing her Dalmatian costume, a black and white spotted cape that tied around her neck and under her stomach. A little firefighter helmet came with the costume, but she kept shaking it off. Mae's father was meeting her at the school, having promised Ben to take lots of photos. Between his campaign and the murder investigation, her fiancé would miss today's Halloween parade. She pulled into the busy parking lot and found a space near the back.

"Hey, Daddy!" she called out her open window.

The tall, middle-aged blond man with a camera strap around his neck waved and went to the passenger door of Mae's Explorer. She rolled the window down on that side and her father laughed. "Hello, Cupcake. Aren't you a sight to behold?" The dog put her front feet up and stuck her head out the open window. Mae's dad snapped several photos before lifting her out through the window. Mae shut the car off, hurried around, and clipped a red leash to Cupcake's collar.

Don December put Cupcake on the ground and kissed his youngest on the cheek. As they walked toward the school, he said, "Beautiful day for it. Do you think I could get some shots outside after the parade? The light's perfect out here."

Mae nodded, hurrying to keep up with her dad's long strides. Even though she was 5'10", her father towered over her and she couldn't walk nearly as fast as he could.

"Matty's teacher emailed that they're bringing the parade outside since it's such a nice day. If you want to save a place right here," she indicated a spot near the back door, "this is where they'll come out. I'll take Cupcake inside and be right back."

"In that case I'll go get my tripod from the car."

Mae and Cupcake entered Matty's classroom to a chorus of "awws."

"Over here, Miss Mae!" A small fireman waved enthusiastically from his desk.

Mrs. Duncan clapped her hands loudly. "Quiet, please. Line up at the door. It's time for the parade." She smiled at Mae. "We have two special visitors today, Miss Mae December and Matthew Bradley's dog, Cupcake the basset hound."

A little girl dressed as Tinkerbell ran over and looked up at Mae. "Are you Matthew's mommy?"

"She's my daddy's fancy," Matthew informed Tinkerbell. "That means they're going to get married. She sleeps naked!"

God, I'm glad my own daddy's outside right now. Mae looked helplessly at Mrs. Duncan, who seemed to be stifling a laugh. The princesses, minions, witches, and various superheroes who made up her class were not even trying to stifle theirs.

"That's enough, everyone. Quiet down. Matthew, the word is 'fiancée,' not 'fancy.'" She turned to Mae. "Is there anything you'd like to tell the class before we start?"

"Um, what?" Mae's mind was a total blank.

"About the dog," the teacher murmured. "Not feeding her candy."

"Oh, right." Still blushing, Mae turned to face the line of kindergarteners. "It's very important that you don't give Cupcake anything to eat while she's here today, okay?" Mae gave the leash handle to Matthew, who stood near the front of the line. "Especially chocolate. It could make her really sick."

"Is she 'lergic?" a small Superman inquired.

"Yes, chocolate is bad for all dogs," she answered. "If you have dogs at home, you should be very careful that they don't get into your candy from trick-or-treating tonight."

Mrs. Duncan led her class out the door, where they joined the parade behind another kindergarten class. Mae watched them leave and went outside to join her waiting father. *I think I'll skip parent-teacher conferences this year. Matthew calling me Ben's 'fancy' and the 'sleeping naked' comment will probably be the talk of the teachers' lounge before the day is over.*

Rather than leaving after the parade when her dad did, Mae stayed for the class party. She felt bad for Matthew that both his parents were working and unable to be there. Once she got over her embarrassment at the "she sleeps naked" comment, she really enjoyed herself watching Matty and his friends. They were so cute in their costumes and so excited about Halloween. Some of the other parents had made adorable treats for the kids— eyeballs in Jell-O (actually green grapes in strawberry Jell-O squares) as well as pumpkin-shaped orange cookies. The teachers had hung apples by their stems from the ceiling. The kids had fun trying to catch the apples with their mouths, especially kids with missing teeth. At three o'clock, she loaded Cupcake and Matthew into her car and drove back to Little Chapel Road.

BEN CAME HOME at five o'clock. They planned to take "Fireman Matthew" trick-or-treating on their street, very briefly. When Katie picked him up, she would transform him into "Batman Matthew" and she and her son would make the rounds in her neighborhood. Mae and Matthew's mom had finally worked out the best solution for the both of them and Matt, who was happy to have two costumes to wear.

Mae and Ben walked along Little Chapel Road with Matt and his costumed puppy. Ben's son was one of only a few children who lived on the street and the earliest trick-or-treater, so everyone wanted to see Matt and take pictures of him and Cupcake. It was also a good opportunity for Ben to shake hands with all the residents and have them wish him luck. As Matt got into Katie's car and Mae and Ben waved goodbye, the little boy held a plastic Halloween pumpkin stuffed with candy.

Ten minutes later, a Wild West sheriff and a saloon dancing girl climbed into Ben's truck for the short drive into town. Mae flipped the visor mirror down and applied bright red lipstick. A dot of black eyeliner made a convincing beauty mark on her cheek, and she'd piled her wild blonde curls on top of her head.

"You look very pretty, Ma'am."

Mae put the mirror back up and smiled at her fiancé, batting her eyelashes. "Why, thank you kindly, Sheriff. You make a mighty handsome lawman in that ten-gallon hat."

"Speaking of being a lawman," Ben said, "I talked to Jeanie and Caroline today—the cocktail waitresses who worked with Zoé at Randall's Tavern."

Sigh. So much for his party mood. "Did they give you any useful information?"

"Some. It sounds like Zoé and Darnell did have a fling, but it ended a while back. They both confirmed that Randall Perdue, the owner of the bar, had been after Zoé for years, even though he'd been married most of that time. His wife left him several months ago and he got even more obnoxious after that."

Mae looked out the window at a decked-out Main Street, complete with a portable stage and amazing carved pumpkins, cornstalks, and black and orange streamers festooning the lampposts. The street was blocked by barricades at both ends, and costumed revelers were everywhere.

"Sounds like you need to talk to both those men. And we probably have to park behind Patrick and Tammy's place and walk back."

Ben nodded. "Good thing it's such a nice night; otherwise you'd be feelin' a tad nippy in that skimpy dress, Miss December." Ben backed up the truck and turned down a side street. "You're right about Darnell and Randall. I'm having them brought in tomorrow."

TWELVE

Sheriff Ben Bradley

BEN WAS WORN OUT. Last night's Halloween party had been fun for a little while, dancing with Mae and passing out the "Team Bradley" buttons that were shaped like a sheriff's badge, but then one person too many had commented favorably on Ramsey's TV interview and debate performance and wondered aloud just why Ben had left the debate so early.

By ten o'clock he'd had enough; his fiancée wanted to party on. He'd been surprised she wasn't ready to quit, but realized it was probably a way for Mae to put aside the stress she was under from running his campaign and worrying about the murder case. He had gone home by himself, deep in thought about the Canja case, after Mae said she'd catch a ride with one of their neighbors. She'd fallen into bed after one, mumbling something about sore feet.

Mae had lifted her head from the pillow when he was about to leave the room this morning and given him a sleepy smile. "You're going to win the election; don't worry. Everyone I talked to last night said they were going to vote for you."

"What else are they going to say to my fiancée?" He bent to kiss her bare shoulder. "I'm afraid people don't feel as safe as they used to in Rose County—especially after Zoé was killed. And Ramsey's exploiting that for all it's worth."

Mae rolled over. Yawning, she pulled the covers up to her chin. "You're going to win, *and* you'll solve the case. I have faith in you."

"I know you do," he told her. *Wish I had that much faith in myself. Or the voters in Rose County.* "Go back to sleep, babe. I'll call you later."

YESTERDAY'S WARM, CLEAR WEATHER had been replaced by clouds and chilly mist. Rosedale was quiet and disheveled after the Halloween revelry the night before. After parking his truck, Ben walked up to the door of the empty sheriff's office building, unlocked it, and flipped on the lights. Wayne and both his deputies had worked last night, so he hadn't expected any of them this morning.

I wish Sophie had come in and started the coffee.

He'd started to fill the water tank on the coffee machine when his cell phone rang. "Hi, Rob. Where is everybody today?" he greeted Detective Fuller.

"Good morning, Sheriff. It's Saturday, remember?"

"Oh, right. Are you coming in?" There was a brief pause.

"I'm picking up Darnell and Randall like you told me to. Should be there in an hour or so."

"Okay, see you then."

Ben put his phone back in his pocket and finished filling the coffee maker. Lost in thought, he stood and watched it brew.

"Anybody here?" Dory stuck her head around the corner. "Hey there, boss man, how're you? We missed you last night. Mae invited us in, but it was pretty late. We made sure she got in the house safely and then went home ourselves."

"I thought she got a ride from one of the neighbors."

Dory shook her head. "By the time Miss Dancing Girl was done dancing, all your neighbors were gone. Al and I were happy to run her home."

Ben looked at Dory with admiration. At twice Mae's age, she'd had a late night and was still here early, perfectly groomed and stylishly dressed. "Thank you, and tell Al thanks as well. I'm glad you're here."

"You don't know the half of it." Dory set her tote bag down and opened it to reveal a plastic container full of muffins. "If you pour me some coffee, you can have some of these pumpkin cream-cheese muffins. I was afraid Al would eat them all if I left them behind."

"Guess it's time to quit feeling sorry for myself. I was just too stressed out to enjoy the party. I clearly missed out on a good time." Ben poured two mugs of coffee, put sugar and creamer in Dory's, and carried them both to his office. "C'mon, Investigator Clarkson, bring in those baked goods."

By the time Rob Fuller arrived with Randall Perdue and Darnell Williams, Ben was feeling considerably better. And a whole lot fuller. Three muffins and two cups of coffee, plus talking through the case and his campaign worries with Dory, had perked him right up. He knew it would be a close race, but hopefully his devotion to doing his job as opposed to campaigning would win the voters over. Or maybe not. The timing of this murder case could not have been worse.

In the absence of both deputies and his office manager, Dory had graciously agreed to answer phones for the rest of the morning, even though she did feel the need to re-mind him it was a Saturday. Walking back to his office, Ben heard Rob greet her and Dory tell him to take the men to the conference room. When Ben neared the con-ference room, his young detective was leaning against the wall, waiting for him.

"Hey, Rob, thanks for rounding them up. Did they say anything of interest in the car?"

Rob shook his head of close-cropped, golden-brown hair. "Not unless you count Randall's whining. Very busy man, apparently. Darnell's a different story; you can tell he's been inside. Not a word out of him—just stared out the window the whole time."

"All right, let's put Darnell in the interview room and talk to him first. Wayne's on his way in and Dory knows to send him to the conference room to interview Ran-dall."

Rob opened the door to the conference room. "Mr. Williams, could you come with us, please?"

The tall African-American man with tattoos on his neck stood up and walked over to them.

Ben stuck out his hand. "I'm Sheriff Bradley. Thanks for coming in today, Darnell."

"Like I had a choice, right?" His rueful smile took the sting out of his words.

"You had a choice. And I do appreciate you coming in willingly. Follow me, please." He turned to lead the way to the interview room when Randall spoke up.

"What about me? I have a business to run, you know. I can't sit here all day."

Ben looked back at the heavyset man who was slumped on one elbow at the conference room table. He had dark, greasy hair and pasty skin. "Oh, don't worry,

Mr. Perdue. I called my chief detective to come in and interview you. He'll be along soon and he just *loves* to work on Saturdays. You sit tight." Randall opened his mouth but then closed it without further complaint. Ben was gratified by the quick flash of fear in his eyes.

"CAN I INTERVIEW DARNELL?" Rob asked Ben after installing the barkeep in the interview room. "Detective Nichols said you were going to let me try a serious interview."

"Oh, sorry, Rob. We did talk about it, so let's do this together. You can start out with the demographics—age, address, and so on. You can take a supportive position reiterating that we're sorry to bring him in on a Saturday. Sound good?"

Rob nodded, a bit glumly, and they went into the interrogation room.

"Mr. Darnell, I read you your Miranda rights in the car on the way over here, but for the audio recording I need you to say you've been cautioned. Okay?" Rob said.

"I understand my rights," Darnell said, "and I don't need an attorney."

"We're just confirming for the records. You're thirty-five years old?" Rob asked.

"I am." Darnell said.

"And you're employed as a bartender at Randall's Tavern in Richfield, Tennessee?"

"Yes," Darnell answered.

"How long have you worked for Mr. Perdue?"

"Three years now."

"We pulled your sheet, Darnell. You have priors for burglary and possession with intent. And you did a nickel for them at Morgan County Correctional, correct?"

"Yes, that's right."

Rob continued to verify the suspect's jail time and previous employers. After confirming that he'd been out of jail for four years and seemed to be getting his life back on track, Rob stopped talking and Ben took over.

"Tell me a little bit about yourself, Darnell. Did you grow up near Richfield?" Ben asked.

"No, Sheriff, I grew up in a rough neighborhood in Memphis, and I did what most of the guys I knew did back then. I got in with a rough crowd and started doing drugs. You may not believe me, but I found Jesus when I was in jail." He smiled at Ben and Rob. "Or he found me, I guess. Either way, I'm staying out of trouble from now on."

Ben did believe it. Darnell's gaze was clear and steady, with no evasion. One of the neck tattoos, upon closer observation, was actually a cross. "That's good to know," he said. "Now, what can you tell me about Zoé Canja? Miss Canja was murdered late Thursday night or early Friday morning."

"Awful thing," Darnell said. "Caroline called to tell me."

Ben watched the man's face closely. He seemed genuinely saddened.

"What was your relationship with Miss Canja?" Ben asked.

For the first time, Darnell paused and looked down at the table. After a moment, he replied quietly, "I loved her. Thought she was the one. But she never would introduce me to her family, and after a while I figured it out… I was only a pastime for her." Ben could see the pain in the man's hazel eyes. "She wasn't serious about me, and so I stopped asking her out. But my feelings didn't go away."

"Did Zoé have someone new in her life after you two broke up?"

"Naah. Just worked a lot, went to church. She loved her dog and she was going to sell those puppies, get some money together. I don't know what she needed the money for." Darnell sighed. "That girl had some heavy shit on her mind, though. I know that. Always so serious."

"So she wasn't dating Randall?" Rob asked.

"No. God knows the man tried. Zoé told me he'd been after her for years, but she never paid him any mind."

Rob frowned. "That make him mad? Her blowing him off like that?"

"Probably." Darnell shrugged. "Everything pisses that man off. But Zoé, she ran that place—he couldn't do it without her—so he had to be careful. That's why he's all stressed out now. Not upset about what happened to her, just worried about his bottom line."

"What were you doing Thursday night? That would be this past Thursday, the twenty-third," Rob asked.

"I was back home in Memphis. My mom's not feeling so good, and I went to visit her at my sister's. Didn't come home until Friday afternoon." Darnell was looking Rob straight in the eye while he answered the question.

"Can you prove that, Darnell?" Rob Fuller asked quietly.

"I'll give you my sister's phone number and you can ask her what time I left."

"Rob, why don't you go join Detective Nichols and Randall in the conference room?" Ben said. "I'm going to run Mr. Williams home, and I'll get the phone number for his sister. Tell Wayne to call me when you're done."

"Yes, sir." Rob stood up and started to walk out. "Thanks, Detective Fuller. See you Monday."

BEN DIDN'T LEARN much more from Darnell on the drive, but it gave him time to think. Wayne called on the way back.

"I emailed my notes to you. Don't like that Randall at all, but I didn't have any reason to hold him. We'll have to double-check his alibi for the time in question, but he said he was working in the kitchen at the tavern most of the night. They don't stop serving food until pretty late, and his cook, Carlos Rivera, wasn't feeling well. Randall said Carlos was gone by ten. I called George, and he drove Randall back to Richfield for me. Is there anything else you want me to do today?"

"Not that I can think of. Dory still around?"

Wayne's laugh was a low rumble in his ear. "No. She got bored, switched the phones over to dispatch, and went home to boss her boyfriend around. That woman has energy to spare."

"She's a force of nature, all right. Thanks, Wayne. I'll read your email when I get home. Bye." Ben drove home in a funk, wondering if he would be able to solve this one before Ramsey Tremaine took over as sheriff of Rose County.

THIRTEEN

Chief Detective Wayne Nichols

WAYNE DIDN'T FIND Ben alone in the office again until the afternoon before Election Day. The sheriff was stressed out after his long campaign. Once the votes were counted, Wayne assumed things would settle back into their usual groove of policing the trivial crimes in Rosedale, but the Voodoo Village murder had tongues wagging all over the county.

Carrie Allen, the television news reporter and Tremaine fan, was their top critic. Both Ben and Wayne were frustrated by the lack of solid leads. Wayne couldn't turn on the news without seeing the lovely exotic face of Zoé Canja. Some crimes that couldn't be solved stayed with detectives their whole lives. He had begun to fear that Zoé's murder was going to be one of those. He shook his head, trying to focus on what he had to say to his young boss.

He felt bad about his timing. Sticking his head around the corner of the open doorway, Wayne asked, "Can I talk to you a minute, Ben?"

Sheriff Bradley raised his face from the computer. He looked drained. At the beginning of the campaign, Ben was the odds-on favorite to be elected sheriff. As a prominent defense attorney, his opponent Ramsey Tremaine looked like a pretender who defended criminals and got a lot of them off. But since the Voodoo Village murder had hit the press, the race was too close to call. Dory told Wayne that she had overheard Ben talking to Captain Paula Crawford in Nashville about an open position on her staff.

Wayne wished he could have delayed this trip until after the election. If Ben didn't win, what would he do? He wouldn't work for Ramsey Tremaine. What path would he take? He thought of the cold beaches of Lake Michigan in the winter and the clear, wintry air that always made him feel so alive. He could join the police force in Marquette or work private security, but what would that decision mean for his relationship with Lucy? He was concerned about Ben too. He had been a good friend and boss. They worked well together and had solved a number of murders in the area. He would have some big decisions to make if Ben didn't win.

"What's up?" Ben was obviously glad to distract himself from what seemed like a campaign circling the drain. "I don't suppose you've got anything new on the Zoé Canja murder?" A brief hopefulness crossed his features. Making an announcement that they had arrested the killer would certainly help him keep his job.

"Sorry, boss. No. We're still waiting on some studies from forensics and trace. And I have more bad news. Remember the other day at the Donut Den—I said I needed to talk with you? I'm sorry about this, but I have to leave the office for a few days. It's a personal matter."

"Oh, man, that's not what I want to hear today. What the hell can be more important than the Canja case? Or the election?" Ben ran his hand through his curly, dark-brown hair.

"I know. This isn't a good time for either of us—for me to leave Rosedale and for you with the election. I have to go to the Upper Peninsula. It's for my family." Wayne could not bring himself to share more of what was going on until he had executed his plan in Michigan.

Ben frowned. "I seem to recall one other time when you asked me for leave to attend to a personal matter. That concerned finding your foster mother. Now that she's passed away, I didn't think you had any family left. What's this about?"

Wayne just shook his head, fearful that if he started talking, the whole decades-long debacle of his young foster brother's murder would come tumbling out. He didn't respond.

Ben looked irritated. "I had a feeling the other day when you said we had to talk that it was going to be about your past." He sighed. "Listen, Wayne, I've got to have something to go with here or I'm just going to have to say no this time."

"It's an old case, a cold one that's heating up." Wayne felt the blood drain from his face as he said the words and saw his little brother begging him not to leave on that foggy morning so long ago. He had left anyway, promising to return, but when he came back three years later, the boy was dead. The guilt and loss he felt at abandoning the boy and the horror at finding his body buried on the Outinen farm hit him again. He felt a cold knot in his stomach. Seeing what was left of Zoé Canja emerge from the leaves brought back the revulsion he felt the day he and his foster mother had unearthed his little brother's body and saw the evidence of multiple gunshots to his thin torso. "I caught a break on a cold case from my past. But there's some evidence that's about to be destroyed and I need to take care of it."

Ben sighed, looked back at his computer, and then at his watch. "How long do you need to be gone?"

"I think I can do it in three days."

"Can it wait until after the election at least?" Ben's frown showed his frustration. "I need you here working the case, and I could use the moral support."

"I'll be here until early tomorrow morning, but I just learned that the house where the crime took place is going to be changing hands and will probably be demolished soon," Wayne said.

"Fine." Ben stood up, irritation and worry plainly written on his face. "I'm not happy about it, but go. Just keep in touch. I know some of those remote areas have minimal cell service, but if we catch a break in the Zoé Canja case, I want you back here and focused on that crime. And Wayne, do me a favor. Vote before you leave, okay?"

Wayne nodded. "I already did—used an absentee ballot so I could vote early. I hate going to the polls when it's crowded. I'll be thinking about you guys and hoping for a decisive victory." He gave a sketchy salute and walked away. Wayne hated abandoning his young boss with the unsolved crime, but the old house was about to be razed. Before that happened, the gun he had taken from his foster father's bedside table decades ago—the gun with Aarne's fingerprints on it; the gun that brought his brother's life to a premature end—had to be planted where it would be found by local law enforcement. He had considered flying up north to save driving time, but the regulations concerning carrying firearms on airplanes would make it too easy to trace if anyone ever looked into his role in this old business.

HE LEFT THE OFFICE, thinking about what he was going to tell Lucy. That conversation would be even harder than the one he'd just concluded. Driving to the hospital, he

mentally ticked off the details of the trip. It took close
to sixteen hours to drive from Rosedale, Tennessee, to
the Potawatomi Reservation in Michigan's Upper Peninsula. His cousin and her daughter lived there. He could
visit her and stay overnight at her place. Then he'd have
twenty-four hours to plant the gun and could head back
to Rosedale the following day. He didn't want to involve
his cousin, Waseta Bourcier, but she was going to be
critical to his alibi. He'd called and left a message. She
called back before he reached the hospital.

"Hi, Cousin," he said, seeing the distinctive 906 area
code on his phone display. Waseta was the only person
left who would call him from Michigan's Upper Peninsula.

"You said you were thinking of coming for a short
visit. We would love to see you. Is there a reason this
time?" He pictured her as she was speaking—tall with
silver streaks in her long black hair, narrow facial planes,
and a nice smile. Wayne respected her intellect and was
fond of her.

"Yes. I'm sure you remember I didn't learn about
Joci's passing until it was too late for me to attend her
funeral. Anyway, I'd like to see where she's buried and
the stone I commissioned. I've never seen Kurt's stone
in place either."

"So we will be visiting the cemetery then?" she asked.
Wayne heard a little clink. She often wore a silver and
turquoise squash-blossom necklace. It suited her, but
bounced against things, making that distinctive sound.

"Yes, and I want to see Mr. and Mrs. Wilshire while
I'm there too. They were our neighbors when I was growing up."

"Are you going to see the old place before they knock it down?" she asked.

"No Goddamn way," he said gruffly. "I *never* want to see that place again. Too many bad memories." He spoke loudly, wanting her to remember his denial, in case law enforcement contacted her.

"What time will you be here?"

"Before nine tomorrow night, unless I run into the predicted snowstorm." He bid her goodbye.

NEXT HE PLACED a call to Northwoods Place in Escanaba, an independent living facility. He wanted to check that Mr. and Mrs. Wilshire were still alive. They had been Aarne and Jocelyn's neighbors in the years when Wayne was young. Mr. Wilshire was the closest thing there was to a witness. He hadn't actually seen the killing of Wayne's brother by their foster father, but he had heard the three shots. It hadn't been hunting season, and they weren't rifle shots. A few minutes later, he saw Aarne dragging something through the tall grasses in the field. He called out to Aarne, asking what he was dragging. Aarne said it was a coyote he had shot, but Mr. Wilshire had caught sight of something that looked a lot like denim, like the blue jeans a young boy would wear.

The last time they talked, Mr. Wilshire said he planned to inform the sheriff's Office in Escanaba about what he had seen. If he had done that, everything was in place for the final act in this play.

"Northwoods Place," the young receptionist chirped.

"Are Mr. and Mrs. Wilshire still living there?" Wayne asked.

"I'm sorry, sir. Only Mr. Wilshire lives here now. Mrs. Wilshire passed away a few months ago. He's not in the facility, though. He went out to do his daily swim at the Y. Did you want to leave a message?"

"No. I'll call back." He hung up before she could ask for his name.

WAYNE PARKED HIS car in the 'Reserved Police' space near the entrance to Rosedale General's ER and walked inside. Lucy was seeing a patient, but when informed he was there, she joined him in the waiting room. It was filled with people either injured or ill, some coughing loudly. Seeing her in her long white coat, her shiny brown hair just touching her shoulders, he felt a surge of pride to have this woman as both lover and friend.

"Hi," Lucy said, surprised to see him. They were living together now and only a few hours previously had shared an early breakfast at her place. Although they'd agreed to move to a new house, they hadn't gotten around to looking. "Has something happened on Zoé Canja's case?"

He took a deep breath and asked if they could talk in a nearby conference room. She led the way. Once they were seated, he cleared his throat and began.

"I have to go up to the Upper Peninsula for a few days," Wayne said.

"Really? When? You know I'd love to go. The fall leaves might still be on the trees. I can probably get a few days off next week..." she trailed off, seeing his expression. "You weren't planning on taking me." Her voice was flat.

"Sorry, babe. I just can't this time."

"Why?" Her face registered dismay and something like suspicion. "What's going on?"

"There was a case I was involved in up there," he admitted.

"Okay, so tell me about it."

"I can't. I just can't talk about it. I'm sorry. I'm going to be gone for three days is all."

"When are you leaving?" The cold note in her voice was hard for him to hear.

"Tomorrow morning."

"Well, it's not you being gone, Wayne. You know that perfectly well. I thought we agreed to share this old stuff. Frankly, that agreement was the basis for us getting back together and for me wanting to live with you. You're treading on unstable ground here." She was getting mad now and shook her head, her fair skin flushing from her neck up to her cheeks.

"Please, Lucy. The day will come when we can talk about it, but not now. I am asking for your understanding and trust."

She looked at him for a long time and he felt the strings that bound them together start to fray. There was a coldness in his chest.

"Wish me luck?"

"No, my friend. I won't wish you luck, not for keeping me in the dark about something that's obviously important to you."

"Kiss me goodbye then?"

"Are you leaving right now?"

"In the morning."

She stood up and went to the door, giving him a fierce look over her shoulder. "Then I'll see you at home."

FOURTEEN

Chief Detective Wayne Nichols

THE MORNING OF the election was cool and clear. Whatever happened today, Ben was still sheriff until January. *I really hope he wins, though.* Wayne checked his phone and the long-range weather forecast predicting snow in the western part of Michigan's Upper Peninsula. The storm would reach the Escanaba area by the following day. Six to eight inches of snow were expected. Anyone who went out to the old place would see his footprints embedded in the snow. It was the only aspect of his planned alibi that was not under his control, and as such, it was worrisome.

He knew the route to Michigan and only rarely had to refer to his GPS. He pushed Ben's irritation with him being gone out of his mind. It was a little harder to stop thinking about Lucy. She hadn't been willing to make love with him the night before and had continued to be cool and distant, pretending to be asleep when he left their warm bed before five a.m. He hoped that once he got back, her arms would be open to him again. He decided not to call.

The droning of the wheels on the Interstate helped him think. He rarely listened to music in the car, and sometimes the answers to questions he'd been obsessing about came to him while driving long distances alone. He needed to decide where he would put the gun. If he made a mistake, the bulldozers would take the old place down, nobody would spot the weapon, and his brother's murder would never be pinned on Aarne Outinen. The case note would still read, "Murder by person or persons unknown." He took a deep breath. Those were the most horrible words Wayne knew.

By the time he crossed the Mackinac Bridge, it was getting dark. A few maple trees were still ablaze with autumn color, flickering in and out of his headlights as he passed. The white birch trees quaked in the wind, their last yellow leaves looking forlorn. He turned west, driving along Route 2 toward Escanaba. The coarse beach grasses bordering the northern shore of Lake Michigan grew in the sand right up to the partially frozen water.

In his coldest and most rational moments, Wayne knew he should turn the car around and give this mission up. Aarne was long dead. Kurt's pitiful bones lay in the Potawatomi Cemetery. His headstone, reading, "His was the valor of the lion" was the only evidence that he had ever lived. Even his foster mother Joci was gone now. But the gun with its bullets that would match those taken from his little brother's chest was in a paper bag in the glovebox of his car. He felt briefly grateful for the long memory of the law. The bullets taken from Kurt's body would still be in old police storage, and the rifling in the barrel of the gun would be a match. If he succeeded in this risky venture, the decades-old murder would be solved. Setting the record straight was the only way he could forgive himself.

When he turned on the road that led into the reservation, he felt his breathing slow. *Coming home is always good.* He parked his truck under the streetlight closest to his cousin's home, a three-bedroom ranch with peeling paint. He wanted the vehicle in full view all night long. The wind was rising and snowflakes swirled in the air. He'd planned originally to drive to the Outinen property in late evening, parking on neighboring land and walking across the field to the house. But in order to have witnesses say his car never left the reservation, he was going to have to walk all the way. It was nearly ten miles there and back, a brutal walk in a winter snowstorm for an older guy with bad knees.

Waseta came out on her porch and called to him. "*Bozo Nikan.*" The words meant *Hello, friend.* "Come on in. It's getting colder out here. A storm is coming. I can smell it on the wind."

Grabbing his duffle bag from the backseat of the truck, Wayne headed down the street to his cousin's house. He walked inside the small home, appreciative of Waseta's welcome and the aroma of beef stew he knew she had prepared just for him.

"Tell me, why are you really here, Wayne Nighthawk Nichols?" Waseta was giving him her full attention.

"To pay my respects to my mother and little brother and to give my condolences to Mr. Wilshire. I just learned that he lost his wife a few months ago."

"Nothing else?" she asked, her look penetrating.

"Should I need more than that to visit my only family?" Wayne smiled at his cousin. After a moment, she smiled back.

"Do you have any signal here, Waseta?"

"It's not very good for cellphones. If you need to make a call, you can use the land line."

"I just want to find out if my boss will still be sheriff next year. I can send a text. It's fine." He got his phone out and saw that it only had one bar. "He probably can't talk anyway, since it's election night. I'll ask Dory."

"Come in the kitchen, Wayne. Better signal there."

He followed his cousin into her small, warm kitchen, where the screen on his phone showed two bars. After quickly tapping in his text to Dory, he pressed send. Waseta filled a glass with water and handed it to him. Wayne gulped it down and handed it back to her as his cellphone dinged.

"It's still too close to call," he said, reading the message out loud. "Will text you when I know. Fingers crossed." With a sigh, he typed a quick "thanks" and put his phone back in his pocket.

"He's a good man, your boss?" Waseta asked.

"He is." Wayne took a seat at her kitchen table. "And I like working for him, even though he's a lot younger than I am. Somewhere along the line, we've become good friends as well."

His cousin sat down across the table from him. "Then we must pray your friend wins the election and keeps his job."

He reached across the worn wood of the table and gave Waseta's hand a quick squeeze. "Yes, we must."

Pray for me, too. Pray that I can pull this off and that Aarne Outinen goes on record for his crime.

FIFTEEN

Mae December

MAE GOT UP early on Election Day, but Ben was already gone. His absence was something of a relief, since he was so keyed up that it was starting to rub off on her. It was another crisp, fall morning, and she pulled on jeans, warm socks, and a sweatshirt before going downstairs. Her cellphone was on the kitchen counter with a text from her fiancé. "Fed our dogs, on my way to vote and then the office. Love you," it said. She looked at the empty dog dishes and her four dogs and shook her head. "Good thing he texted me," she said out loud. "I would have fed y'all again."

Erzulie wandered into the kitchen. The big, gray Weimaraner was looking better. She wouldn't be putting on much weight until her puppies were weaned, but she was less gaunt than she had been when Mae brought her home. She stroked Erzulie's velvety ears and head, then poured herself a cup of coffee. "Let's go see your babies, girl."

Erzulie gave her a quizzical look, her golden eyes sparkling with intelligence. "Oh, I know, you want scrambled eggs first." Mae laughed. She was going through a lot more eggs trying to fatten Erzulie up, especially since her four dogs all wanted some whenever she gave them out.

Mae finished her coffee, cooked a dozen eggs, and ate some herself. She put a good-sized serving in a bowl for the nursing mother dog and divvied up the leftovers between Titan, Tallulah, Tatie, and Cupcake. When her dogs were finished, she ushered them out to the backyard. Leaving them outside, she went down the hall with Erzulie for a puppy visit. Ben had built an enclosure in one corner of her studio. The walls kept the pups contained but were low enough that their mother could step over them and come and go at will.

Erzulie sniffed her offspring, who responded with squeaks and tiny growls. The puppies were all nicely rounded, with glossy coats darker than their mother's. Their eyes had opened since Mae brought them home, but they were bluish, rather than the hazel color they would attain at maturity. She knelt down and cuddled each one for a minute, then Erzulie stepped back into the enclosure and lay down. The pups swarmed her and began to nurse vigorously, stubby tails swishing back and forth. Mae smiled, delighted at their obvious health and vitality. "I could watch you cuties all day, but I need to check on my boarders and go vote. Oh, and have at least one more cup of coffee."

THE METHODIST CHURCH on Hillsdale Pike was the designated polling place for the residents of the Little Chapel Road area. The line wound out from the front door, snaking into the parking lot. Several of her neighbors greeted her when she walked up with smiles and nods of encouragement.

Neesy Dennis stood at the end of the line. "What should Joe and I bring to the victory party tonight?" Neesy's husband Joe was the contractor who had remod-

eled Mae's house and worked on many other houses on
Little Chapel Road.

"Just yourselves. I'm having it catered. Any time after
six. Did you get a babysitter?"

"Yes, thank goodness!" Neesy gathered her red hair
into a ponytail. "She's coming at three thirty today so I
can get these split ends cut off, and then I'm going dress
shopping. I may just go back to Birdy's Salon and change
there and meet Joe at your house. He already voted, by
the way."

"Oh, good. And you don't have to be fancy for the
party, you know." Mae smiled at her petite and pretty
friend. "Unless you just want to be."

The line was moving forward quickly. Mae pulled her
voter-registration card out of her wallet.

"I want to." Neesy gave an emphatic nod. "We've been
so busy between the kids' activities and the renovation
business that I can't remember the last time Joe and I
went on a date. I thought my life would get easier once
the older three were all in school, and I do have a little
more time free during the week now, but it's been crazy
recently. My mom's watching the baby today until the
sitter arrives."

They entered the community room and walked over
to the table marked D, E, and F. "Dennis and December," Mae said. "See you tonight, Neesy." She took her
ballot to the booth, placed her vote for Ben and walked
back out into the sunny parking lot. Talking to Neesy had
given her an idea, so she called her best friend Tammy
as soon as she got back in her car.

"Hi, Mae, just a minute." She heard loud crying in the
background, followed by Patrick's voice, saying he'd take

NB and put him down for his nap. "Okay, let's try this again. Hi," Tammy said.

"Hello. When did you start calling the baby NB?"

"Just recently. Patrick's mom kept using his full name and Noah Bennett is kind of a mouthful, so we've all agreed on NB, at least for now."

"That's cute," Mae said. She started her Explorer and turned toward Rosedale as she left the parking lot. "Did you vote yet?"

"We did. Took the baby with us this morning. He'll sleep for a few hours now and Patrick has some writing to do, so I'm free. Are you busy, Mae-Mae?"

"That's why I called. I was hoping you could go shopping with me. I need to pick up some things for tonight and maybe get something new to wear for the party. I'll treat you to lunch if you'll be my fashion consultant."

Tammy and Mae agreed to meet at Valid, a trendy new boutique on Main Street, where her best friend assured her that she'd find the perfect outfit. Mae drove the rest of the way into town trying not to worry about the election. She wasn't quite as confident of his victory as she had led Ben to believe, but there was nothing more they could do now except wait for the votes to be counted. *He's going to win. He's got to.* She did her best to put it out of her mind and appreciate the glowing leaves and clear blue sky of the glorious autumn day.

SIXTEEN

Sheriff Ben Bradley

BESIDES THE MOMENT that Ben actually cast his vote, he'd passed most of the morning in a distracted blur. Mae called him around noon to see if he wanted to meet her and Tammy for lunch, but he declined.

"My mom already brought me some food, and Dory and Sophie have been mother-henning me to death around here," he told her. "You two have fun and I'll see you at home later."

He tried to concentrate on his computer screen, where all sorts of administrative tasks awaited him, but couldn't focus for more than a few minutes at a time. Though he acted annoyed, it was a relief when Dory interrupted him for the fourth time with a question about the Zoé Canja case.

"Can I at least read the coroner's report?" his investigator whined.

"Nope. It'll just make you want to run out to the Voodoo Village, and you're not safe there." He shut down his computer. "Tell you what you can do, though. Call Channel Four and ask them to run the tip-line info. And put something on our Facebook page too. As long as you promise to stay here, you can monitor what comes in, all right?"

Dory nodded. "Thanks, I'll do that." She paused half-way out of his office door. "If you don't mind me saying—"

"Like I could stop you from saying anything, Clarkson. Go ahead."

"You're like a bear with a sore head. I know you're nervous, but you're so grumpy.... I think the office might function better without you for the rest of the day."

Standing up, Ben grabbed his jacket, pocketed his cellphone, and stepped around her. "I think you're right about that. Later."

He walked past his office administrator, Sophie Coffin, without a word, got in his truck and slammed the door. *Now what? I don't feel like going home yet or being around anyone.* He fired up the engine in his F-150 and noticed the time—only twelve thirty. He could be at the cabin in an hour and have plenty of time to be home before six o'clock tonight. He sent Mae a quick text about his plans, fastened his seatbelt, and headed for the county line.

BEING AT THE cabin calmed his mind, as it always had. When his grandfather—known to all as Gampy—passed away, he'd left his house in Rosedale to David, Ben's older brother. Ben had inherited the old hunting cabin on fifty acres. He had loved the place from the first time Gampy brought him here, when he'd been an awkward little kid with allergies and glasses. Over the years Ben and his grandfather had compiled lots of wonderful memories here. After the cabin came to him, Ben made minor electrical and plumbing updates, but it was a time capsule in most respects.

Ben removed the spider webs from the corners of the wraparound porch and swept the leaves away before going inside to empty the mouse traps. That done, he opened all the windows to let in the fresh air. Taking a beer from the ice chest, he sat in his favorite mismatched rocker from the row on the porch and took in the panoramic view. He smiled, remembering the first time he brought Mae here. Unlike Katie, Matthew's mom, Mae had loved the place on sight. Watching her face light up as he gave her a tour had solidified his feeling that in her he had found the right one. Unfazed by dirt, bugs, rodents and Spartan facilities, she made herself at home right away. Of course she brought her dogs out here, and they loved it too.

He was exhausted after the campaigning and pulling double shifts to identify Zoé Canja's killer. He moved the rocker and a foot stool into a bigger patch of sunshine and went inside to find a hat. Returning to the porch with an ancient ball cap low over his eyes, he sat down, put his feet up, and tried to doze. It didn't work. He was too antsy.

Looking around, he noticed that the forest was once again encroaching on the walkway he had cleared around the cabin. Since the old place was not lived in fulltime, the fire department encouraged the clearing of growth close to the house.

He walked to the shed and got his tree clippers. As he was cutting off the lower limbs of a cedar tree, he felt the hair on the back of his neck rise. Someone was watching him. He turned his head in slow motion with his hand on his gun and heaved a sigh of relief when he saw a beautiful doe and a late fawn standing in a clearing. The sun lit their ears from behind, and they almost glowed. He smiled, and just as suddenly as they had appeared, they vanished. Seeing them lifted his spirits.

He remembered the time when he was about ten when Gampy first took him deer hunting. Gampy had missed an easy shot at an eight-point buck that day and Ben was young enough to be relieved. Later he asked him what made him miss.

"Oh, I guess I'm getting old, son. I'd rather see the deer than shoot them. Plus, if hunters killed all the big bucks, we wouldn't have them romancing the females and we'd not have the little spotted fawns in the spring." From then on, they "hunted" with an old camera.

Now Ben's own son was nearly old enough to bring out to the cabin to photograph wildlife. He decided if he lost the election he would try to get a few days free after his term ended in January to bring Mae, Matty, and the dogs to the old place. *Maybe it will snow this winter.* He envisioned them sitting in front of the old stone fireplace in the evening, watching a snowstorm swirl around the cabin and drinking wine. *If I lose the damn election, at least I'll have plenty of time to fix up the cabin while deciding what to do next.* He put the clippers away, slamming the shed door and startling a squirrel who thought he was alone in the world.

Ben pulled his cellphone out of his shirt pocket and set the alarm for four thirty. Settling back in his rocker, he finished his beer and finally drifted into a half-sleep in the warmth of the afternoon. When his phone alarm chirped, he closed the cabin back up and drove home, much refreshed and ready to face the evening.

"GLAD YOU'RE BACK." Mae greeted him with a quick kiss when he walked into the kitchen. "You've got time to shower and change before everyone starts arriving."

"I think I better," he told her. "Otherwise I won't be worthy of my fiancée. New outfit?"

Mae spun in front of him, the long skirt of her denim dress flaring around brown cowboy boots. "New dress and earrings—old boots. You like?"

"You look great. So does the house," he added. "And where are the dogs?"

"Our four are out in the kennels, and I closed Erzulie into the studio with her puppies. They're still too young to be handled much and if people see them, they'll want to hold them. You like all the banners and posters, right?"

"I could do without all the posters of myself, but I like the red, white, and blue—looks festive and patriotic."

"Good. The caterers are setting up in the backyard and I'm going to go check on them. She winked. "See you after your shower, Sheriff."

THREE HOURS LATER, Mae walked through their crowded backyard, hugged her sister, July, and her husband, Fred, who had just arrived and approached Ben with a downcast look on her pretty face. "Ninety percent of the vote is in," she said quietly. "It's really close, but…."

"But Ramsey's in the lead?" She nodded and a sick feeling flooded up from his gut. His eyes found his dad, deep in conversation with Mae's parents near the back door. He noticed Mae's sister and her family who had just arrived and nodded to Dory, and Rob. Ben's dad glanced up and started toward him, eyebrows raised. Ben shook his head and pulled Mae in close. "You're my campaign manager," he murmured in her ear. "Is it time for my concession speech yet?"

He heard her draw in a deep breath. "I'm so sorry, honey. I think it is."

Ben climbed up on the picnic table closest to the house. A gradual silence fell over the crowd as everyone turned their faces toward him. A few calls of "Go Team Bradley!" were quickly muffled as people noticed his unhappy expression. Mae went to the back door and called for everyone inside the house to come out. "Sheriff Bradley's going to say a few words," she said.

Ben cleared his throat. "I want to thank everyone here for their support, my family, Mae's family, our friends and everyone who works for me, and my lovely campaign manager. I can't thank you enough for all your hard work, and I'm so sorry to tell you that come January, Rose County will have a new sheriff."

There were scattered boos and cries of "No!" Raising his voice, Ben went on, "It's true. I've loved serving as your sheriff, and I wish I could keep doing it, but ninety percent of the votes are in, and I think it's time to concede."

Tears were sparkling on Mae's cheeks. *I love you*, she mouthed, looking up at him.

"I don't know what else to say, except thanks and goodnight." Ben started to climb down as Dory hustled through the crowd.

"Not so fast, boss man."

"What is it, Dory?" he asked wearily.

His investigator gave her trademark sassy grin and looked around, pausing for dramatic effect. "Well…" she drawled, "your campaign manager left her phone on the kitchen counter and I heard it ring, so I answered it."

"Clarkson, I swear to God, if you don't spit it out, you're back answering phones in the office for the rest of your life!"

"All right, calm down. You young people are so excitable, I swear. It was the county commissioner. Seems the votes from the Methodist church on Hillsdale Pike just got counted. Ninety-nine percent of the votes are in and you did it. It was awful close, Sheriff, but you won!"

He jumped down. Grabbing Dory in a bear hug, he kissed her on both cheeks. Then he bent his campaign manager back for a thorough kiss on the lips as everyone cheered and his dad thumped Ben on the back.

SEVENTEEN

Evangeline Bon Temps

EVANGELINE LAY STILL, not even opening her eyes. She was trying to recall something just out of reach—a faint remembrance she couldn't quite recapture. Then she heard it again; the morning *cock-a-doodle-doo* of a rooster. A rooster! In their city neighborhood? It was his call that had woken her. It reminded her of the trip she and her mother had taken to Haiti to visit her grandmother so many years ago now. Her bedroom had been a tiny upstairs room under the eaves. Her grandmother kept chickens and a single rooster in her backyard. He was black, she recalled, with a bright red comb. Her grandmother had told her with a giggle that it was his call that drew the lady chickens to come to him for a little romancin'.

She sat up, reached for her robe at the bottom of the bed and put it on. Jason was still sleeping. Getting out of bed, she walked to the window and looked out. Crossing their fenced backyard, stepping lightly through the dew, was a black rooster. She wondered if she was dreaming. She glanced back at the bed and saw that Jason had woken and was propped up on one elbow. The sheet had fallen off his chest and his beautiful brown torso was visible.

"Come back to bed, honey," he said, pulling the sheet

back to welcome her. "It's way too early to get up yet. It's only five o'clock in the morning, girl."

"Did you hear the rooster, Jason?" she asked.

"I did. Wonder who let that fool out in this neighborhood. Should I get my BB gun and shoot him?"

"No," she said. "Wouldn't do any good. He's gone now."

She got back into bed then, snuggling against Jason's warmth and letting his hands take her thoughts away.

When they got up together later, she knew why the rooster had come. A black rooster was the familiar of Maman Brigitte. He was the harbinger of her Loa, the spirit that warned a person of a coming death. Such a warning came in accord with the rhythm of the universe, following the instructions of the Creator. In Voodoo ceremonies, the rooster only appeared in a celebrant's vision. But this rooster was real. He had deliberately been planted in their backyard. It was a warning. She was being told to leave the Zoé Canja case alone. For a moment, Evangeline tasted fear like a copper penny on her tongue.

AFTER HER MORNING SHOWER, Evangeline dressed in a navy suit and a bright-yellow blouse, had cereal for breakfast, and drove to her office, all the while thinking of the black rooster threat. This campaign of fear had begun with the red veve painted on Dory's sidewalk, she realized. There had to be a reason her dear friend Dory had been threatened first. Dory's insistence that Zoé's disappearance be investigated wouldn't have been enough to elicit a death threat. Since the two of them visited the village together, both she and Dory should have received the same threat. Yet only Dory had been targeted...until now.

She tried to reach Dory on her cellphone with no luck, and then called the sheriff's office from the car, expecting to hear her friend's familiar voice say, "Rose County sheriff's office." But it wasn't Dory. Evangeline had still not adjusted to the new receptionist, Mrs. Coffin.

"Is Dory in?"

"Who's calling?" Mrs. Coffin asked.

"Evangeline Bon Temps," she said.

"I'll put you through, Counselor."

"Good morning, Evangeline." Dory sounded better than she had in days. Apparently she had gotten over her fear of the death threat.

"So, are you still staying at Al's place?" Evangeline asked.

"Yes, and I'm ready to be back home. The problem is that Attila the Hun, otherwise known as Sheriff Ben Bradley, won't give me an okay to return."

"He's just worried about you," Evangeline said soothingly.

"I know, I know, but here's the other thing. My dog, True, turns out to be a traitorous Jezebel and a hopeless flirt. I obviously misnamed the little strumpet. She follows Al all over the place. He so much as crooks a finger and she's all over him. He decided, foolishly in my view, that she's a frustrated lapdog and lets her sit in his lap all the time. She's a full-sized pit bull and way too heavy to sit in anyone's lap. It's starting to get old. True and I need to get back to our house so I can exert a little authority here."

"I get you, my friend. But the reason I wanted to know is that I woke up this morning with the feeling that there had to be some reason for the Voodoo people to place the veve on your sidewalk. I don't think it was just you insisting on having Zoé's disappearance investigated. It had to be because of something you saw or heard that I missed completely. Do you have any idea what it might have been?"

"You know, I do remember something I didn't mention to you before. It just didn't seem important at the time. When we were leaving and walked through that living room, do you remember the old guy watching television?"

"Of course."

"He had a sort of guilty look, and I saw him fold some papers in half and tuck them inside his shirt."

"That has to be it, Dory. What did the papers look like?"

"It was the kind that banks or law offices use—several sheets of white paper with a blue cover."

"That's how a lot of legal petitions are prepared," Evangeline said thoughtfully. "The exterior blue paper was included originally so your important papers wouldn't get lost in your ordinary correspondence."

"Well, I certainly didn't get enough of a look at it to identify it later," Dory said. "What do you think this means for me getting back home to the Flower Pot district?"

"When I asked my mother, she said if you just stayed out of the Zoé Canja case, you would be okay." The Voodoo people had moved away from Dory. Now Evangeline was the target.

"I haven't done a darn thing to help the sheriff with the case." Dory sounded exasperated. "He hasn't so much as let me look at the postmortem report. I'm happy he was reelected, of course, but he's so stubborn."

"Sorry, Dory, but I think he's right to keep you out of it. However, it's been almost a week and nothing has happened, so if you want me to talk to Ben and try to re-assure him it's safe for you to go home, I will."

"Thanks, Evangeline. I would really appreciate your intervening here. If I don't get back home soon, I'm afraid True will just decide to be Al's dog instead of mine."

They said their goodbyes as Evangeline pulled her car into the parking lot at her law office.

SEVERAL HOURS LATER, Evangeline had a break between appointments and decided to call Ben. This time she was prepared for the crisp delivery of Mrs. Coffin.

"Hello." The sheriff sounded tired.

"Ben, it's Evangeline," she said. "I wanted to congratulate you on last night's victory."

"Thanks," he laughed. "That was a close one."

"I also need to tell you what Dory and I figured out this morning. As we were leaving the home of Marie Canja on our first visit, we walked through the living room. There was this old guy who was watching television there. Anyway, according to Dory, he looked guilty. He had a folded set of papers with a blue cover that he quickly hid in his shirt."

"Go on," the sheriff said.

"I think that must have been the reason Dory was threatened. They obviously thought she saw something they didn't want her to see."

"Interesting. Dory's been working it hard to go back home. What do you think? Would she be safe now?"

"I think if she takes reasonable precautions, like lock-ing her house and leaving her outdoor lights on, she will be," Evangeline told him. She had decided by then not to tell Ben about the black rooster, which she would deal with in her own way.

"She's been pretty adamant that I have no authority in this matter." Ben spoke slowly, obviously considering his decision.

"If I'm right, perhaps Dory catching sight of these papers threatened the Voodoo people in some way. In any case, it might be an important clue."

"What do you think it means?" Ben asked.

"I'm thinking that these papers, whatever they were about, could have something to do with the motive for Zoé's death. In which case, much as I hate to say it, the perpetrator might be one of the Voodoo people. Of course, an outsider could also be using the Voodoo community and its practices to hide their own criminal actions."

"That's an important distinction, Evangeline. I'll keep it in mind. Perhaps Zoé saw something she shouldn't have in those papers and was silenced because of it. We're struggling to identify the motive in this crime. And as you know, we need the big three—means, motive, and opportunity—to figure out how to proceed. But I'm not convinced that Dory's safe to go home just yet, sorry."

"Well, I tried," she said. "Thanks for hearing me out. Goodbye."

A few minutes later, Evangeline buzzed her secretary, Kimberly Reed, and asked her to come to her office.

"Yes, Miss Evangeline, did you need something?" Kimberly asked. She was a soft-spoken young woman with ivory skin; her hair was gathered into a single long dark braid that hung down the middle of her back.

"I'm looking for a document. Not any particular document, just a document that's comprised of several pages of white paper with a blue cover stapled over it. Do you know what I mean?"

"I think so," Kimberly said. "You were recently copied on a petition for a client that looked like that. Plus, you know my husband and I recently bought a new house. I think the Quit Claim deed for our mortgage was prepared with a blue cover. If you like, I'll bring it to the office after lunch."

"That would be very helpful," Evangeline said, wondering how on earth a property deed or a legal petition could constitute a motive for murder. But if the blue cover on the papers the old man hid meant the document was a legal brief, it made sense. The Voodoo people had given her a warning with that black rooster. Perhaps they didn't want a lawyer involved—a lawyer who might be able to help the sheriff's office obtain and interpret the legal documents that would tell them the motive for Zoé Canja's murder.

EIGHTEEN

Detective Wayne Nichols

THE PHONE CALL Wayne had been dreading came early. He hadn't been able to sleep much last night, keyed up after returning to Rosedale from Michigan. Slipping out of bed before five in the morning, he'd arrived at the office hours before anyone else. Lucy hadn't spoken to him, although he knew she was awake when he got out of bed. She was waiting for him to tell her about his trip. He felt like he was walking on ice around her—half-melted spring ice that was not only slippery but soft and could break at any time, dumping him in dark, cold water.

"Sheriff's office," Wayne answered when the phone rang around seven o'clock.

"Good morning. I'm wondering if Detective Nichols is around." It was a man's voice and the display screen on the phone showed a 906 area code. He was calling from Michigan's Upper Peninsula. Wayne felt a fine sheen of sweat forming on his forehead. Good thing the man couldn't see him.

"This is he," Wayne said. He tried hard to make his voice sound confident but a wisp of fear circulated in his gut.

"This is Sheriff Easterbrook from the Escanaba post in Michigan. I want to know where you were on November fourth and fifth." Wayne recognized that tone of voice; it was the tone a lawman took when questioning a person of interest in a serious crime.

"I was in the Upper Peninsula on those days."

"Do you mind telling me why you were here?"

"Not at all, Sheriff. I drove up to visit my cousin, Waseta Bourcier. She lives on the Potawatomi reservation. I arrived around eight thirty in the evening on the fourth and left early the morning of the sixth."

"And I presume she could attest to you being there?" The sheriff sounded doubtful.

"Of course," Wayne said. "I'll be happy to text you her contact information. And now, if you don't mind, our staff meeting is starting and I need to review some notes preparatory to that meeting."

"Hold on, Detective. I find it interesting that you haven't asked *why* I want to know where you were," the sheriff said.

"I presumed if you thought I needed to know, you would tell me." Wayne kept his voice calm, as if gentling a dangerous animal.

"I'm telling you now. Turns out that some new people purchased the old Outinen place. You were a foster kid there until you were seventeen, right?"

"Right," Wayne said.

"The new folks had to tear down most of the house since it was condemned, but there was an old stone fireplace in the living room they wanted to keep. They had a chimney sweep come to see if the chimney was salvageable before the rest was torn down."

Wayne waited, superstitiously crossing his fingers behind his back. He felt sweat forming in his armpits and was glad Sheriff Easterbrook couldn't see him. There was a reason they called it "sweating a suspect."

"Turns out, right after you were up here, the chimney sweep found an old gun in the flue. Somebody had stuck it up above the damper, and when he cleaned the chimney, his brush dislodged it. It was an old .38. He brought it straight to the office."

"What does this have to do with me?" Wayne asked, gruffly. "I haven't lived in that house for over forty years."

"The gun was legally registered to Aarne Outinen and used to commit a murder. Did you ever see him use the pistol when you lived there?"

Wayne took a shaky breath before he replied, saying that he had not seen Aarne use the gun. It was true. He had seen Aarne use his rifle, but not the .38.

"You know, Detective, I hate to accuse a fellow law officer of a crime, but your being up here just before the property was demolished is suspicious. It's coincidental and I don't believe in coincidence. Did you plant that gun at the Outinen place on the night of November fourth?"

All Wayne's training screamed at him not to lie to the police and battled against the need to keep his midnight walk in a blinding snowstorm a secret. But the man had given him an out. It was well past midnight when he had reached the place. He had planted the gun on the fifth, not the fourth.

"I did not, sir," Wayne said, keeping his voice convincing and sincere. "I spent the night of the fourth with my cousin, as I told you. There was a bad snowstorm. Parked my truck in front of her house. You can ask her or any of her neighbors. It was there all night, right under the streetlight."

"You could have walked over there and planted the gun," the man insisted.

"I'm closing in on sixty and I've got bad knees. Don't know how old you are, but walking that distance in a snowstorm would have been impossible for me."

His ten-mile walk in the snowstorm had been a nightmare. He kept to the little gravel roads for most of it, but when he set off cross country to cover the last mile, he was almost immediately disoriented by the darkness and blowing wind. At one point, he stepped down into a ditch filled with water and covered over by snow. His right foot felt like a block of ice when he pulled it out.

When he arrived at the old place, he had experienced a moment of intense dread. What if it was locked up? But the back door was open, and using his flashlight, he quickly found the fireplace and stuffed the gun up inside above the flue. Then he paused and said a quiet prayer for the souls of his foster mother and Kurt. When he got back to the reservation, it was nearly five o'clock in the morning. The gray light of dawn outlined the blocks of small houses. Coming down the street he stopped in his tracks. There was already a light on in Waseta's house and he could smell coffee. When he went inside she looked up at him, her eyes asking where he had been. He told her he had woken early and needed something from his truck. She looked at his snow-covered clothing but didn't say a word. He knew that if anyone ever questioned her, Waseta would keep her suspicions to herself.

"Yeah, my knees are none too good either," Sheriff Easterbrook finally said.

"You said the gun was used in a murder?" Wayne asked.

"Yes, it was. We matched the gun to some old bullets we had in conjunction with the murder of Kurt Outinen. Your brother, right?"

"No. I always thought he was just another foster kid they took in, but I later learned he was my foster mother's biological son from a relationship she had prior to her marriage to Aarne Outinen. He wasn't my brother."

"So you weren't related?" The sheriff's voice was dubious. "Why then would you pay for an expensive gravestone? And why does the stone read, 'His was the valor of the lion'? Pretty personal inscription for a kid you're acting like you hardly knew." His voice was accusing now, intent and focused.

Wayne tried to slow his breathing to bring his heart rate down. In fact, he and Kurt were related. Joci Outinen, Kurt's biological mother, was Wayne's aunt. He hadn't known that when he was a kid, believing her to be simply his foster mother. Telling Sheriff Easterbrook about the complicated family relationship would only add to his suspicions. "My cousin was close to the boy. She took care of him before he went to the Outinen's. That's the reason I had the stone commissioned. I did it for her." He stopped himself from saying another word about Kurt. "Do you have all the information you need, Sheriff Easterbrook? I do need to get going."

"Not yet. What did you do on November fifth?"

"My cousin and I went to the Indian cemetery so I could see the gravestones the stonemason carved for my foster mother and Kurt. I hadn't seen either stone since they were set in place. Waseta and I had lunch in a little cafeteria in town called the Copper Mine Diner. You can check with them. In the afternoon, I went to see Mr. Wilshire, my old neighbor. We talked and I joined him for dinner at the Northwoods assisted living facility. I returned to my cousin's house afterwards and stayed there the rest of the night. Left early on the sixth to return home."

"You see, Detective, that's what's confusing to me. Why would you drive all the way to the U.P. from Tennessee on November fourth—a drive of fifteen or sixteen hours—spend just one day here and then leave early the morning of the sixth? It's a pretty long drive to stay only one day. And the weather was bad. Why come when you did?"

"November fourth was the election day for sheriff in Tennessee. It usually takes a day or two for the votes to be counted, so it seemed like a good time to be away. When Sheriff Bradley called to say he'd been reelected and wanted me back there as soon as possible, I left for home."

There was a long pause. "Somehow I get the feeling you wanted this case—Kurt's murder—closed. And pinned on Aarne. We only found one person's fingerprints on the weapon, just Aarne's. He killed the kid all right. Interesting that we never found the weapon when we did the search before. Pretty convenient all around, I'd say." He was still sounding distrustful but less accusatory.

"Always good to get a cold one off the books," Wayne said, heartily. "Congratulations." Relief was starting to rise from his chest. He felt lighter than a balloon. Lighter than air.

"Thanks," the man said. "I'll call you back if there's anything else we need, but as long as your alibi checks out, this seems settled. I'll let you go."

The gray load of suffering Wayne had carried for so long suddenly seemed inexplicable and unnecessary. According to a priest Wayne knew long ago, there does occasionally appear, in the lives of even the darkest sinners, a shaft of light that pierces the clouds—a moment of the purest joy, a moment of grace. That such a thing had been granted him seemed incredible. He quietly hung up the phone, threw his head back, and laughed out loud.

A few minutes later, Wayne called Lucy's pager. When she called back ten minutes later he said, "I'm ready to tell you everything, Lucy. Can we talk tonight?"

She hesitated such a long time he wondered if she'd hung up on him, but there hadn't been a click. He waited.

"Took you long enough," she said at last, and he heard amusement in her voice.

Her words were like sunshine melting the patch of ice between them. And Wayne hadn't fallen into dangerous waters, not at all. He was standing on solid ground.

THAT EVENING, AFTER they shared takeout Chinese around Lucy's coffee table and each had a glass of white wine, Lucy leaned back against the couch cushions. "You said you were ready to tell me about what happened to send you scurrying up north." Her lips quirked into a grin. Wayne knew she was putting him on the spot and enjoying it, too. He took a deep breath.

"You already know I lived with Joci Outinen and her husband Aarne when I was a kid."

Lucy nodded, her hands folded in her lap.

"A week before the sheriff's election, I learned from my cousin, Waseta, that the old house we lived in was about to be torn down by the new owners. I hoped that they would want to save the stone fireplace and that the chimney would be a perfect hiding place." Wayne stopped.

"Okay," Lucy said, looking perplexed. "What would you want to hide in a chimney?"

"A gun," Wayne said and took a shaky breath. "When I was twenty, I went back up north to see my little foster brother. It turned out that Joci had killed Aarne just hours before I arrived."

"Was it because of the abuse?" Lucy's eyes were narrowed in concentration.

"No. It was about Kurt. You were with me when we picked out the headstone for my little foster brother, but you never asked me how he died."

"I assumed it was an accident. You told me he was only fourteen. Teenage deaths are usually accidental, or suicide."

"Aarne shot and killed the boy. That's the reason Joci killed Aarne. I've had the gun ever since the night Joci and I buried Aarne. I didn't turn it in to the authorities because I feared they would focus on my foster mother for both Aarne's and Kurt's murders."

"My God, Wayne, you've had the gun for almost forty years?" Lucy's eyes widened.

Wayne nodded, looking down and feeling shame cross his face. "I had only three days, you see. I had to drive up there, plant the gun, establish an alibi, and drive back. That's why I couldn't take you." The brutally cold night and the long hike in the snow and darkness had been a terrible ordeal. His knees still ached. "It was a crime to conceal the evidence. Please promise me you'll never tell anyone I did that."

"Well, first off, you kept the gun to pin the murder on the right guy. So, in my mind, you were on the side of the angels. And now you're hoping that someone will find the gun, turn it over to the authorities, and you'll be able to place the blame for Kurt's death on Aarne. It's such a long shot." Lucy shook her head, her long brown hair swinging.

"But it paid off already. A chimney sweep did find the gun. He turned it in to the sheriff. They called me and it's over. It's finally over, Lucy." Wayne stood up and pulled her to her feet, his warm hands on hers. He drew her close in an embrace. "I did it, honey. Aarne has officially been listed as Kurt's killer."

"His was the valor of the lion," Lucy said, remembering Kurt's headstone inscription. "Come to bed with me, King of the Jungle, but no roaring or biting." She smiled mischievously.

"They say the only member of the pride the King of Beasts will bow down to is his queen," Wayne said.

Smiling, he bent down to kiss her.

NINETEEN

Evangeline Bon Temps

EVANGELINE WAS WORKING on a motion for the judge in a domestic assault case when her secretary buzzed her, saying Detective Nichols was on the line.

"I'll take it," she said. She punched line two and greeted the detective.

"I just learned that Dr. Estes has released Zoé's body," Wayne said. "Apparently Ms. Canja wants to hold her funeral. Can't say as I blame her. It's been two weeks since she was killed, although I have to say it feels much longer, with the election and everything else that's happened. Anyway, the remains have been transported to the funeral home in Richfield. She's to be cremated. The church memorial will take place on Sunday. I assume there will also be a ceremony in the Village."

"It feels like it's been at least a month since that poor girl was killed." Her eyes strayed to a petition on her desk. "Anything else I can help you with, Detective?"

"Yes, I'd like to go out to the Voodoo Village today— with you, if you can manage it. We're not getting very far with the case, and I could use your help. There's also a missing piece of information I'd like to obtain from Zoé's grandmother."

Evangeline looked at her in-box, which was piling up, but agreed, telling Wayne to pick her up after lunch. Sher-

iff Bradley had offered to pay her as a consultant on the
Zoé Canja case, but Evangeline turned him down, saying
she would help without any remuneration. If anyone from
the Voodoo Village asked if she worked for the police,
she wanted to be able to say, truthfully, no.

DETECTIVES ROB FULLER and Wayne Nichols arrived at
Evangeline's office shortly after one o'clock in the afternoon. Kimberly buzzed her, and Evangeline came out
into the reception area, picking up her coat and purse
before following the detectives to the car. Rob took the
backseat and Wayne held the door open for Evangeline
to get in the front.

"Come on, Dorothy, we're off to see the Wizard,"
Wayne said and smiled his crooked grin. Evangeline
frowned at him.

"Detective Nichols, you mentioned that there is a missing piece of information you need from Zoé's grandmother. What is that?" Evangeline asked as she buckled
her seatbelt.

"On the timeline we created for the Canja case, Zoé
made a call Thursday night before leaving Randall's
bar. Caroline, the waitress, thought Zoé had called her
grandmother. She overheard her say something about
'Grand'mère,' then 'hello,' like she got another call. What
we're going to do today is find out whether Zoé called
her grandmother that night and if so, get Ms. Canja to
tell us about that call. We need you to find out what they
talked about, and if possible, who else might have called
her at work that late."

"I'm confused. I thought law enforcement could get
cell phone records," Evangeline said.

"Zoé had an iPhone with a four-digit lock code. We

haven't gotten into the phone yet, and unless we figure out the code, we never will."

"Well, regardless, I'm happy to talk to Ms. Canja about that call. Maybe she knows the code. I presume she'll be planning the funeral in the Village as well. I'll find out when that's happening and whether it'll be held in the Voodoo Village or somewhere else."

Evangeline was quiet the rest of the way out to the Voodoo Village, thinking about the black rooster and whether she was putting herself at risk by going back to the village or even talking with Mira Canja.

IT WAS MID-AFTERNOON when the threesome arrived at the top of the hill above the Voodoo Village. The day was blustery, with looming dark clouds, and a misty rain. Evangeline spotted Mira Canja slumped in a rocking chair on her front porch. She was wearing a long skirt and old gray cardigan.

"Evangeline and I are going to talk to Ms. Canja," Wayne told Rob when they got out of the car. "I need you to go to the house across from Zoé's—that's where they hold the Voodoo services. If there is any sort of kitchen there, and you can do it without attracting much attention to yourself, look around for a bottle of scopolamine. Or any bottles of scent or perfume. We're looking for a perfume called Voodoo Love. Take pictures with your cellphone of anything that's of interest and then we can get a warrant. Let's go, Evangeline."

Ms. Canja saw the twosome approaching and stiffened. She didn't stand up or welcome them into the house.

"Good afternoon, Mira," Evangeline said in her warmest voice and reached out to clasp Mira's hands with her own. "This is Detective Nichols from the sheriff's office in Rosedale. We just need to ask you a few questions."

Mira Canja stood up and without a word led the way into the house. Once they were inside, Mira looked back at Wayne. It was obvious to Evangeline that the detective frightened the poor woman. He seemed too big for the little house, which was completely silent. No old man watching television, no scent of catalpa-flavored honey for tea in the air.

"Could we have tea, Mira?" Evangeline asked gently. She thought if Detective Nichols sat down, he might seem less threatening.

Mira didn't speak, but put the kettle on and took a jar of homemade honey from the cupboard. "You may sit," she said when the kettle started to whistle.

Evangeline and Wayne sat down at the same square kitchen table where she and Dory had learned Zoé Canja was missing. It was hard to believe only two weeks had passed since then.

Sipping the fragrant tea, Evangeline asked, "We believe the last phone call Zoé made was to you, Mira. Did she call you from work two weeks ago Thursday?"

Mira nodded. She was obviously keeping her responses to a minimum. Wayne sat restively in the chair that was too small for him.

"She called you that night?" Evangeline asked again.

"She did," Mira said, and tears formed in her eyes. Evangeline handed her a tissue from her coat pocket.

"We're going to find out who did this to Zoé, Ms. Canja," Wayne said in a surprisingly soft, gentle voice. "We intend to get justice for you and for her. But we need to know why she called you that night and what you talked about."

Mira just looked down at the floor. She was crying silently.

"Please tell us, Mira," Evangeline said.

Sitting up a little straighter and wiping away her tears, Mira Canja said, "She called to say she had gotten a message from her friend Virginia earlier that night. Zoé calls her Ginny. They've been friends ever since Zoé started working in Richfield when she was eighteen. They met at the restaurant near Randall's Tavern. Ginny was working there as a waitress then. Now she works for a Realtor."

"Go on," Wayne said. He had leaned forward and was focused on Mira.

"Ginny told Zoé that she'd seen an Offer to Purchase Real Estate on her boss' desk. It was listed as eighty acres of vacant land and the price was a million dollars." Mira paused to sip her tea. "Ginny thought it seemed like a lot of money for vacant land in Tennessee. Then she looked up the legal description of the property. It was the acreage surrounding and including our village."

The blue-covered legal document Dory saw the old man hide had probably been a copy of the Offer to Purchase. Somehow, Evangeline realized, that old man had discovered the real estate deal that could wipe out the Voodoo Village.

"So Zoé said she got this message earlier, right?" Wayne's hazel eyes were focused intently on Mira's. She nodded. "Why do you think she called you so late?"

"She said she overheard some man—a customer at the bar—talking about bulldozing the village. Then she said she had another call coming in." Mira stopped talking and wiped the tears from her cheeks. "That was the last time I heard her voice."

"And did you tell your sister about the phone call?"

"She heard the first part of my conversation with Zoé and then she left to talk to the Houngan and his wife, the Mambo, about it. You see, only a few of us own our homes here. The Houngan owns the rest of the land."

"Did you tell anyone else about this?" Wayne asked.

"No," Mira said. "I was too upset."

"Did you pay for your house on a land contract?" Evangeline asked.

"Marie and I both did," Mira said. "She owns this house, and I own Zoé's. We bought them from the Houngan."

Evangeline and Wayne locked glances. Wayne had gotten what he wanted and seemed poised to leave. "We need Ginny's last name and address if you have it," he said.

"I'm sorry. I don't think Zoé ever told me her last name. It's best you go home now." She was echoing what she'd said to Dory and Evangeline on their earlier visit. Evangeline got the distinct impression from Mira's body language that if she came back, she would no longer be welcome. "Do you know the code for Zoé's phone?" she asked quickly.

Mira shook her head with a frown.

"One more thing," Wayne said. "We know the pathologist released Zoé's body to the funeral home in Richfield. When is the funeral taking place?"

"There will be a memorial service day after tomorrow, at Zoé's church in Richfield." Mira turned and looked out the window, shoulders hunched as if bracing for a blow.

"Won't the village also have a ceremony?" Evangeline asked gently, but Mira didn't answer. "It's Saturday night then?" she persisted.

Mira glanced at her, gave one sharp nod, and then looked away. It was clear from Mira's demeanor that Evangeline was not invited to Zoé's service. The rejection left her close to tears.

TWENTY

Detective Wayne Nichols

WAYNE AND EVANGELINE were walking to the car when Rob came running up, his hair windblown and wet. The rain was falling harder now.

"I found it," he said, satisfaction animating his boyish face. He took off his glasses, dotted with raindrops, and attempted to dry them on the lining of his jacket.

"We can talk on the ride back," Wayne said. "Let's get going." He glanced down the street toward Zoé's marigold-colored house and saw Marie Canja come out through the front door, turn, and lock it with a key. *The dogs are at Mae's. What would the woman have to do now in that house*? He frowned.

None of them spoke until they reached the top of the hill. They stopped under an elm that still had most of its leaves, providing some shelter from the rain.

"Okay, what did you find, Rob?" Wayne asked.

"I found the bottle of scopolamine. It's a clear liquid and it looked like nothing but a little glass bottle of water until I read the label. It had a drawing of a plant on it with the label 'Belladonna.' That's the plant scopolamine comes from, according to the research I did on the drug after I read the coroner's report. I took a picture of the bottle showing the surroundings and a close-up of the label. Didn't find any perfume though. Sorry."

"Okay," Wayne said. He knew he should be acting more enthusiastic about Rob's find, but the image of Marie Canja locking Zoé's door was troubling him. Marie had learned about the real estate purchase offer on the night Zoé died. She had left the house to speak to the Houngan before Mira and Zoé were off the phone. And now Rob had found the scopolamine in the area where the Voodooists held their ceremonies.

"Maybe we can get Emma to check for fingerprints on the scopolamine bottle from my photo. If the prints on the bottle are the same as those on Zoé's eyelids, would that be enough for an arrest?" Eager for action, Rob slid into the backseat and drummed his fingers on the seat in front.

"It's possible," Wayne said, starting the engine, "but we have to get a search warrant before we can do any of that. You need to know what Evangeline and I found out. Zoé got a message the night she was killed from her friend, Ginny. We don't have her last name, but she works in Richfield for a Realtor. There can't be that many real estate offices in a town that small."

"Should I start working on that?" Rob asked as they drove out of the village.

"No," Wayne said, "hold off until I can discuss all this with Ben. Ginny's message for Zoé was that she found an Offer to Purchase the entire tract of eighty acres that includes the Voodoo Village. The offer was for a million dollars. The night Zoé died, she heard a customer at the bar say something about bulldozing the village. She called her grandmother about it." He glanced at the rearview mirror, watching the village disappear behind them. "I just saw Marie coming out of Zoé's house. Now that the dogs are being fostered by Mae, she has no reason to be in that place, unless she's removing evidence."

"Or planting it," Evangeline said with a grimace. "We discovered that all the land belongs to the Houngan or Mambo—that's what they call the Voodoo priestess."

"Sounds like we have three prime suspects," Rob said. "Marie Canja, although unless she stands to benefit from the real estate sale, she might not have a motive. But the Voodoo priest or priestess would become millionaires overnight if the land deal went through."

Evangeline cupped her cheeks in her hands, shaking her head. "A person who disrespects their family, especially to satisfy their own greed, commits the gravest sin in Voodoo."

Wayne saw the tension her face. Even the thought of such a sin seemed to terrify her.

"All three of these suspects are worth more investigation. However, I don't want to eliminate anyone yet," Wayne said. "Rob, didn't you and Cam do a house-to-house the day after we found Zoé's body?"

"We did, but we were completely shut out. The people here obviously know their rights and refused to speak to us. Nobody let us into their house, and the few people who would talk gave us the usual. 'I saw nothing, I heard nothing, and I know nothing.'" Rob blew out a puff of air in disgust. "I just wish people would help the police more. How can we investigate crimes if nobody will tell us anything?"

Wayne understood his frustration. "It's part of the job. Lots of perfectly law-abiding people are reluctant to talk to the cops. Now we know there were two places Zoé's killer could have come from—the bar or the village. We've eliminated Darnell the bartender, but the sheriff and I want to keep Randall Perdue in the frame. Did we ever fully vet his alibi?"

"I guess we didn't. Where did Randall say he was around midnight Thursday night?" Wayne glanced in the rearview mirror to see Rob flipping through his notes. "Oh right, here it is. He told us he was in the kitchen cooking all night because his cook was out sick. The cook's name is Carlos Rivera. Did you talk to him personally? I didn't. With all the attention focused on the election, I forgot to follow up." Rob looked sheepish.

"I didn't follow up either, Rob. I think we may have dropped the ball on that one." *It was just before I took those three days off to go up to Michigan.* "The sheriff needs to know all this. He can divvy up the jobs between you, Cam, and George."

"If it's okay with the boss, I'd like try to identify this friend of Zoé's," Rob said. "All this would sure be easier if we could get into Zoé's cellphone records."

"Sure would," Wayne said. "While I'm not ready to dismiss Randall Perdue as a suspect, I'm leaning toward the murder being committed by someone in the village. A million dollars constitutes a hell of a motive. Either the priest or the priestess could have killed Zoé to stop the news that they were planning to sell from traveling like wildfire through this little town."

"But both Zoé's grandmother and great aunt knew about the Offer to Purchase and they weren't killed."

"You're right, Ms. Bon Temps," Rob said. "Both women would profit from the sale and they're still alive."

"One step at a time," Wayne said, turning the wipers up to high against the rain. "There will be two services for Zoé. Someone needs to attend the memorial that will take place Sunday at the Catholic Church in Richfield.

Could you go to the funeral in the Voodoo Village Saturday night, Evangeline?"

"To tell you the truth," Evangeline said, "I'm not comfortable doing that. Not alone, in any case. I got the distinct impression from Mira Canja that I'm no longer welcome in the village."

"Any of the white men from the sheriff's office would stand out like sore thumbs at the ceremony," Wayne said, deep in thought.

Evangeline sighed and folded her hands in her lap. "I doubt they would let you in anyway."

They drove in silence for some time before Wayne spoke again. "If the fingerprints from the bottle in the kitchen of the sanctuary…. Is that what it's called, Evangeline, a sanctuary?"

"It's called a peristyle," Evangeline said. "I know it would be a help to have someone at the funeral…" her voice trailed off.

"I'd like to see whether anyone from the outside shows up, especially from Randall's Tavern. Won't you reconsider, Evangeline, and attend the Voodoo service?"

She threw up her hands in a helpless gesture. "I'm sorry, Detective; I can't go by myself. You see, there was a black rooster in my yard this morning."

"A black rooster?" Rob echoed. He was frowning.

"Yes. It's the familiar of Maman Brigitte, the Loa whose emblem was placed on Dory's sidewalk. I'm afraid whoever is behind this killing is now targeting me."

"The sheriff's not going to let you go then," Rob said.

Wayne gave her a searching look. "Actually, you probably shouldn't go back there at all."

Wayne was surprised by the sadness he read in Evangeline's face. The Voodoo Village obviously had a strong hold on Counselor Bon Temps.

TWENTY-ONE

Sheriff Ben Bradley

THE GLOW FROM winning the election had worn off quickly for Ben, thanks to a lack of progress on the Canja case and their inability to get into Zoé's cellphone. As he sat at his desk, he wished he had gone out to the Voodoo Village with Wayne, Rob, and Evangeline. Four would be too many, but he wasn't accomplishing anything here. He felt a vibration and took his phone out of his breast pocket.

"Hi, Mae."

"Hi," his fiancée sounded breathless, "I have an idea about Zoé's phone—her code, I mean."

"You must be psychic, girl. I was just thinking about it," Ben told her.

"I'm not psychic. I just got my new phone, and I had to come up with a new passcode because it's a six-digit number instead of four."

"You're not running up credit card debt, are you?" He tried for a light-hearted tone and failed. "New outfit for election night, new phone...."

There was silence on Mae's end; then she cleared her throat. "No, don't worry. I was due for an upgrade anyway, and I paid cash for the outfit."

"That's good." Ben opened the Canja case file on his computer. "Anyway, Zoé's phone is older, so it's definitely a four-digit code. What's your idea?"

"I figure it's a date that has something to do with her mom. Maybe her mother's birthday, or the year of her disappearance. My old code was my birthday, but it sounds like Zoé was obsessed with her mother...."

Ben felt a surge of hope. "You could be right, babe. I'll get those dates." He scrolled down through his notes. "Hmm, let's see...here it is. Her mother, Laure, left twenty years ago, so 1994. I'll have Emma try that, and if it doesn't work, we can ask Mira Canja for Laure's birthdate. I'll let you know."

"Okay, hope it works! Bye."

Due to an ill-considered remodel in the '80s, it was necessary to exit the sheriff's office, go outside, and then reenter the building through the back door to get to the lab. Ben hurried through the reception area past a startled Sophie Coffin and was almost running by the time he hit the parking lot, cursing the rain. He slowed just a little at the lab doors and called for Emma as soon as he got inside.

"She's not here." Hadley Johns, Ben's senior CSI tech, unfolded his tall lanky frame from behind his desk and walked over to Ben. "Anything I can help you with, Sheriff?"

"I hope so. Do you know where Emma put Zoé Canja's cellphone?"

Hadley tilted his head to one side, lips pursed. "Last time I saw it, she had it on her desk. She tried a few codes with no luck. She knows if you try ten, and none of them work, the iPhone wipes its hard drive clean. The phone's probably in one of her desk drawers." He gestured to a desk opposite his own. "She just went out to lunch with Mark. Let's have a look. If we don't find it, I'll call her."

Ben and Hadley searched Emma's desk thoroughly.

There were numerous tools of the trade and various personal items, but Zoé's phone was nowhere to be seen.

"Should I call her?" Hadley closed the bottom drawer.

"No, I'll do it. You can get back to work." Ben retraced his steps around the building, shielding his face from the rain, and dialing Emma's phone. He hit the off button in disgust when it went to voicemail, burst back in the front door, and stopped at Sophie's desk.

She looked up at him with a slight smile. "Hello there, Sheriff. You should have worn a coat."

"Could you keep calling Emma Peters' cellphone? Maybe she'll pick up when she sees the office number. Patch her through to me when you get her, please."

She nodded her permed gray head and picked up the phone with customary efficiency. "I will."

Ben thanked her and went back to his office. Closing the door behind him, he started at the beginning of Zoé's file and read it through carefully. Nothing else was jumping out at him in the way of ideas for the code. *Damn it, what is taking so long?* His desk phone buzzed.

"Emma?"

"Yes, Sheriff Bradley, it's me. Sorry I missed your call earlier. I just—"

"That's all right," he broke in. "Do you know where Zoé Canja's cellphone is?"

"Umm, yes. It's in my purse," she said after a short pause.

"Mind telling me why? No, never mind. You aren't driving, are you?" He thought he remembered seeing her beat-up old Subaru in the parking lot.

"No. Mark picked me up for lunch. I thought he might have some ideas about the passcode."

"Try one-nine-nine-four. I'll wait."

A few seconds went by before Emma Peter's excited

voice came back on the line. "That's it. It worked! How did you know?"

Ben smiled. "It was Mae's idea—that's the year Zoé's mother disappeared. Listen, sorry to interrupt your lunch, but I need you to bring that phone back here right away."

"It's practically dead. Want me to pick up a charger first?"

"Good idea, Emma. See you soon."

He sent Mae a quick "You're a genius, code worked" text and got a smiley face in return; then Ben left his office in search of his deputies. He had an assignment for them. Before he reached George Phelps' desk, his cellphone rang again. This time it was Rob Fuller.

"Sheriff Bradley, we're going to need a search warrant for the area where they hold the Voodoo ceremonies, especially the little building that houses the altar. I found a bottle there labelled as belladonna. It could be the scopolamine Zoé was dosed with. The door to the building was open and the bottle was out in the open, so I took a picture."

"Wait, belladonna is scopolamine?" Ben asked.

"Yes. If I send this picture to your phone, could you start the warrant process? We're on our way back to the office. Should be there in twenty minutes or so."

Ben thought quickly. "Tell you what, Rob…send the picture to Dory's phone. She can work with Wayne on requesting the warrant. Sounds like you're more than halfway back, right?"

"Yes, sir. I'll send this to Dory with some notes right now."

Rob Fuller ended the call before Ben could relay the news about unlocking Zoé's phone. Pudgy, red-haired Deputy Phelps was in his office with the door open. He opened his mouth to ask a question but Ben held up a finger for him to wait and went past George's desk to talk to Dory.

"Rob's sending a photo to your cellphone, Dory. As soon as you get it, start developing a list of the probable cause points for a warrant to search the area where they hold the Voodoo services. Wayne will be back here in twenty minutes. Work with him on the argument. We need the thing airtight. And see what judge is available to sign it. We need it ASAP."

Dory pulled her phone out of her desk drawer and nodded. "Finally need my expertise on the investigation, I see. It's about time, Sheriff." She narrowed her eyes at him, but she was smiling. "There are two photos with a text here already." She gave a half smile, shaking her head. "Hope I can rustle up a judge on a Friday afternoon."

Ben smiled back at her. Besides being able to pass as a "mature" model, with her smooth caramel complexion and stylish outfits, Dory had worked in the office for decades and had connections throughout the community. "Thanks, Dory. I think I mentioned that my aunt, Judge Cochran, is on vacation right now, or I'd call her. One of the other judges should be around, though."

He turned back to George, his less-than-model deputy, who had followed him to Dory's office. "I need you to go to the Voodoo Village and ask Mira Canja to let you into Zoé's house. There are boxes of photo albums under the bed in the upstairs guest room, and a bunch of old postcards in one of the boxes. If it's okay with Ms. Canja, bring me those postcards."

George was shaking his head. "You want me to go

by myself? That's no place for a good Christian alone, you know."

Ben frowned. "This is non-negotiable, Deputy Phelps. I was planning to send Cam with you, but she's on patrol right now. I don't have anyone else available, and I'm busy. I'm sure your faith is strong enough to spend a few minutes in the village. This is a murder investigation, remember?" At George's terrified expression, he added, "You can take your gun, I guess."

"Really?" George perked up.

"No ammo, George," Ben said, wagging his index finger.

George stood, squared his unimpressive shoulders and gave a martyred sigh. "Guess I'll get going now."

"Now's definitely the time, George." Ben heard a suppressed giggle as he walked away, but he wasn't sure if it came from Sophie or Dory.

TWENTY-TWO

Mae December

MAE HADN'T BEEN entirely forthcoming with her fiancé about her finances when they'd spoken on the phone. While she had been due for an upgrade, and had indeed paid cash for her new clothes, she had received a windfall she hadn't told Ben about. Now she stood in her kitchen, watching Erzulie eat her second bowl of dogfood of the day, wondering again how to break the news. *Maybe I'll start by telling Tammy about it. She'll be happy for me.*

She called Tammy West, her best friend since seventh grade, but it went straight to voicemail. It was probably a sign. Ben really should be the first to know about her upgraded financial situation, even if it was going to be awkward telling him about it. He had told her once that if she had bad news for him, she should break it while he was chewing on a steak. Mae escorted Erzulie back to her puppies, grabbed her purse, and headed to the grocery store.

Ben got home after seven, full of good and bad news about the Zoé Canja case. He filled her in, between bites of salad. "Rob found a bottle of scopolamine out at the village, but he could only take a picture of it. Dory tried to get a warrant and couldn't find a judge to sign it—Friday afternoon, so nobody was available."

"That's too bad. When does your Aunt Cornelia get back from London?" Mae asked.

"My mom said late tonight. Hopefully we can get it signed tomorrow and have that bottle fingerprinted before someone gets rid of it." He stood up and carried their empty salad plates to the sink. "I thought about what you said—that Zoé was obsessed with finding her mother—so I sent George out to her house to get the old postcards. They were in a box under the bed the night Zoé's body was found, but George said they're missing. Mira only had one left. It's frustrating, but I can't do anything about it tonight. Want me to grill those steaks now?"

Mae smiled at her fiancé, still in uniform after a long day. "I'll do it. You can go change and then pour us some wine. The potatoes are done and I just need to steam the broccoli when the steaks come off the grill."

Erzulie and Cupcake followed her when she went outside with the steaks. Tatie followed Ben upstairs. It was dark already, and Titan and Tallulah, her two oldest dogs, were asleep in their beds in the laundry room. She put the steaks on and stood there, looking up at the star-filled sky. After a few minutes, Ben and Tatie appeared and he handed her a glass of the Cabernet she'd left out on the counter.

"Thank you." She gave him a kiss, and he responded enthusiastically. "About four more minutes and they'll be done. Did you get much from Zoé's phone?"

"We did. Now we need to track down her friend Ginny to explain some things about the message she left. At least we know her last name now. She's in Zoé's contacts as Ginny Burke."

Mae took a sip of wine, inhaling its blackberry aroma. "It's strange that Ginny hasn't contacted you, isn't it? If something happened to Tammy, I'd be in touch with the police right away, wanting to know how the investigation was going."

Ben laughed. "Wanting to take over the investigation, you mean. You didn't even really like Ruby Mead-Allison, but you got right in the middle of that case."

She opened the grill and took the steaks off. "They're almost done; just need to put foil over them and let them rest while the broccoli cooks." She gave Ben a sideways look. "I did find Ruby's body, after all. It wasn't like I was just being nosy, you know."

He held the door open for her. "Um-hum, I know." They went inside, followed by the dog procession.

"Would you put Erzulie in with her pups and close our dogs in the laundry room for the night? I'm going to trip over one of them and they'll get our dinner."

Ben nodded and returned to the kitchen after a moment, sans canines. He sat down at the counter and gave her a serious look. "You're right, though. It's weird that her friend hasn't come forward. She left a voicemail for Zoé that said she was going camping with Josh—must be her boyfriend—but it seems like she would be back by now." He cut a bite of steak and began to eat steadily. "This is great." After pausing for a sip of wine, he asked, "What's the occasion?"

Mae took a deep breath. "I have some news. I think it's good, but you might not."

He raised his eyebrows and continued eating, his dark blue eyes fixed on her.

"When you asked about my spending…well, you know the kennel business isn't all that lucrative."

"I know. I thought you must have sold some paintings."

Mae looked down and took a bite of her baked potato. "Not since September. I did sell something else, though."

"Now you're making me nervous. What did you sell?"

"There's a new music publishing company in Rosedale, and they contacted me a month ago about some of Noah's songs. One of the filmmakers they work with is making a movie—a murder mystery set in Nashville. They offered me thirty thousand dollars for his whole catalogue. I told them I'd think about it…then I asked Uncle Phil if he'd ever—hypothetically—sell his catalogue. He said he'd just license it to whoever wanted to buy it because recurring revenue is better than one big check."

Ben swallowed, put his fork down and stared at her. "A month ago? Why didn't you tell me?"

"With your reelection campaign going on, I thought you were stressed enough, Ben. And I was worried it might be uncomfortable for you."

"Because a sheriff doesn't make a lot of money like your first fiancé did? Give me some credit here; my ego isn't that fragile." He stood up and looked down at her, his expression hard to read. "I suppose Tammy and Patrick know all about it. I don't appreciate being the last person you tell."

Mae touched his arm. "I haven't told anyone else. For a while it didn't seem real, but I actually got a check last week."

"For how much?" One corner of his mouth went up.

"Five thousand," she beamed, "with more to come."

He stepped back. "How much more?"

"Well, I told them I also wanted a percentage from the movie revenues, and they agreed. If it does well, we could 'get a lot more.'"

Ben pulled her to her feet, grinning now. "You really

are a genius, like I said in my text. I can't believe you were nervous about telling me. And it's nice of you to say 'we could get a lot more,' but it's your money. Noah wanted you to have it, not me."

"Noah wanted me to be happy, and sharing it with you will make me happier than keeping it for myself. I thought about giving some to NB, for a college fund or something."

"NB...is that what they're calling the baby now?"

"It is. He's Noah's nephew, so I think that giving some of the money to him is the right thing to do."

"You always do the right thing; that's one of the reasons I love you," Ben said. "But I doubt Patrick and Tammy would accept. They have plenty of money from his trust."

"I know, they probably won't," Mae agreed. "I also want to start a college fund for Matthew, if you haven't already."

"When I sold my house and moved in here, I put a good amount of the profit into a tax-deferred college savings account for him. So thank you, but we'll have to do something else with the money."

"What do you think we should spend it on?"

He kissed her thoroughly. "I'd really like to spend the rest on an amazing honeymoon with you, Mae December."

TWENTY-THREE

Chief Detective Wayne Nichols

WAYNE AND BEN were once again discussing the question of whether they should ask Evangeline to attend the Voodoo funeral for Zoé Canja. Both men felt she would be the perfect person to observe and report back to them, but they were reluctant to put her at risk.

"Tell me again about this black rooster that appeared in Evangeline and Jason's backyard. What did she say about that?" Ben asked. It was Saturday, and the two men were having lunch at a local sandwich shop.

"Not much, really," Wayne said as he put extra mayo on his ham sandwich. "According to Evangeline, the black rooster is the 'familiar' of Maman Brigitte, one of the Voodoo spirits. She thinks someone from the Voodoo Village, probably the same person who put the design on Dory's sidewalk, has now turned their attention to her." He took a large bite.

"But this rooster...it was real, right? Not some sort of ghost or spirit?" Ben's forehead wrinkled in a perplexed frown.

"Right," Wayne said after he swallowed.

"So, it might've been an escapee from a farm or somebody who keeps chickens."

"It could," Wayne admitted, "but nobody in their neighborhood keeps chickens. I checked. And the nearest backyard chicken farm is fifteen miles away. I drove out there and asked the farmer if he had sold any black roosters recently. He said he only keeps Orpingtons. He showed them to me. They're gray and white speckled. There's a black chicken breed called Ameraucana, but he didn't know anyone who raised them around here."

Ben drummed his fingers on the restaurant table and took a sip of his coffee.

"We need to make a decision about this funeral in the Voodoo Village and who should attend," he said.

"Evangeline might feel more comfortable if her husband, Jason, went with her," Wayne suggested.

"That's a good idea. He's ex-military, isn't he? A Marine?"

"He is. If I'm not mistaken, he has a concealed carry permit. His Military Exemption would have allowed him to skip the eight-hour State training course, but he took it anyway. I think he was an MP in the service. He's a solid guy."

Having finished off his potato chips, Ben wiped his hands and his mouth with his napkin. "I'm reluctant to ask Evangeline to go, even with her husband, but we could really use her help. The Catholic ceremony is on Sunday?"

Wayne nodded and finished the final bite of his sandwich.

"I'd like Rob and Cam to go to that one. I particularly want them to look at the funeral guest book and bring it in as evidence once the service is over. Have them tell the Canja family that we'll return it later. Maybe Zoé's friend Ginny will show up. If they hang around the table with the guest book, they could ask her some questions.

We called Ginny's number, but it went straight to voice-mail. What're you working on right now?"

Wayne pushed his empty plate away. "Rob and I both screwed up on fully vetting Randall Perdue's alibi. Neither of us checked it carefully. According to Perdue, his cook left work around ten p.m. because he wasn't feeling well, and Perdue had to step in and finish up orders for the night. I'm going to talk with the cook and see what he remembers. I also want to find out when they close the kitchen. What are you focusing on, Ben?"

"I had an idea about the postcards Zoé got from her mother in the years following her disappearance from the village. I sent George out to the village to get them. There were quite a few in the box under Zoé's bed the night we found her body, but Mira said she only had one. I wanted to check them for fingerprints. If Laure Canja's in the system, we can possibly track her down that way, assuming she's still alive." He tapped his fingertips together thoughtfully. "Oh…we did get my aunt to sign a limited search warrant this morning, so Rob went to get the belladonna bottle."

Wayne folded his arms across his chest and leaned back in his chair. "Good, hope he finds it. And I did wonder what Marie was doing in Zoé's house when I was there last. She has no reason to be in there now that Mae has Zoé's dogs. Maybe she was after those post-cards." Wayne was thinking out loud. "Well, gotta go," he said, rising to his feet. "Thanks for lunch. I'll call you if I learn anything."

Ben nodded, a discouraged frown creasing his brow.

HALF AN HOUR later Wayne sat in his patrol car, consulting his notes on the man who cooked for Randall's Tavern.

His name was Carlos Rivera. He was pleased to find that the man still had a listed address and a land line. Wayne decided he'd drive over and talk to the guy. He always preferred a face-to-face interaction with any known associates of the victim.

The address was for a manufactured home park on the outskirts of town called Rosedale Estates, a new development. He drove slowly down several roads within the park until he found the Rivera residence at 1256 Gilmore Street. Pulling in to the short driveway, he parked beside a blue Saturn Vue. He knocked on the door and a little girl with shiny dark curls who looked to be around seven or eight answered.

"Are you Mr. Rivera's daughter, honey?" Wayne asked.

"Granddaughter," she replied, and turned to call out, "*Abuelo!*"

Carlos Rivera was short, round, and smiling. "Can I help you?" he asked, hitching up his jeans over a round pot belly. He had dark hair and eyes with large white sclera. His dark irises were completely surrounded with white, giving him a childlike aspect.

"I'm Detective Wayne Nichols with the Rose County Sheriff's Office. I have some questions for you. Could I come in?"

"*Sì*, come in, come in," he said. "Marisol, please bring your *Abuelo* and the Detective some coffee, will you? Just pour it from the thermos on the counter. Do you take it black, sir?"

"I do. Thank you, Marisol," Wayne said as the little girl scampered from the room. The front door of the manufactured home opened directly into the living room that was open to the eating area and kitchen. There were two chairs and a couch that faced a flat screen TV. A large crucifix hung on the wall behind the couch.

"Have a seat. What can I help you with, Detective?"

"As you probably know, we're investigating the death of Zoé Canja. She worked with you, I believe, at Randall's Tavern?"

A spasm of sadness crossed the man's face, and he turned away briefly. It took him a moment to regain his composure. "Yes, of course I knew Zoé. She was a fine young woman."

At that moment, Marisol came back into the room carefully balancing a tray with two mugs of coffee. She placed it on the coffee table between the men, spilling a little.

"Thank you, *mija*. That's fine," he told the child who was mopping up the coffee with a napkin.

"I thought her name was Marisol?"

"It is. *Mija* means little sweetheart in Spanish." Mr. Rivera smiled at her.

Wayne took a sip of the coffee and thanked Marisol, who left the room beaming.

"I need you to think back to October twenty-third. It was a Thursday night and you were supposed to cook at Randall's Tavern. According to Mr. Perdue, you left work early that night, around ten o'clock."

He shook his head. "Actually, I didn't work that night. I was on the schedule but I had a bad cold—sneezing and coughing. I won't prepare food when I have something I might give the customers. Mr. Perdue wasn't happy with me, but he knows I won't work at those times." A little trace of pride was in his tone of voice. "Ever since I found out Zoé had been killed that night, the events of the evening have been stuck in my head."

"So you didn't go in at all?" Wayne frowned. Randall Perdue told them he had taken over for the cook at ten o'clock. He had lied to them. "What time would your shift have ended that night? It's critical that we trace the whereabouts of everyone associated with the bar that entire evening."

"Are you suspecting me, Detective?" Carlos looked shocked. "I would never kill anyone. Even back on the farm I couldn't kill, not even a chicken. My father called me *cobarde*—it's Spanish for coward. I get sick when I see blood. And killing is a sin. It is written in the Bible. I cared about Miss Zoé. She had a hard life—no parents, and with Randall chasing her, always trying to touch her. It was disgusting."

"I see. So you were home all evening?"

"Yes, my wife, Juanita, is a nurse at the hospital. She came home early that night, around five, because I was sick. I was here with her the whole night."

"Fine," Wayne said, folding his small notebook and putting it in his jacket pocket. He would check with Mrs. Rivera, but it was just a formality. "One last thing. What time do you usually close the kitchen on Thursday nights?"

"If people are in the bar, we normally keep the kitchen open until one a.m."

"And who decides if there's enough business to warrant keeping the kitchen open?"

"Mr. Perdue does." Carlos Rivera's expression was serious as he looked at Wayne. "You should ask the dishwasher, Brandon Jenks. He's always there later than the rest of us. He'll know when Mr. Perdue left."

"I'll do that. Thank you for your time, Mr. Rivera." *I don't think anyone talked to the dishwasher yet.* He left his card with Carlos, asking him to call if he thought of anything that might be helpful. Back in his patrol car, he called Darnell, who said he'd text him the number for the dishwasher.

Wayne was driving when his cellphone buzzed with the text from Darnell giving him the dishwasher's phone number. He pulled over and called Brandon Jenks, who said his boss was there most of that night, but had stepped out for a while. When pressed to be more specific, he said Perdue was possibly gone for an hour or so around midnight. Wayne looked out the window of the car while he considered whether he needed to meet with the dishwasher in person. He decided not to. It was unlikely Jenks could be more precise about the times. His estimate of how long his boss was gone certainly wasn't definitive, but Randall Perdue might have had enough time to kill Zoé before coming back to the bar to lock up. He quickly called Ben's cellphone and told him what he had discovered.

"Do you think we have probable cause to bring Perdue in?" Wayne asked.

His boss gave a noncommittal "hmm."

"He lied to us about the cook leaving at ten," Wayne pressed his point. "The cook was out the whole night. And Randall's alibi isn't rock-solid." Wayne wondered again if he should talk to the dishwasher in person, but decided there would be time for that if their other leads came up dry.

"I just talked to Evangeline," Ben said. "She and Jason are going to the Voodoo service tonight. Rob and Cam are going to the service at the Catholic Church in Richfield tomorrow. I have a feeling that by Monday we may have a pretty good idea of who killed Zoé Canja. Then you can use your signature interrogation technique to get a confession."

Wayne felt his mouth crook into a fierce smile. "So you'll let me off the chain on Monday?"

"That's right." Ben laughed. "See you then."

"Looking forward to it," he told his young boss. "A lot."

TWENTY-FOUR

Mae December

ON SATURDAY MORNING Mae found herself at loose ends. Ben had gone to the office and she had already completed her kennel chores. Matthew was with his mother for the weekend and for some reason she didn't feel like painting. She was staring out her kitchen window when Erzulie nudged her leg. Mae looked down into a pair of golden-yellow eyes.

"You can't be hungry," she said. "You already had your eggs and you haven't nursed those puppies in two days."

The big dog sat down, regarding her unblinkingly. Tilting her head to one side, she made a sound deep in her throat that sounded like a question.

"Want to go for a run?"

Erzulie's tail thumped on the floor.

"All right, we'll go in a minute. First, it's time to relocate those puppies of yours out to the barn." *Maybe I'll feel more like painting when they're not tussling under my feet and chewing on my easel.*

After putting on shoes and her barn jacket, Mae opened the bottom half of the Dutch door to her studio. All four pups scampered over and she picked the two females up. In honor of their Voodoo heritage, she'd given them French names, which they had already learned.

Tucking Cosette under one arm and Felicity under the other she headed out to the barn. "Come on, Jacques. You too, Pierre." She made a kissing sound at the two males. Erzulie, who seemed to understand what Mae was trying to do, chivvied them along, and eventually the four puppies were ensconced in a large, straw-filled kennel.

Mixed-breed Snickers, Mae's only paying guest at the moment, started howling when the young Weimaraners began to growl and yip. Erzulie gave five loud barks, lashing them with her gaze. A hush fell over the barn and Mae looked at her with admiration. "That's some powerful juju—enough to quiet all of them. Good girl."

Sweeping the barn with another glance, Erzulie ran out into the yard. Mae filled water dishes for Snickers and the puppies, turned off the lights, and followed her. It was time to exercise that dog, before she took over the world.

AFTER HER RUN, Mae showered, dried her hair, and applied mascara and lip gloss. She dressed in jeans, a blue-green sweater, and brown boots. As often happened while she was outside, an idea had popped into her head. She'd been thinking about what would prevent Zoé's friend Ginny from coming forward. *I'd have to be in the hospital to keep me away if something happened to Tammy....* The stray thought gave Mae an idea. She inspected herself one last time in the mirror before going downstairs to make a call.

"Dr. Ingram," Lucy Ingram answered on the second ring. Then, obviously realizing the call was not a page, she said, "Hi, Mae." Not only was she a friend and neighbor, Lucy was Wayne Nichols' girlfriend and an ER physician at Rosedale General.

There was a long silence after Mae explained what

she needed to know. "I can't tell you who I've admitted to the hospital lately," Lucy finally said. She was apparently choosing her words with care. "That's a HIPAA violation." She cleared her throat. "The only thing I can advise you to do is call the hospital and ask to be connected to Virginia Burke's room. If she's there, and I'm not saying she is, the switchboard will connect you."

"Thanks, Lucy. I'll tell Ben if I find her."

"Good luck. Bye." She was gone.

Mae called the main line for the hospital and asked to be connected to Virginia Burke's room. "Please hold," the woman said.

After three rings, a youthful-sounding man said hello.

"Is this Ginny's room?" Mae asked, startled by the male voice.

"Yes. Who is this?"

"My name is Mae. I'm a liaison with the Rose County Sheriff's Office. We've been trying to reach Ginny for a while now. Can I talk to her?"

"It's about Zoé, isn't it?" He sounded even younger now, and very sad. "I'm sorry, but Ginny can't talk. She's got a broken jaw and some other injuries."

Mae thought fast. "If you tell me the room number, I can come there. Can she communicate at all? And who am I talking to?"

"This is Josh, her boyfriend. She can communicate a little bit—mostly she just nods or shakes her head to yes or no questions. We're on the orthopedic trauma floor, room three twelve."

"Thank you, Josh." Mae grabbed her purse and car keys. "I'll be there just as soon as I can."

She called Ben from the car. When he answered, her words came out in a rush. "I found Ginny. She's in the hospital and I'm on my way to talk to her right now. Do you want to meet me there?"

"What? Wait a minute. I'm with Emma and Hadley, going over some evidence that just came in. I'll send Dory to meet you, babe." He laughed. "You never cease to amaze me, but you'll have to fill me in later on how you figured this one out."

"That's fine. I'll call Dory. Could you text me the questions we need to ask?"

"Will do," Ben replied.

"I'll let you know what we learn. See you back at the house."

Mae reached Dory on her cell. "Can you meet me in the main lobby at Rosedale General? I found Zoé's friend."

"I'd love to," Dory answered. "But other than paperwork, your fiancé's been making me stay out of the case. Not sure I'm *allowed* to go."

"It was his idea, so I think you're allowed."

Mae heard a loud "Woo-hoo!" and smiled.

"I'm on my way," Dory declared. "See you in ten minutes."

MAE WAS LOOKING out through the glass doors of the hospital lobby when she saw Dory's red Thunderbird come flying in. Dory normally had good parking karma and today was no exception. She pulled neatly into a front row space that had just been vacated and entered the lobby at a fast clip.

"Hey, Miss Dory." Mae gave her a quick hug. "We're going to the third floor. Ben just sent an email to my phone with the questions he wants us to ask. Zoé's best friend Ginny and her boyfriend are both here."

The two women got on the elevator and Dory pushed the button for the third floor. She asked, "Should we each question one of them, or talk to them together?"

They got off the elevator and walked toward the nurses' station. "Let's play that by ear," Mae said. "They're not suspects, and we may need the boyfriend to help us communicate with her."

An older nurse with dark hair pulled back into a short ponytail adjusted her glasses and looked up from her keyboard at their approach. "May I help you?"

"I'm Mae December, and this is Investigator Dory Clarkson. We're here to see Ginny Burke in three twelve."

"Are you from the insurance company?" The nurse frowned.

"The Rose County Sheriff's Office." Dory started down the hall to the left. "Is three twelve this way?"

"It's the last room on the right." She looked at her monitor and then at Mae. "You've got fifteen minutes. Her nurse will be in to check her vitals and give her pain meds."

Mae nodded and followed Dory down the tiled corridor. She put her hand on Dory's arm as she was raising it to knock. "We've only got fifteen minutes, so let's talk to them together. When Ginny's nurse comes in, we can ask Josh—that's her boyfriend—to have coffee with us. Then we can ask him more questions if need be."

"Sounds like a plan." Dory knocked on the door and a young, blue-eyed man with cropped auburn hair, wearing tracksuit pants and a sweatshirt, opened it.

"I'm Josh Harnett. Come in." Josh held the door open with his right foot and shuffled out of the way so Mae and Dory could enter. He was on crutches with a pressure bandage on his right ankle and small cuts all over his face and hands, but he was in far better shape than the young woman in the hospital bed.

Mae and Dory exchanged a glance, then introduced themselves to Josh and Ginny. Ginny's brown eyes moved between their faces. Her jaw was bandaged and her right arm was in a cast from shoulder to fingertips. Her fine blonde hair fell limply to her shoulders.

"What happened to you?" Mae asked Josh.

"We went on the camping trip from hell." He laughed, then winced. "Oh, my ribs are sore. Actually, the camping itself wasn't too bad. We went to a campground in a state park in North Carolina."

"Excuse me," Dory interrupted, pulling a small recording device out of her purse. "Can I tape this for Sheriff Bradley? It's for the Canja investigation."

Mae looked quickly at Ginny to see her reaction. The injured girl blinked, her eyes glistening with tears. "We are so sorry about your loss, Ginny," Mae said.

Dory set the recorder on a metal shelf and pushed the record button. "So Ginny lost her phone—the first day, Friday, right?" Josh looked to Ginny for confirmation. She held up one finger on her left hand, presumably to indicate "yes."

"It must have fallen out of her pack, but we didn't have service out there anyway," Josh said. "So our phones weren't making any noise. We didn't realize it was gone until we stopped for the night." He cleared his throat and lowered himself into the room's only chair. "So…after that everything was fine for a few days; then a bear got into our food one night and we decided to cut the trip short." Ginny's expressive eyes widened at this, as did Dory's.

"Did the bear do this to you?" Mae asked.

"No. We went up a tree and waited until morning. I know that bears can climb trees. Fortunately, this one didn't. He left and we hiked out." He sighed and gestured at his bandaged ankle. "That's when I dropped my phone in a stream. Ruined it. I twisted my ankle trying to get it, so it took a long time for us to hike out. Ginny drove into Asheville and took me to an Urgent Care and they patched me up. We went to a hotel there, intending to spend the night, and that's when we called Ginny's mom and found out about Zoé."

Ginny blinked and made a whimpering noise as tears formed and fell unchecked, rolling over her bandaged lower face.

Josh continued in a quiet voice, his blue eyes resting sadly on his girlfriend. "We decided to come back that night. Ginny was driving, because of my ankle, and a semi-truck came across the median and hit us. We were almost home, so the ambulance brought us here. It's the closest trauma center."

Walking closer to Ginny's hospital bed, Mae touched her gently on the shoulder. Then she checked the email that Ben had sent to her phone. There were only four questions he wanted them to ask, and Josh had answered all but one. Taking a tissue out of the box on Ginny's bedside table, she put it in the girl's left hand. Ginny dabbed at her eyes and nose and looked at Mae expectantly.

"So now we know where you were, when you learned about Zoé, and why you didn't come forward to help us in investigating your friend's murder. We already knew about the message you left Zoé on the day you left to go camping. The sheriff wants me to ask you some questions about the document you saw on your boss' desk, was there a purchaser's name?"

Again, Ginny raised a single finger.

Dory put a notepad on the bed beside the battered girl. She placed a pen on top of it and stepped back. Ginny picked up the pen and in shaky capitals wrote two words: VALHALLA DEVELOPMENT.

"Thank you so much," Mae said, picking up the pen and paper as a male nurse entered the room. "Feel better, Ginny. We're both so sorry about your friend."

Dory switched the recorder off and put it back in her purse. Josh followed Dory and Mae out into the hall. "Do you need anything else?"

"Who does Ginny work for?" Mae asked.

"Main Street Realty, in Richfield. Miss December, do you know what's happened to Zoé's dog…and her puppies?"

Mae smiled at Josh. "I'm taking care of them for Zoé's grandmother." She took one of her business cards from her purse and handed it to him. "You and Ginny can come visit them when she's out of the hospital. Thanks for all your help."

TWENTY-FIVE

Evangeline Bon Temps

EVANGELINE HAD GIVEN much thought to the matter of attending Zoé Canja's funeral in the Voodoo Village. She wanted to help the sheriff's office, to find something that would bring Zoé's killer to justice. And, at a deeper level, she wanted to honor Zoé by being present at the final celebration of her life. She also felt it might be the last time she ever attended a Voodoo service.

She had been sitting in front of her muted television for over an hour when her cellphone rang. It was Ben Bradley, asking for her final decision.

"Hang on, will you?" Evangeline asked as Jason walked into the room.

"It's Sheriff Bradley on the line. He'd like me to attend Zoé's funeral, but I'm scared to go alone. That black rooster shook me up."

"Did you really think I'd let you go alone?" Jason asked. "Girl, if you're going, I'm going, too."

Evangeline listened as the sheriff talked about the need for them to be observant and careful.

"My husband runs his own company, you know. Cyber *and* personal security."

"Oh," Ben said, "that's all right then. But take care. Thanks, Evangeline. Bye."

She set her phone down on the couch and turned her

energies to reassuring Jason. "You know I'm not a fan of guns, but I'll make an exception tonight," Evangeline told her husband.

"Good." He gave her a half-smile.

THE SUN HAD already set, but there was a glow in the air and a slight breeze when Evangeline and Jason got into his car around seven that evening. Evangeline was dressed entirely in white; even her hair was covered with a white cloth. She wore white sneakers and a necklace of white cowry shells, a gift from her grandmother many years ago.

"It's a beautiful night for the service," Jason said, expertly shifting the gears on his bright yellow vintage Camaro as they drove away from their subdivision and headed toward the Voodoo Village.

"It's called a *fête mori*, Jason. A festival honoring the dead. I'm sure you remember attending the ceremony we held for my grandmother. It will be similar, with singing, special foods, dancing, and an invocation for the Loa to take Zoé's spirit into the next world."

"I remember that day well. It reminded me of the Mexican Day of the Dead."

"Yes, it's important that we remember those who came before us and that one day we will be with them."

"I'm fine with that part, Evangeline, but your grandmother's celebration was my first taste of Voodoo. It made me uncomfortable, as you know."

Evangeline nodded and took his hand. "I'm hoping we see something or someone that will help solve this murder, or I wouldn't have agreed to go. Stay close to me tonight."

"I'll be right beside you. What are we looking for? And how long do we have to stay?" Jason asked.

"These *fête mori* can last until dawn."

"We're definitely not staying out there all night." Jason frowned.

"No, but we'll stay a couple of hours. If we leave too soon it would be considered an insult. I'll let you know when it's been long enough."

"At least tell me they aren't going to sacrifice an animal."

"Such a sacrifice is mandatory," Evangeline replied. Her voice carried ominously in the darkness inside the speeding car.

JASON PARKED THE car in a field just outside the village. The moon was rising. The field held quite a few cars and they could hear the sound of drums resounding on the night air. The voice of a singer rang out. The cadence was rhythmic—with one voice calling and a response following—creating a melodic tapestry. Evangeline couldn't understand the words, but it was a melody she remembered from her childhood. Evangeline felt drawn to the people, the tradition and the ceremony, as if led forward by an invisible thread.

They reached the outskirts of the peristyle with its center pole, the *poto mitan*. For this night, it had been draped in black. Plants and flowers in pots interspersed with burning candles surrounded the beaten earth space of the peristyle.

"Is this outdoor space the temple?" Jason whispered.

"Yes," Evangeline replied in a low voice. "Voodoo ceremonies are almost always held outdoors. Libations must be given back to the earth."

Although there were many attendees, they moved back to make room for Evangeline to stand at the edge of the space. Jason stood behind her with his hand on her shoulder. A slim, white-robed girl came out of the darkness into the peristyle. She spun clockwise and then counter clockwise before placing a white candle on the ground and lighting it. Another woman blew cornmeal from her mouth, creating an intricate design on the ground.

"She's making the veve of Maman Brigitte, like the one on Dory's sidewalk," Evangeline whispered to Jason, who shifted his position, patting the inside breast pocket of his jacket where she knew he kept his gun holster.

A man came forward and lit a small fire of charcoal briquettes at the base of the *poto mitan*. Another woman presented a container of water to the cardinal points and then poured small amounts of the liquid into each, creating the axes along which the spirits would enter the sacred space. The drums beat louder and the tempo of the song increased. Simultaneously, both the singer and the drummers came to an abrupt stop. The people were silent; only their gleaming eyes showed in the dark.

A great stir ran through the assembly then, like wind blowing through a bank of rushes, and the Mambo, high priestess of Voodoo, emerged from the darkness and leapt into the center of the temple. She began to dance, rotating faster and faster. Her long red skirt flared out as she moved closer and closer to the fire. She was barefoot, and sparks hit the earth from the small blaze. Evangeline thought the Mambo must have stepped on some hot coals, but if so, she was past reacting.

The night wind rose and the trees wrestled in the dark sky. The moon showed her pale face from time to time behind the layers of clouds that raced across the sky. The priestess spun counterclockwise in a pirouette, hurtling around the peristyle, stumbling, falling. She called out, invoking the Loa with her body moving in a syncopated rhythm.

"The Loa have arrived," Evangeline whispered to her husband. She was trembling.

One by one, the Voodooists were seized by the spirits and danced wildly. The singer's voice was joined by a second singer and their harmony graced the night. The resonant pounding of the drummers was so powerful that it seemed to grab hold of the dancers, claiming their spirits. The Mambo danced for what seemed like forever and then staggered. She collapsed just as the Voodoo Priest darted forward to catch her. The spirit had left the Mambo's body. Evangeline knew that only the priests could handle the spirit's arrival and departure to ensure that nothing would put the dancers in peril.

Holding the priestess in his arms like a child, the priest moved closer to the firelight and began to speak. "This night we honor the spirit of our daughter, Zoé Canja."

Evangeline heard Mira begin to wail but couldn't see her among the sea of people dressed in white. "She has gone from this place into the spirit world. Tonight we celebrate her life and ask the Loa to take her spirit into the realm of the beyond."

Two men carried in a white stretcher, on which lay a photograph of the dead girl and a white box containing her ashes. They placed the stretcher atop the veve and moved back. The priest continued speaking, saluting the Loa the ceremony had invoked, especially Maman Brigitte and Baron Samedi. "Her family members will now come forward," the priest said.

Mira and Marie Canja entered the sacred space. Mira

seemed inert, boneless. Only her sister's arms kept her from falling. Both women were sobbing. The singer began a low keening, and Evangeline felt tears on her face. She found herself falling into Voodoo, into the deep dark night. She was pulled back from her absorption by Jason, who grabbed her abruptly by the arm. She shook her head, clearing her thoughts as one by one each member of the village solemnly stepped forward to pay tribute to the dead. Each took a lighted candle from a platter of votives held by a woman in white. The people holding the candles spaced themselves around Zoé's remains, creating an oval of glowing light. The drums beat so softly then, it was like breathing.

"Look at the house," Jason hissed and pointed at what she knew to be the home of the Voodoo priest and priestess. Upstairs a tiny blue light flashed occasionally. A person was walking from room to room. Evangeline caught a glimpse of a figure hesitating behind some sheer curtains. Then the light went out and they saw nothing else.

Falling to her knees, Mira moaned a ritual recitation to the Loa to take Zoé's spirit to the next world, the one that lies beyond ours—invisible to the living. The priest was holding a clear glass pitcher and pouring drinks into small cups. More women in white began moving among the celebrants, offering everyone a beverage. Evangeline reached for one but Jason took it, and a few minutes later surreptitiously poured it on the ground. He slipped the cup into his pocket.

"The priest's fingerprints are on this," he whispered to Evangeline, who nodded.

The drums rose to a crescendo and then stopped abruptly. The Voodoo singer, her voice harsh as a peacock's, began a plaintive hymn of supplication. The Mambo called out loudly, "Even as you see her, she passes beneath the earth."

The pallbearers lifted the stretcher with Zoé's picture and ashes on it above their heads and carried her out of the temple. A procession formed behind them.

"They're going to bury her cremated remains now," Evangeline told Jason. She moved to follow the retreating Voodooists, but Jason stopped her, pointing at the house. The back door opened, and a dark figure emerged on the stoop. Grabbing Evangeline by the hand, Jason darted toward the house. The man was still there when they arrived and grunted harshly as Jason wrestled him to the ground. Jason pulled him to his feet, holding his hands behind his back.

"Who are you?" Evangeline asked. When she held her burning candle up to the man's face, she recognized the old man she had seen in Marie Canja's house on the day of her first visit.

"I am Papa Febron," the old man declared proudly.

"What were you doing in that house?" Her voice was harsh. "Who killed Zoé Canja?"

"Go away, *blanc*. It's the job of the Bokor to punish the evil ones." He twisted out of Jason's grasp and fled into the night. Jason stood still, breathing hard. Evangeline's feet were rooted to the ground. She remained in that position for some time.

A few of the women returned and began getting the food ready. Evangeline could smell sweet potatoes, aubergines, and pumpkins cooking. One woman held a chicken in her hands, and with a quick swipe of the knife, cut off its head. Blood spurted on the ground.

"I think we've stayed long enough," Jason murmured. Evangeline nodded in agreement and he took her hand. Pulling her behind him, Jason moved through the white-robed women as if fording a river.

TWENTY-SIX

Sheriff Ben Bradley

BEN FINALLY FELT they were making progress on the Canja case with the scopolamine bottle and the one postcard George was able to retrieve being analyzed in the lab, enough so that he decided to spend a quiet Sunday at home with his fiancée. The early November weather was cooperating, sunny and cool. After a late breakfast of waffles, fruit, and bacon, he and Mae decided to get dressed and take a walk. Titan and Tallulah had no interest in long walks at their age, but Mae wanted to take Erzulie and Snickers, as well as Cupcake and Tatie. Ben watched Mae shimmy into her jeans in their bedroom and shook his head.

"What?" She pulled a long-sleeved, tangerine-colored Henley over her head and her blonde curls popped out, corkscrewing in every direction. "It's not like we haven't walked four dogs at once before."

"I know. But Erzulie and Snickers are both so big. They'll be much faster than our two shorties."

Mae's brown eyes sparkled. He loved the way she looked with no makeup, her hair tousled. "How about a short walk with Tatie and Cupcake," she said. "We'll take the other two on a hike this afternoon when it's a little warmer. After that breakfast I can use the exercise."

By the time they walked Tatie and Cupcake down their

driveway and to the corner of Little Chapel and River Road, the two short-legged dogs were panting.

"Guess they're ready to go home." He took Mae's hand in his and they headed back to their driveway. "We learned a lot about the case yesterday, but what we learned raised even more questions."

The tip of Mae's nose was pink and she sniffled in the cool air. "So, explain why you said Zoé's mother might have had something to do with her death, which is just a horrible thought."

"This has always seemed like a woman's crime to me, and I thought a mother would close the eyes of her daughter if she was murdered."

"Hmmm," Mae said, doubtfully. "So what have you got so far that points in that direction?"

"After we got the limited warrant, Rob got the bottle of scopolamine from the village. And George, believe it or not, got one of the missing postcards that Laure wrote to Zoé after she left the village. Wayne saw Marie coming out of Zoé's house a while ago. Turns out it was the day the Mambo asked for the postcards. She said she needed them for a ritual to find Zoé's mom."

"I'm with you so far," Mae said.

"So the postcards are gone, except for one that Marie kept in her pocket—smart woman. She gave it to her sister and Mira gave it to George. The lab is working on the postcard now. When the lab checked the fingerprints on the bottle of scopolamine, they matched the prints on Zoé's eyelids. Nobody in the system, though."

Mae frowned. "I don't see how this means Laure Canja is involved, Ben. She left here twenty years ago."

They started up the long, steep driveway to their

house. "There were four sets of prints on the postcard: Zoé's, which we got from her autopsy, two others probably belonging to Mira and Marie, and a fourth set that matches the ones on the bottle and on Zoé's eyelids."

"And you think this fourth set belongs to Laure Canja? But you don't have any proof, do you? They could be anyone's." Mae opened the front door and they went inside, unclipping the dogs' leashes and removing their coats. She looked at Ben, a frown marring the smoothness of her forehead. "If the fingerprints on Zoé's eyelids are Laure's, that would mean she was there that night. Why didn't anyone see her?"

"Or tell us, if they did." Ben's voice was grim.

Mae hung their coats on the rack by the back door. "Want some coffee?"

"Yes, please. It's cold out there." He looked at Cupcake and Tatie, sprawled, panting, on the floor. "Guess we could use some fur coats like these two."

Mae handed him a cup of hot, black coffee. "What are you going to do next?"

He sat down at the counter. Lost in thought, he burnt his tongue on his first sip. "Ow!" He blew on the coffee. "For a start, we need to get exclusion prints from the Canja sisters."

"Probably wouldn't hurt to get the Mambo's prints as well." Mae added cream and sugar to her coffee and took a small sip. "She *is* the one who wanted the postcards, right?"

Mae instincts had already helped them decipher the code for Zoé's phone. Then, after Ben got home last night, she had explained the intuitive leap that lead her to Ginny's hospital bed. Although her methods were a mystery to him, he knew better than to question her conclusions. Maybe he was wrong about Laure being involved in Zoé's murder. He really hoped so.

"I'll send someone out to fingerprint Mira and Marie tomorrow, and per your suggestion, I think we'll bring the Mambo in for questioning—get her fingerprinted too. Why do you think she might be involved?"

"I just can't see Zoé's mother, with all the guilt she must have felt about abandoning her six-year-old, being involved in her murder. Besides, as you've told me many times, you need opportunity, means, and motive to trap a killer. As I see it, Laure had none of those."

"Just when did you pass your detective's exam, Miss December?" Ben asked, amused.

Mae rolled her eyes and grinned.

AFTER LUNCH THEY ventured out again. This time Ben led the sleek and lovely Erzulie, and Mae walked the shaggy black-and-brown Snickers, a collie mix.

"She's a beautiful dog, isn't she?" Mae said looking at Erzulie.

"Oh no you don't. That innocent act doesn't fool me for one second, Mae December."

She giggled. "I have no idea what you mean."

"What I mean is that Erzulie needs to go back to Mira now that the puppies are weaned."

Mae nodded and was quiet for a few minutes. They walked on, and Ben savored the autumn breeze and Mae's seeming acceptance of returning Erzulie.

"But what if Mira doesn't want her back?" Mae asked. "Couldn't we keep her?"

"Absolutely," Ben winked. "We'll have five dogs in the house just as soon as you learn how to put the Voodoo on me. Maybe you can get Mira to teach you. But it'll have to be some pretty strong Voodoo to talk me into that."

"Five Dog Voodoo." Mae smiled. "I'll see what I can do."

101

me. Maybe ... on can get Mrs. so-and-so ... loo, if I have
to be some pretty simple Vaudoo to talk me into that?"

"You'd ... Voodoo." Max chuckled. "I'll see what I
can do ...

TWENTY-SEVEN

Chief Detective Wayne Nichols

WAYNE FOLLOWED EVANGELINE BON TEMPS' trim figure into
the conference room at seven thirty on Monday morning, surprised to see Ben already seated at the head of the
table. Dory, Cam, and Rob were all in their accustomed
seats, and even George was present and in uniform. The
mood was somber. Nobody had brought donuts. Wayne
pulled out a chair for Evangeline and then sat down with
a nod to the sheriff.

"Good morning, everyone," Ben said. "Ms. Bon
Temps, thank you for coming. The purpose of this meeting is to get everyone up to date on the investigation of
the murder of Zoé Canja." He stood and pointed to the
white board where the timeline for the last day of Zoé's
life was outlined. "We purposely did not put up any pictures of the girl *after* her death. I want all of us to remember her as she was in life, a beautiful, family-oriented
girl who worked hard and tried all her life to locate her
missing mother, Laure." The sheriff pointed to the picture of Zoé sitting in her mother's lap. She looked about
six years old.

"I would also call your attention to the pictures of the
Voodoo Village on the right-hand side. The photo on the
left shows Zoé entering her house."

While the staff looked at Don December's photos of

the village, Mrs. Coffin entered the room silently, distributed cups, and poured coffee.

"Now, I'd like everyone to imagine Randall's Tavern on Zoé's last night working there. It's a blue-collar bar that employs a cook, Carlos Rivera, two waitresses—Jeannie and Caroline—a dishwasher, and two bartenders. Zoé was the head bartender and by all reports virtually ran the place. On October twenty-third, Zoé's friend Ginny Burke left her a message about a developer buying land that she thought included the Voodoo Village. Later that night, Zoé overheard a conversation between three men seated at the bar. They were discussing the purchase of a large tract of land in Rose County. At one point Zoé overheard the words 'Voodoo Village' and realized they were talking about buying and tearing down her entire town. With the exception of a few of the houses, all the land belongs to the Voodoo priest, the Houngan, and his wife, the Mambo. Evangeline, even though most of us already understand why you were brought in to help with this case, could you please explain your history with Voodoo and why this purchase would have been so devastating to Zoé."

Evangeline Bon Temps straightened her shoulders and took a sip of coffee. She wore a black-and-white patterned dress with a black suit coat. After briefly touching her throat, she began to speak.

"Certainly. Good morning, everyone. As most of you know, I'm a family attorney in Rosedale. I handle mostly domestic matters—divorce, pre-nuptial agreements, child custody—and do some estate work as well. Before I moved to Rosedale with my husband Jason eight years ago, I lived in New Orleans, where I went to college at Xavier University and law school at Tulane. My mother is a famed Voodoo singer and I was introduced into the religion at an early age."

Cam crossed herself. George made a faint sound, and when Wayne looked at him, he was very pale.

"It's important to understand that Voodoo is an ancient religion. Some estimate, conservatively, that it has existed for ten thousand years or more. But Voodoo is more than a religion; it's a way of life that encompasses every aspect of one's existence from before birth and long after death. Voodoo adherents believe in spirits called Loa, which are consulted on matters of daily life. Once a Voodoo colony has been established for some time, most adherents believe the Loa cease to wander the earth and become settled. Our Voodoo Village has existed in one form or another in the same general area of Rose County for over a hundred years. It once burned to the ground and was once moved because of river flooding, but everyone who lives there now was either born there or came as a young person." Evangeline took a sip of her coffee.

"Although the Voodoo Village is a curiosity to most of us, to the people who live there it's a paradise, a sacred space of safety and community. To have the houses bulldozed, the sanctuary destroyed, and the land sold is the most awful desecration imaginable. And the town exerted even more of a magnetic pull for Zoé Canja because she believed that her mother, Laure, would return someday. She could not leave, not ever, in case that happened."

Wayne was entranced by Evangeline's powerful narrative. Although he had solved many murders, most of the time he concentrated on the perpetrator. This was one of the few cases where it was the victim he saw day and night in his mind.

"Thank you, Evangeline," Ben said. "I believe everyone here knows that Zoé left Randall's Tavern around eleven o'clock on the night of October twenty-third. She drove straight home, parked her car in the outbuilding behind her house, and left her phone in the car. After that, she either took scopolamine or was dosed with it by someone else. The amount she had in her system would not have killed her, but it almost certainly would have rendered her unconscious."

Ben paused, glanced at the pictures of Zoé and then went on in a quiet voice, "Sometime after that, she was strangled with a red scarf and buried in a shallow grave in the woods behind her house. The scarf itself must have been carried off by the wind, because it was found snagged on thorns some distance from her body. After she was killed, someone closed her eyes. The lab was able to get a partial print from her eyelids, but there were no hits on AFIS. Whoever felt badly enough about Zoé's death to close her eyes is not in the system.

"We have three prime suspects in this case. They are the Houngan, the Mambo, and Zoé's boss." Ben nodded at Wayne. "Detective Nichols will review what we know about our third suspect."

Wayne scanned his notes as he stood up and walked over to the white board. Pointing to a picture of the man, he said, "Randall Perdue, the owner of Randall's Tavern, has been Zoé's employer since she was eighteen. Mira Canja, Zoé's grandmother, said he was obsessed with her, and several people have corroborated that. There's evidence that he stalked Zoé. She rejected him repeatedly, but according to Darnell, the other bartender, she was tactful about it. She didn't want to offend her boss and lose her job. Randall's alibi for the night in question is that he had to take over for the cook who was ill. He claimed that he was in the kitchen until closing. However, according to the dishwasher, Brandon Jenks, Randall wasn't in the kitchen the entire time. He was gone for about an hour or so around midnight. So he could have followed Zoé to the Voodoo Village and killed her before returning to the bar." Wayne resumed his seat.

"Thank you, Detective." Ben turned to Evangeline. "Could you please tell us about the Voodoo service for Zoé you attended on Saturday night?"

"Yes." She cleared her throat. "I went with my husband, Jason, and it was a lovely final tribute. In recent visits to the village, I got the distinct impression I wasn't welcome. That was difficult for me because I still miss some elements of Voodoo, especially being part of that community." Evangeline closed her eyes for a moment and laid a hand on her breastbone. Picking up the thread of her account, she continued, "Nonetheless, I chose to attend in hopes of seeing something that would be of help in catching Zoé's killer. Two things of note happened. Drinks were passed around by the Houngan, who poured a clear liquid into each cup. Jason took his cup, poured the liquid on the ground, and put it into his jacket pocket. It had the Houngan's fingerprints on it and I gave it to Wayne yesterday so he could take it to your lab."

"Excuse me, Evangeline," Wayne said. "I'm sorry to interrupt, but we ran those prints through AFIS. We didn't get a hit on him in the FBI database, but found something from Interpol. The Houngan came to the States from Haiti in the 1980s as a child. He inherited the land from his childless uncle who was the Houngan then. While in Haiti he was arrested for breaking and entering, but was never convicted. He has a thorough knowledge of the Voodoo ways, so he must have apprenticed as a Houngan in Haiti."

It was clear from Evangeline's face that she hadn't known about the man's criminal background and that it troubled her. Wayne touched her arm gently. "I'm sorry I wasn't able to tell you earlier."

"Evangeline, you said there were two things that happened at the Voodoo funeral?"

"Yes, Sheriff. During the service, we noticed a little blue light bouncing around the upper floor of the Houngan and Mambo's house. When the intruder came out, Jason tackled him."

At this, Dory pumped her fist in the air. Cam clapped quietly.

"While Jason held him down, I asked who he was and if he knew who killed Zoé Canja. His name is Papa Febron. He's the same man Dory saw with the legal papers the first time we visited the village. Papa Febron told us to leave. He said the Voodoo court would punish the wrong-doers. Strict Voodoo believers hold no respect for the white man's law." Evangeline smiled a little pensively as she said these words.

"Thanks, Evangeline. We'll check him out. Now, Cam and Rob, you attended the Catholic memorial service in Richfield at St. Francis yesterday, right?"

"We did, Sheriff," Cam said. "The priest gave a nice eulogy about Zoé and her quest to find her mother. There was a soloist who sang a French funeral song and a song from the musical *South Pacific*. Translated, it means, 'Tell me why, oh why, my life is wonderful. Could it be, possibly, that you love me?' Mira Canja told me it was a song Laure taught Zoé when she was just a little girl. We were trying to locate Zoé's friend Ginny and hoped to see her there. However, we now know that she couldn't have attended because she was in the hospital. We got permission to bring the guest book back here. I copied it and returned the original to Father Thomas yesterday evening."

Cam turned to Rob, who continued, "Although the turnout was light, Randall was there. Cam and I talked to him as he was leaving the service. He seemed uncomfortable and was in a big hurry to get away. On another point, our George here was able to get one of the postcards Laure sent to Zoé."

"Good work, George," Ben said, and George reddened.

A scowl marred Rob's boyish face. "Apparently the Mambo asked Marie Canja to bring her those postcards. She said she needed them for a ritual that involved burning them, apparently in an attempt to locate Laure."

Evangeline waved her hand in the air. "Excuse me, Rob, but there's no such ceremony in Voodoo. They would consult the Loa for such a search or perhaps do the string-tying ceremony that connects the soul to the body, if the person is alive."

Rob raised an index finger, indicating he wasn't done. "We were lucky that Marie found the Mambo's request suspicious and slipped one of the postcards into her pocket," he said.

At these revelations, everyone in the conference room was quiet for a bit. Finally, George said, "So this Mambo woman destroyed evidence?" He looked at the sheriff with wide eyes.

"She did," Ben confirmed. "Luckily not all of it. We need to get fingerprints when we bring her and the Voodoo priest in for questioning. The Houngan's prints don't match any of the ones on the postcard, the scopolamine bottle or Zoé's eyelids, but Wayne and I definitely suspect him of being involved. I'd also like to get exclusion prints from Mira and Marie Canja. Dory, please tell everyone else about your meeting with Ginny Burke and her boyfriend Josh."

Restless after the long meeting, Wayne tuned out Dory's account of how Mae had located Ginny and their subsequent interview. He leaned closer to Ben and said quietly, "Do you want me to start rounding up suspects?"

His boss gave a sharp nod. "Bring them in, Wayne," was all he said.

TWENTY-EIGHT

Mae December

BEN'S SIDE OF the bed was cold by the time Mae woke up on Monday morning. Today was the day she had agreed to return Erzulie to Mira Canja, and she was dreading it. The puppies were weaned, but Mae had become attached to the mother dog and was saddened at the thought of saying goodbye to her. She lay in bed for a few minutes longer and then put her bare feet on the cool wooden floorboards of her room. She wrapped herself in her robe and went downstairs, shivering a little. The weather had turned the corner toward winter. It was time to light the furnace.

She picked her cellphone up off the kitchen counter and checked her messages. There was a "What are you doing today?" text from her mother that gave her an idea. *Maybe Mama will go with me to take Erzulie back.*

"Good morning, sweetie," Suzanne December answered on the first ring. Much more of a morning person than either of her daughters, she sounded alert and wide awake.

"Morning, Mama. I saw your text. I've got to take Erzulie back to the Voodoo Village today and I was wondering if you'd like to ride along with me. I could use the company."

"Absolutely," her mother answered. "What time are you going to leave?"

"Around eleven. I'll text you when I'm leaving here and come pick you up."

"Great, see you soon." She was gone.

As Mae sipped her first cup of coffee, she got food and water for her dogs and Erzulie, who all ate quickly. Then she released them into the frosty backyard. She watched from the doorway, and when they had all relieved themselves, she called them back in. After a bowl of cereal and another cup of coffee, she went to the mechanical closet off her laundry room. She lit the pilot light, set her hall thermostat to heat, and cranked it up. The first stirrings of warm air began to emerge from the vents, accompanied by a hot, dusty smell. Mae went back upstairs to take a hot shower and put on warm clothes before going out to the barn.

THE PUPPIES AND SNICKERS, her only boarding dog, were in fine spirits, and after she fed and watered everyone and cleaned the kennel that the little Weimaraners had completely trashed, she went back to the house. It was time to get Erzulie loaded into the car, along with the surprise she had for Zoé's grandmother.

At ten forty-five she texted her mom that she was on her way and pulled out of her driveway onto Little Chapel Road. Erzulie sat up tall on the backseat. Mae could see her in the rearview mirror, golden eyes fixed on the barn where her puppies were. As they turned the corner, the big, gray dog whimpered and then lay down with a sigh.

Ten minutes later, Mae pulled into her parents' driveway. Her mother was out of the front door like a shot and climbed into the passenger seat with a smile. "Beautiful day for a drive," she said. "Thanks for inviting me."

Mae looked at her mom, so pretty with her sparkling brown eyes and smooth dark hair with a sheen of silver. "You look cute, Mama. Is that a new coat?"

Suzanne December fastened her seatbelt, looking down at the caramel leather jacket she wore with jeans and a green sweater. "Not at all," she laughed. "It's really old. I was cleaning out the guest-room closet and I found it."

Mae drove out of her parents' neighborhood and headed toward the Voodoo Village. "You're in a good mood," she said.

"I am," her mother agreed, reaching in the back to pet Erzulie. "I got my next three 'Suzanne About Town' columns done yesterday, so I now have some time to do what I want around here. Your sister told me it's called a stay-cation." Mae could feel her mother's keen eyes on her. "You, on the other hand, don't seem like you're in such a great mood."

Mae shook her head. "Nope. That's why I wanted company on this errand. I know it's silly—she's not my dog—but I'm going to miss her."

"You've been this way your whole life, Maeve Malone. Never enough animals for you. You've got the puppies for a few more weeks, don't you? And didn't your fiancé just win reelection? All in all, things are going well for you."

It's true. I need to cheer up. And Mama doesn't even know about my little windfall. Mae filled her mother in on that good news, and the rest of the trip went by quickly. She paused her Explorer at the top of the hill overlooking the village.

"Don't you just love this view?" Mama asked. "I'm

surprised Ben let you come out here without a police escort, by the way."

"We talked about it. He said as long as we didn't leave Rosedale before ten, there'd be plenty of law enforcement here when we arrived." She drove down the hill and parked in front of Marie Canja's turquoise house, right next to the Rose County Sheriff patrol car. "I think we'll be safe." She looked back at Erzulie. "You're home, girl." The big dog was cowering on the seat, making herself as small as possible.

"She looks terrified," Mae's mother said. "Poor thing."

Mae got out, opened the back door and attached Erzulie's leash to her collar. "Her food's in the back. Can you get it, please?"

Her mother popped open the hatch and gasped. "Why is this painting back here? This is breathtaking, by the way."

Mae was trying to coax Erzulie out of the car, but she wouldn't budge. "Thanks, I'm quite happy with that one. I'm giving it to Mira." She gave up on getting the dog out and closed the car door. "Let's take her food and the painting in and see if Mira or Marie can persuade her to leave my car. Hi, Cam. Hi, George."

The two deputies, who had just emerged from the car, greeted Mae and her mother.

"I love that painting!" Cam exclaimed. "Can George and I give you a hand with that, Mrs. December?"

"Call me Suzanne," she said briskly. "And if you have a minute, we'd appreciate some help." She handed the large bag of dog food to George and gestured at Mae and Cam to take the painting. Walking toward the front door, she asked over her shoulder, "What brings you out here today?"

Mae laughed. Mama's journalist instincts had obviously kicked in. She winked at Cam.

"Sheriff's office business, ma'am. Can't talk about it," Deputy George Phelps said officiously.

Suzanne raised one elegant brow and tapped on the orange-painted door. "That's fine," she said. "Even though my daughter is marrying the sheriff, I'm sure you can't tell us anything."

George blushed but didn't say another word.

"We're just doing some evidence collection, Suzanne," Cam said smoothly. "We'll stay in the car while you're here. Call my cellphone if you have any problems, all right, Mae?"

"I will. Thanks, Cam."

George put down the bag of dog food and the deputies went back to their car as Marie answered the door.

"Hello," she said, but her eyes were not welcoming.

Mae and her mother exchanged glances. "Hello, Marie, do you remember me?" Suzanne asked. The woman nodded, unsmiling, and Suzanne soldiered on. "This is my daughter, Mae. We're returning Erzulie to Mira. Is she here?"

Marie turned and walked back into the house. Mae and her mother followed, carrying the painting upright between them. There was a choked cry from the kitchen as Mira caught sight of the painting.

"My Zoé! Oh, did you bring that for me?"

They leaned the painting against the wall. "I did, Ms. Canja," Mae said with a smile. "I wish she'd been coming out the door in the photo, instead of going in. Then I could have painted her face."

Mira stared down at the painting, her gaze soft and unfocused. "No," she shook her head. "This is right...she is

LIA FARRELL   205

going inside, where she thought she would be safe. Come
and look, Marie. Look at what this girl made for me."

Marie took her sister's hand and together they gazed
quietly at the painting. Mae blinked back tears. She heard
a sniff from her mother and cleared her throat.

"I'm so glad you like it," she said. "Erzulie's in the
car. If you could help me get her out, I'd appreciate it."

Mira tore her eyes from the image of her granddaughter and dropped Marie's hand. She gave Mae a short,
fierce embrace. "Yes, yes. Of course we will help you."

Erzulie was still reluctant, but eventually she suc-
cumbed to Mira's cajoling and went into the house with
the Canja sisters. Mae carried her food in and told Mira
that she would be back in a few weeks to bring her the
money after the puppies were sold. As Mae and her
mother said their goodbyes, Marie, Mira, and Erzulie
didn't seem to notice. They simply stared at the painting.

TWENTY-NINE

Chief Detective Wayne Nichols

WAYNE WAITED IN the patrol car while his partner, Detective Rob Fuller, walked up the courthouse steps to get the expanded search warrant. According to Mrs. Coffin, it had been executed and was waiting in the chambers of Judge Bryant. Wayne felt a rush of adrenaline. He was itching to get Zoé Canja's killer in their interrogation room. He could feel the pressure to lock the bastard up building inside his body. He flicked the radio on and then turned it off again. Finally, he got out of the vehicle. Taking deep breaths to calm himself, Wayne leaned against the car until he saw Rob's thin frame emerge from the portico of the courthouse.

As Rob walked out, he flashed Wayne a quick thumbs up indicating that he had the warrant—that little piece of paper that would allow them to officially search the residence of the male and female religious leaders of the Voodoo Village. He had a feeling today was the day they would close the case.

"Any problems, Rob?" he asked as the young detective climbed into the shotgun seat of the car.

"Nope, just had to wait while the clerk logged it into their system. Judge Bryant strongly supports law enforcement. He doesn't dick around asking a bunch of questions like some of them do—like Judge Cochran, the sheriff's aunt, does sometimes."

Wayne backed out onto Main Street and drove toward the Voodoo Village. He hit the gas before he got to the city limits sign, urgency driving his heel down. "She's a stickler, all right, but I've learned a lot about probable cause from her. And she did give us the limited warrant so you were able to get the bottle of scopolamine finger-printed before anyone could destroy it."

Rob glanced at the speedometer, then looked at him with wide eyes.

Smiling, Wayne dropped his speed slightly and said, "I wrote up the request for Judge Bryant listing any bot-tles of Voodoo Love perfume as well as the legal docu-ments pertaining to the million-dollar Offer to Purchase the land the Voodoo Village sits on. I included the infor-mation that it's the priest who owns the property. I also included a description of the Voodoo symbol on Dory's sidewalk and the black rooster that was planted in Ms. Bon Temps' yard, warning both women to stay away. The symbol and black rooster had to have come from someone in the village. All of that must have been suf-ficiently convincing, because I didn't get a call asking for more information."

They hit the freeway ramp, gravel spraying from the tires. Rob said, "I know that private citizens whose homes and offices are being searched can challenge probable cause for the warrant, but since the Voodoo priest wasn't there when the warrant was issued, we should be good. What are we looking for today, specifically?"

"This warrant's broader in scope, so just trust your gut. If something strikes you as funny or out of place, signal me and we'll both look at it. Obviously, any documents relating to the property or any other legal papers, any additional scopolamine bottles and Voodoo Love perfume need to come with us."

They were quiet until Wayne turned onto the gravel road and then braked abruptly to head down the tiny lane, its tall dried grass topped with white seed heads on each side. Oak and pecan trees bordered the trail that turned and twisted back and forth, finally rising up a hill. When they reached the crest of the rise, the Voodoo Village lay in a green bowl of fields below them. The bright colors on the houses made Wayne think of a set of blocks a child could use to build a little play town. He took a deep breath, dampening the urge to pick a fight that always rose inside him when he was near to closing in on a killer. He didn't want to be accused of using excessive force.

THEY PULLED UP in front of the home of the priest and priestess of Voodoo, directly across the street from Zoé's house. Unlike any of the other houses, the Voodoo priest and priestess' house was painted white. The shutters on the windows were in the colors of the other houses on the street—reds, blues, and purples. They got out of the car and strode up an old brick walkway. It was uneven and grass had shouldered up between the bricks. Rob had the warrant in his hand. Wayne knocked on the front door and a woman answered.

"Yes?" she asked. Although she could have been anywhere between her forties and early fifties, she was slim and attractive. Her hair was arranged in tiny tight braids tied into a thick ponytail with a green and gold cloth. She wore a loose caftan and her small brown feet were bare.

"What is it?" she asked in a honey-smooth voice, surprisingly deep for a petite woman.

"My name is Wayne Nichols and this is my partner, Rob Fuller. We're detectives from the Rose County Sheriff's Office investigating the murder of Zoé Canja. We have a warrant to search your home."

The expression on the woman's face, which had been neutral, changed abruptly. Something flashed quickly across her fine mahogany features—emotions Wayne read as fear and then resignation. She stepped back, and although she didn't invite them in, she opened the door wider. Both men came inside.

"Would you tell me your name, please, ma'am?" Wayne asked, gesturing to Rob, who was poised to enter the information, tablet in hand. "We need it for the record."

"My name is Ardra Flambeau." She stood taller and said, "But I am known as the Mambo. I have earned the *asson*, the sacred rattle of Voodoo, and have risen to the level of priestly authority." Pride seemed to emanate from her with these words.

"What should I call you, ma'am?" Rob asked, politely.

"You may call me Mambo," she said and smiled briefly. The smile did not reach her large eyes.

"We would like to be taken to the Hounfour, if that is all right," Rob asked tentatively. "I understand Hounfour is the name for the sanctuary where Voodoo ceremonies are held. Is that correct?"

"Yes, but you have been there before," the Mambo gave the young detective a sharp glance, "when you took my belladonna."

"I have, yes, ma'am, I mean Mambo. I knocked on the door but no one answered, so I left the warrant and went around back."

She gave a short and humorless laugh. "There's noth-

ing left there that would interest you, but I'll show you
the way. Follow me."

The detectives walked behind her through the house.
Wayne paused for a moment in the kitchen, looking at
a shelf full of thin bottles with hand-drawn labels with
words like Ogoun, Legba, and Ghede. The bottles contained what looked like creamy lotions. He wondered if
the kitchen served as a small shop where religious adherents could buy supplies. Although the wares were different, he had seen many such shops near Catholic churches
and Jewish synagogues.

The house was very old. The kitchen cabinets had
been painted many times and most of the doors and drawers didn't close properly. Some were askew, slightly open.
The countertops were a tired yellow laminate, rubbed off
in some places where the surface had been scrubbed for
decades. Through an east-facing window, light shone in
at a slant, making squares of brightness on the stained
linoleum floor.

They exited through the screen door at the back of
the house and walked out into a patio space surrounded
by trees. A young girl dressed in white was sweeping
the earthen floor. The Mambo spoke to her quietly and
she set aside her broom and departed, moving silently
between the trees. There seemed to be three exits from
the area, really just paths between the unusual trees. The
openings corresponded to the directions of east, west,
and south. The altar itself was in a small building on
the north side.

"All this is sacred space, gentlemen," the Mambo said,
raising her arms to encompass the air around them. "Our
home, the Houngan's and mine, the ceremonial space…
even the trees are sacred here. They are Mapou trees.

When a Mapou tree is full grown, the trunk will expand to hold vast amounts of water. The blessed Loa enter our ceremonies from their customary places above our earthly realm."

"Tell me about the Loa," Wayne said quietly. The woman interested him, and he wanted to build trust between them. There was a story here and he wanted to hear it. The key to the information this woman held was almost certainly her pride in her role as Voodoo Mambo.

"The Loa are divine quintessence that manifest themselves in the mounting of those who summon them. We call them with dance and song." She swayed a little as if beginning a dance, one she had done many times before.

Wayne narrowed his eyes, watching her. He found the woman charismatic and compelling. He had met a very old Native American woman once who had a similar presence. He forced himself to remain silent. He wouldn't ask for any more information here, not on her turf. If there was sufficient cause to take her into the office, he would wait until then to ask any more questions. Here the Mambo was in her element; all the power was hers.

ROB PULLED ON his latex gloves and approached the little white altar building. He pushed the door farther open and looked inside before turning to Wayne and shaking his head.

"There's nothing here." He frowned. "It's empty."

"We'd like to see your bedroom now, please, Mambo," Wayne said. The woman glanced obliquely at him before reentering the house. When she turned her large amber eyes on him, Wayne felt his spine tingle, as if he were in the presence of a powerful magnetic field. He tried to make eye contact with her, but she veered away, leading them toward the staircase. As she led them upstairs, he noticed that she forked her fingers at him behind her back. It was an old superstition supposed to keep a threat at bay. A protection against *malchance*, he thought, remembering the French word and the Canadian woman who had taught him the gesture.

The Mambo ascended the staircase to a single large room on the top floor. Wayne and Rob followed. They entered a bedroom with four dormer windows and a fine view over the tops of the trees that ringed the Hounfour and the harvested fields of maize and sweet potatoes that surrounded the village. The large bed was covered with a quilt created from many different-colored scarves sewn together. Wayne remembered the red scarf that Rob had pulled from the blackberry canes the night they found Zoé's body. He wondered if it had come from this room and had belonged to this woman.

An elegant French dressing table and bench stood on the east wall in front of a large mirror. Wayne had seen something similar in a wealthy old woman's house. She called it a vanity. The piece of furniture had a glass surface, and many bottles of lotions and scent stood in front of the mirror.

"Do you use perfume?" Wayne asked, and the Mambo walked to the dressing table and picked up an elegant cut crystal decanter. Using her left hand, she pulled the stopper from the top with a little popping sound. The distinctive odor of Voodoo Love floated in the air—pungent, almost palpable.

"Voodoo Love," Wayne said, and the Mambo nodded. She was definitely left-handed. It was nearly automatic, this registering of which hand was dominant. He wondered if the ME could have told him whether the person who strangled Zoé Canja was right or left-handed. He couldn't remember that information being in the report and felt infuriated with himself. He glanced at the Mambo's arms, slim and smooth. He wondered how strong she was.

Seeing the perfume in the Mambo's hand, Rob's posture had changed. He looked alert as a pointer dog standing with a raised paw in front of a hidden covey of quail. Detective Fuller held out a gloved hand. "I'll take that, if you don't mind. Where's your husband?"

"Not here," the Mambo smiled, head tilted to one side. They hadn't seen any sign of him. Wayne wondered if he had fled, knowing the law was closing in. "He will return," she said in a defiant tone, as if reading Wayne's thoughts.

"Where are the rest of the postcards Laure Canja wrote?" Wayne asked suddenly. "Marie Canja brought them to you from Zoé's house. Did you burn them?" When she didn't respond, he said, "You're going to need to come to the station with us."

Gently clasping her upper arm, he escorted her down the stairs. Walking through the kitchen, she asked him to stop so she could leave a message for her husband. Using her left hand, she quickly dashed off a note on a little pad of paper. She made no effort to resist as they left the house, walking toward the car. She even ducked her own head before Rob could do the honors, making sure she did not bump it on the door frame of the vehicle.

"Stay with her," Wayne said. "I'm going back in to look for the real estate papers." He hurried back inside. Ten minutes later he climbed into the car, empty-handed.

AT THE STATION, Cam took the Mambo's fingerprints. Rob rushed them down to the lab, along with the bottle of Voodoo Love they had taken from her house. When Wayne escorted the Mambo past Dory's office, Dory crooked her finger in a "come back here" gesture. Wayne nodded.

"Can I get you something to drink?" Wayne asked the Voodoo priestess after he got her seated. "We have coffee and tea."

"Tea, please," she said in a flat voice. She looked alien here, like a beautiful wild creature that lost all its color when caged. He would use her unsettled state to his advantage, he thought and then felt a touch ashamed of some of the tactics his job demanded.

Carrying a cup of tea and a plate of store-bought cookies back to the Mambo, he stuck his head in Dory's office.

"Looks like a 'person of interest' to me," Dory said and grinned. In contrast to the woman in interrogation, Dory was bright and sassy. She was wearing a pink sweater, black pants, and pink shoes. Clearly Dory belonged here, just as the Mambo did not.

"She certainly stands to make a bundle of money if they sell the village." But he wondered if the Mambo could even survive in the outside world. "Can you get Ben? I want him to help me question this woman."

"I'll think about it," she said. Wayne rolled his eyes.

BEN CAME INTO interrogation and introduced himself to Ardra Flambeau. He had a way of making a person relax in these daunting surroundings. While Ben worked his people skills on the Mambo, Wayne thought through the timeline again. Zoé had left the bar in a hurry, driven home, and probably headed immediately across the street to see the Voodoo priest. She would have been desperate to find out if it was true that he was selling the Voodoo Village land. Some conflict or argument must have broken out shortly thereafter, and it escalated to murder.

"Thank you for coming in today, Ms. Flambeau," Ben said. She nodded. "We have no plans to arrest you at this time, but I need to say that you have the right to remain silent and have an attorney present during questioning. Anything you say could be used against you in a court of law. Would you like me to call someone to represent you?"

"No," she said clearly, her face contorted in rage, "I want no *blanc* lawyer." Wayne sighed in relief. She had declined representation, which freed him to push her hard for a confession. Again he felt a touch of shame.

Someone knocked on the closed door, a quick rat-a-tat-tat. Ben disappeared into the hallway for a moment, and when he returned, he whispered to Wayne, "Only the Mambo's fingerprints were on the perfume bottle. And they match the prints on Zoé's eyelids." Wayne gave a quick thought to his strategy and realized he already had the key. He just couldn't see this woman agreeing to the sale of the village. He felt a flare of satisfaction deep inside.

Once Ben had asked the necessary background questions, he nodded to Wayne to begin the interrogation.

"Were you aware that your husband was planning to sell the Voodoo Village land?" Wayne asked, keeping his voice mild and unconcerned. "Or was it a surprise when Zoé came over so late that Thursday night to tell you?"

The Mambo looked away and then down. She was silent for a few minutes and then began to talk, as if she had bottled up her resentment for a long time. As she did so, her anger surged to the fore. Her face flushed.

"I knew a week before Zoé told me," she said, practically spitting out the words. "The Voodoo people will *die* without the guidance the Loa provide. They will literally *die*. We fought, the man and me, like wildcats. He said we could build a new Voodoo Village with all that money. He could even return to Haiti to study with the adherents there. I cursed his scheme with the rich *blanc*. We have no need of their money. I spit on him." She raised her head and her eyes flashed at Wayne.

"Why did you give Zoé the scopolamine?" Ben asked her gently. "We know she took it. It was found in her system during the autopsy."

The Mambo crossed her arms across her chest and looked away.

"Tell us about what happened that night," Ben said. When the Mambo didn't answer, Ben let Wayne take over.

"Tell me what happened to Zoé," Wayne said, his voice loud and insistent. He hit the table hard with his hand. "Tell me!"

"She asked for the scopolamine," the Mambo admitted. "She wanted the release the drug gave her. She had taken it several times in the past, so I knew it was safe. I mixed it in some tea."

"After she took the medicine, what happened?" Ben asked.

"She went home. But I had to help her across the street."

"Having her drugged made it easy for you to slip your red scarf around her neck and choke the life from her," Wayne said, disgust pouring from his mouth. "You killed her. You didn't want her telling everyone in the village about your plan to sell the land. She had to be silenced until the deal was finalized."

"No. No, that's not true." The Mambo shook her head back and forth.

"We know you were in that house for some time on the night Zoé died," Ben said. "There's no point in denying it. Your perfume still lingered in the closed-up house the night we found Zoé's body."

The Mambo nodded reluctantly. "I was in the house; I told you that. But I didn't kill her."

"I don't believe you," Wayne said, making his voice cold.

"I believe you." Ben's tone was supportive. Wayne flashed him a searing glance. "The detective thinks you're guilty of murder, but I don't. Was Zoé breathing when you left?"

"Yes, she was sleeping quietly on the couch. I am a healer, not a killer."

"Then what happened?" Wayne asked.

"My husband was asleep upstairs when Zoé arrived that night. I was working in the kitchen, making my lotions. My husband never came downstairs while she was there. After I returned from walking Zoé home, I went upstairs to bed. A bit later I woke. My husband was looking out the window of our bedroom. He said he'd seen a van driving away from the village—one that didn't belong to any of us. He thought Zoé might be in trouble. We went over there together."

Ben and Wayne exchanged a look. "And by then she was dead?" Wayne said. He could see the scene in his mind. The two religious leaders bending down over Zoé, pulling the red scarf off her throat. It must have been caught by the wind and blown away when she was carried outside.

The Mambo closed her eyes and blinked back tears.

"Yes, she was dead by then." She swallowed hard. "I felt for her pulse. My husband carried her out to the back of her property. We said a prayer for her and I closed her eyes. We feared that people would think I poisoned her. So not knowing what else to do, we laid her in the leaves behind her house and covered her with leaves and dirt."

"Excuse us just a moment," Ben said and the men left the room.

Dory, Rob, Cam, and George were waiting expectantly in the corridor.

"Do you believe her?" Ben asked Wayne.

"I do," Wayne admitted, reluctantly. "But they still broke the law by burying Zoé."

"'A person who, by concealing the death of another person, hinders a discovery of whether or not such person was unlawfully killed is guilty of a felony and upon conviction shall be punished by imprisonment for not less than one nor more than ten years, a fine of not less than one thousand dollars nor more than five thousand dollars, or both,'" Rob recited. "So do we put her in jail until she can be arraigned?"

His body tense with impatience, Wayne turned to Ben. "She told us her husband was upstairs sleeping when she gave Zoé the scopolamine, but he could have slipped out of the house without her knowledge. He could have strangled Zoé, returned to the house, and told his wife the story about someone else being there. He could be our perp," Wayne said.

"I agree," said Ben. "We could arrest her now, but I'm going to hold off."

His voice gruff with outrage, Rob said, "The woman committed a serious crime."

"She did, and I want her kept under tight surveillance,

but I'm after her husband. He's the bigger fish. She's going to lead us right to him."

"It's risky, Ben," Wayne said, "but I'll take her home and see if her husband's back yet. If so, I'll bring him in. He's the one who's selling the land. He had the most to lose if Zoé told everyone about his plan."

"George, you're going with them." Ben held up a hand to forestall Deputy Phelps' inevitable protest. "Take a separate patrol car. That way, if Wayne can locate the husband and bring him in, your job is to keep an eye on Ardra. Don't let her out of your sight. I'd like to get Randall Perdue in here, too. Rob, you're with me. Let's go pick him up."

"What about me?" Dory asked, "and Cam?"

Wayne tried to hide his smile. Dory hated being left out and she could out-whine a four-year-old when she was.

"Deputy Gomez needs to stay here in case any calls come in." Ben gave her a stern look. "I still need you to stay out of this, Dory. You can take the rest of the afternoon off."

Dory stalked off without a word. Seconds later, her red T-bird flew past the window as she left the parking lot.

"Better call Al and make sure she shows up at home," Wayne murmured to Cam on his way out the door.

"Already called him. He's going to text me when she gets there." Deputy Gomez gave him a wink.

THIRTY

Evangeline Bon Temps

MONDAY AFTERNOON EVANGELINE had an appointment with her investigator, Johnny Burton, whom she had assigned the job of finding Laure Canja ten days earlier. He had called her office to say he was ready to tell her what he had found.

Johnny arrived before Evangeline got back from lunch, and when she walked in her office, she found him seated at her round conference table. "Hey there," Johnny said. He was wearing a blue Grateful Dead T-shirt and blue jeans faded almost to white. He wore his graying hair long, touching his shoulders, and his beard was even longer. While Evangeline often wished he would dress more professionally, she acknowledged he was good at his job.

"How are you, Johnny?" she asked and held out her hand to shake his.

"I'm good, Ms. Bon Temps. I've got some information, but I haven't found her yet."

"Before you bring me up to date, would you like something to drink? Coke, water?"

"Coke would be good," he said. Evangeline buzzed Kimberly and asked her to bring in a cold soda. Johnny took a long grateful swallow and thanked her. "I quit smoking a month ago," he smiled. "This is my last vice."

"It certainly is." Evangeline smiled. She had originally

met Johnny after his second DUI ten years ago. After seeing his drug test results, she'd gotten the prosecutor to give him a deal based on completing rehab and attending weekly meetings of NA and AA. Aside from one relapse, he had stayed on the program ever since. "So tell me what you found out."

"You gave me her birthdate, October 7, 1968, the year she disappeared, 1994, and her full name, Laure Simone Canja. You also gave me a photograph, but it was twenty years old. It wasn't a lot to go on, but I did manage to locate a driver's license that listed her address in the Voodoo Village. It expired in 1996 and has not been renewed in Tennessee or any of the surrounding states."

"What about a social security number?" Evangeline asked.

"Couldn't find one under that name. I needed a birth certificate. You didn't want me bothering the mother, but I figured if anyone had a birth certificate, it would be the birth mother. I went out to the village and found Miss Mira Canja. She said Laure's father's last name was Febron and she gave me a copy of the birth certificate. Mira was married to Luc Febron. He got himself killed in a bar fight when Laure was only five."

Then the man called Papa Febron must be Luc's father and Mira Canja's father-in-law.

"So her birth name was Laure Simone Febron."

"Yes, but she later changed her last name back to Canja," Johnny said.

"Go on. I presume you checked for a social security number under both names?"

"I did, and I found it. Laure worked from when she was eighteen until the night she disappeared—at a hair salon in Richfield called The Sassy Lady. It's still in business, but under new ownership and renamed Shear Reflections."

Johnny had outdone himself. Not that Evangeline was surprised. She leaned back in her chair, smiling, waiting to hear more. "Excellent work, Johnny. Were you able to talk to anyone who knew her?"

He made an ambiguous gesture with his hand. "Yes, but it's been twenty years since Laure disappeared, so it took a while to find anyone who remembered her. I found one older woman in her seventies who was still doing hair. Her name is Bootsie Raine, and she remembered Laure. Apparently, Laure had a mostly African American clientele, and a lot of young black women came to see her. I don't know much about this, Ms. Bon Temps, but Bootsie said Laure used a lot of tiny braids in her styles. The current owner of the salon had to take down a poster that showed one of Laure's styles when she bought the place. People kept asking for appointments with Laure years after she disappeared."

"So is that it, Johnny? Anything else?"

"Yeah, one more important thing. Bootsie Raine was working with Laure Canja the last day she came to work. Laure already had her daughter Zoé by then. Sometimes she brought the kid in to work with her. When Laure never returned to work after that day, Bootsie kept the photo of her little girl at her station. She let me take it. Do you recognize her?" He pulled out his phone and showed Evangeline a picture of a dark-eyed little girl. Her hair had been braided in a complex style, clearly the work of her mother.

Evangeline sighed as she stared at the photo of the lovely child. "That's Laure's daughter, Zoé. I've seen pictures of her when she was that age." She paused and looked Johnny in the eye. "I haven't told you the whole story, Johnny, or the reason I asked you to try to find Laure Canja. That little girl, Zoé, was recently murdered. She spent the last twenty years of her life waiting for her mother Laure to return and looking for her with no success. I was with the police when they found Zoé's body. Since Ms. Canja's only daughter disappeared and then her granddaughter was murdered, I felt terrible for her. I told her I'd try to find out what happened to Laure. I hoped that if you found Zoé's mother, I could convince her to come home to see Mira."

"No luck yet, but I found out a little bit more. Apparently on the last day Laure came in to work, a man showed up. Laure told Bootsie she was going to take a break, and they went out behind the beauty shop. When Laure came back inside, she was upset. Bootsie asked her what was wrong and Laure said, 'That man is the father of my little girl.' So Bootsie asked, 'Were you arguing about custody?' And Laure said, 'No, he's getting married.' Bootsie said she dropped it then. Didn't ask any more questions."

"Did you ask Bootsie if she could describe the man?"

"Yes. She said he was a light-skinned African-American with greenish hazel eyes and straight, black hair. Probably in his mid- to late-twenties then, which would make him mid- to late-forties now."

"Sounds Creole," she said, tapping her pen on the table, her brain whirring as she processed this new information. "So did you find out anything else? Was Laure's disappearance ever reported to the police? Any official investigation?"

"Richfield has exactly one officer to keep the peace, Officer Shaver. First name is Henry. He said Laure's dis-

appearance was before his time. The man who had the
job before him died about five years ago. Henry looked
through the records after I asked him about it. There had
been a report of the disappearance, but since Laure was
an adult and there was no evidence of a crime, the officer's predecessor didn't bother to look into it."

"Sounds like we hit a dead end," Evangeline said,
frowning with disappointment. "I know you'd rather stick
to facts and not speculate, Johnny, but if you were before
a grand jury and the judge asked you what you thought
had happened to Laure Canja, what would you say?"

Johnny grimaced and brushed a stray hair out of his
face. "I'd say she's dead, probably killed by her little girl's
father. You know what the cops say are the big three mo-
tives for murder—lust, lucre, and loathing. My guess is
Laure wouldn't marry him and he was angry. Probably
had been furious with her for years for rejecting him.
Maybe when he told Laure he was marrying someone
else, she threatened to tell his new woman the reasons
she wouldn't marry him. Something like that could have
happened, anyway…" Johnny trailed off. He shrugged
his shoulders.

"Thanks for all this information," Evangeline said, rising to her feet and shaking his hand. "You can give your
hours to Kimberly and your expense receipts. She'll cut
you a check. The sheriff's office has a postcard Laure
sent her daughter. If it turns out to contain any evidence
of interest, I'll call you and you can look into this a bit
more."

AFTER JOHNNY LEFT the office, Evangeline sat back down
at the table and remained there a while, deep in thought.
If Zoé's father had been about to marry someone else,

why would he kill Laure? On the other hand, if Johnny was right and Laure was dead, she should tell Sheriff Bradley their assumptions. The twenty years since Laure's disappearance made it an awfully cold case. It was unlikely the sheriff's office would turn up much more than Johnny had already found.

She called the sheriff's office. Mrs. Coffin told her Sheriff Bradley and Investigator Clarkson were both out of the office, so she called her friend's cellphone.

"Dory, it's Evangeline."

"Hi."

"What's wrong? You sound depressed."

"I'm in a bad mood. Boss man gave me the afternoon off."

"That doesn't sound so bad to me. I'd like an afternoon free—"

"Well, it is," Dory cut her off. "Everyone else is investigating, but Ben Bradley is keeping the investigator out of it!"

"Then I'm going to cheer you up right now, my friend. I've got information on the case that no one else at your office has. I had my investigator, Johnny, look into the disappearance of Laure Canja. The last day Laure came to work at this hair salon called the Sassy Lady, a man she told a co-worker was Zoé's father came to see her. Laure and Zoé's father never tied the knot. He told Laure he was getting married. Anyway, after that day she never came back to work. I'm trying to get the man's name. Could be he's still around the village."

"Excellent work, girlfriend. What's our next step?" Her friend's voice had regained its normal buoyancy.

"I'm betting Mira knows or at least suspects who Zoé's father is."

"I'll go to the village with you, but we have to wait about an hour," Dory said.

"Why?"

"Because Wayne and George are out there now, and I'm not supposed to go near the place…don't want to run into them."

"No problem," Evangeline told her, after pulling up her schedule on her desktop computer. Luckily, her husband was working from home today. "Jason and I will pick you up from Al's in an hour."

AFTER ENDING HER call with Dory, Evangeline decided that if Zoé's father was still around, she would ask Detective Nichols to investigate him. If anyone could get a person to talk about crimes in their past, it would be Wayne Nichols. Almost two years ago, Wayne had come to consult her as an attorney. It was during the Tommy Ferris case. Wayne got Evangeline's assurance that their meeting was confidential before confessing to concealing the crime of his foster father's murder and taking the gun to divert suspicion from his foster mother, Jocelyn, who had killed her abusive spouse. He had tried to get Jocelyn to turn herself in, but when he couldn't convince her to do so, he helped her escape.

Evangeline had often wondered if Wayne Nichols had ever found a way to get that gun he had kept back into evidence and the right man convicted of the crime. If she and Dory could find out who Zoé's father was, she had no doubt Wayne could get the man to tell him everything.

THIRTY-ONE

Sheriff Ben Bradley

"So YOU DON'T think the Mambo or her husband killed Zoé?" Rob asked, fastening his seatbelt on the passenger side of Ben's truck.

Ben drove out of the parking lot and turned to take the now familiar route toward Richfield. "I don't think the Mambo's our killer. Not sure about her husband. But I've had a bad feeling about Randall since the first time he came in. We definitely need to talk to him again."

Rob's phone beeped and he looked at the screen. "It's a text from Emma. But it doesn't make any sense."

"What doesn't make sense?"

"She checked the other two sets of prints on the post-card against the exclusion prints we got from Mira and Marie and they match."

Makes perfect sense to me. "I thought they'd match up." Ben glanced over at the young detective. Rob had removed his glasses and was rubbing his forehead.

"But she also said the fourth set matches the Mambo's fingerprints...." Rob shook his head before putting his glasses back on. "There should be another uniden-tified set. Other than Zoe's, Mira's and Marie's and the Mambo's."

"You're right. If Laure really sent those postcards,

there'd be one more unidentified set of prints, so we both know what that means."

"Yeah, we do." Rob's voice was sad. "It means Laure didn't send those postcards to her daughter…and she's probably dead."

Ben passed the exit that would have taken them to Richfield. "Bringing Mr. Perdue in will have to wait. I think someone in that village killed Laure Canja twenty years ago…maybe the same person who killed Zoé."

BY THE TIME they reached the Voodoo Village, the hollow where it sat was completely in shadow. Ben parked his truck in front of Zoé's house. "The days are getting shorter," he said.

Rob climbed out of the truck. "They're over at the Mambo's house," he said, indicating the patrol car across the street. "Is that where we're going?"

"In a minute. I need to ask Mira a question first."

They walked over to the house shared by the Canja sisters. As they got closer, they heard the howl of a dog in distress. Rob raised his hand to knock on the door but it flew open before he had a chance.

"Are you here to take her back?" Mira demanded.

"To take who back?" Ben asked, although he knew what she was going to say. The howls were deafening now.

"Erzulie must go with you. She has been crying and howling ever since Mae and her mother brought her back this morning."

Mira had seemingly aged ten years since Ben last saw her. On top of the shocking loss of her granddaughter, this new strain was clearly too much. "What happens when you let her out?" he asked.

She started to sway where she stood. Ben and Rob both reached out to prevent her from falling. Mira gasped for breath. "She runs straight to where Zoé was lying. The poor dog...she sits there like she's waiting for something. When I bring her back inside she starts to howl again."

"All right," Ben sighed. "Rob, will you put Erzulie in the back of the cab? Just flip the seats up and she'll have plenty of room. I'll get her food."

Mira walked back through her kitchen. Seconds later, she returned with a now-silent Erzulie. She handed the leash to Rob and invited Ben inside. "Thank you. I did not know what to do." She pointed at a large, full bag leaning against the kitchen wall. "Her food is there."

Ben rolled the top of the bag down and hoisted it under one arm. "You're welcome. But now I need some help from you."

Mira Canja looked up at him, her eyes unreadable in the dim light. "I will help you if I can," she said warily.

"Who was Zoé's father?"

The woman stiffened, but didn't answer.

"Please, it's important."

Mira turned away. "It can't be. He didn't kill his own daughter; he wouldn't."

Ben paused, knowing he was about to break what remained of the poor woman's heart. "Maybe not," he said in a gentle voice, "but what about your daughter, Laure? Would he kill her?"

Mira sagged against the wall. "You found Laure. I knew in my heart that she was dead." She lifted her head and Ben caught the silver glint of tears snaking down her cheeks. "When the postcards started coming I knew they weren't from my daughter. The writing was different. But they made Zoé so happy—"

"We didn't find her, Ms. Canja, not yet. But we did find evidence that proves Laure didn't write those postcards. And I don't think she would have left voluntarily. So I'm asking you again. Who is Zoé's father?"

Mira Canja peeled herself off the wall and stood, straight and dignified, before him. "I can't tell you. I promised Laure I would never tell anyone. But I can show you a picture of Laure and a man. You will draw your own conclusions."

She went to a small dresser that served as an end table by the couch and opened the top drawer. Her hands shook as she rifled through the papers until she found a small envelope near the bottom of the drawer. Wordlessly, she handed it to Ben.

He looked at the photo inside and then slid the envelope into the pocket of his shirt. "Thank you. It won't bring them back, but we're going to find out who's responsible and they'll be brought to justice. I promise you that."

She gave an almost imperceptible nod, turned her back to him, and walked away.

Ben trudged out to his truck and loaded the bag of dogfood into the bed of the pickup. Rob was across the street talking to Wayne, who had gotten back into his patrol car. Ben opened his door and peeked in at Erzulie. Curled up on the floor, she was snoring quietly. Mae would be glad to have her back, but he really didn't want another dog. At least for the moment, it didn't look like he had a choice.

He walked across the street to join Rob at the window

of Wayne's patrol car. "Did Rob fill you in on the finger-prints?" he asked his senior detective.

Wayne's hazel eyes were weary and his face was drawn, the lines around his mouth deep in the last of the daylight. "Yeah. Looks like we're dealing with a double homicide now."

Ben's phone buzzed. "It's Evangeline. Wait here, Wayne." He walked a short distance away to answer, in case she wasn't calling about Zoé.

"Hello, Sheriff. Jason insisted I call you before he brought us out to the village. Do you have a minute?"

"I do. I'm actually at the village right now. What's going on?"

As Evangeline relayed the information she had learned from her investigator, Ben pressed the phone to his ear with his shoulder and took the envelope out of his pocket. He looked at the photo while she finished her account.

"Um-hum, yes, I see why you wanted to come out, but there's no need. I appreciate the info, but I have a picture of Zoé's father right here. Mira won't tell me his name. Is that Dory in the background?"

"It is. We're with her at Al's house right now."

"Right. Tell her I said 'nice try,' and I'll see her to-morrow."

There was a quiet sound from Evangeline that might have been suppressed laughter. "I'll give her your mes-sage."

"Thanks. Can I stop by and show you and Jason this picture when I get back to Rosedale?"

"Of course. Just text me when you're close."

"Thanks, Evangeline. See you then."

Ben returned to the patrol car. "No sign of the Mam-bo's husband?"

"No. But when you combine her admission of helping bury Zoe's body with the fingerprint evidence, we need to arrest her. She must have been the one who wrote those postcards."

"You're right, Wayne. Bring her in. I'll drop off the dog, take Rob back to his car, and go see Evangeline and Jason…need to show them something."

"Okay, will do," Wayne said. "See you tomorrow."

"Or even tonight," Ben said over his shoulder. "Might be a late one."

THIRTY-TWO

Mae December

MONDAY HAD BEEN jam-packed for Mae, bookended by taking Erzulie back to Mira only to have her show up again with Ben in the evening. Mae was thrilled to have her back, but she knew her fiancé was unhappy about it. He had been quite clear about his feelings; in between bites of the fastest meal she'd ever seen him eat. As soon as he emptied his plate of the roast chicken, green beans, and scalloped potatoes, he'd left for Evangeline's with a picture of Zoé's father. He called her an hour later on his way to the office. Jason and Evangeline had both given a positive ID.

The man in the photo, the man who was Zoe's father, was the Voodoo priest.

The weather had warmed slightly on this Tuesday in early November. The sun was bright, highlighting touches of frost in the valley in front of her farmhouse. After finishing her yogurt and fruit, Mae took Erzulie for a run down the driveway and along a route just under three miles. The downside of living on top of a hill was that the end of your run was up a steep driveway, but she wouldn't trade her view for anything. Erzulie wasn't even panting when they got back up to the hilltop, but Mae was winded. She drank a big glass of water before showering.

Mae applied a touch more makeup than usual, dried

and straightened her hair, and put on a long gray skirt with a plum-colored sweater and black boots. She planned to give Erzulie a few days to settle down before finding a new home for her, but having her back had worked out perfectly for today. The governor and her husband were coming to pick out their puppy. Being able to see and interact with the mother dog would be helpful for them. *I wish Ben could meet them. Maybe he can be here when they take their puppy home in two weeks.*

The 'First Couple' of Tennessee had lost their beloved Weimaraner to old age a few months ago. They would be here at eleven to meet the puppies. Greer Patterson, the governor's assistant, had called yesterday to set up the appointment. Mae told her that she recommended at least an hour to choose the right puppy. Greer had sighed, but agreed to block out the time in Angela Featherstone's busy schedule. Since Mae didn't plan to take the couple out to her barn, she decided to let the puppies play outside until just before eleven and then put them back in her studio. Hopefully that would keep the accidents to a minimum.

Mae went back downstairs, leaving Erzulie curled up on her bedroom rug. She closed her four dogs in the laundry room and quickly tidied up her kitchen and living room. The old farmhouse was looking its best in the slanting autumn light, the mellow wood floors and Mae's oil paintings glowing. She fluffed the sofa pillows, fanned out the magazines on her coffee table, and declared victory.

Getting the puppies to follow her out of the barn was no problem. However, the minute they got outside, they all dashed in different directions. She scooped up the nearest and smallest one, Jacques, the runt of the litter.

Holding him to her chest, she called the other three and walked quickly back to the house. As expected, Cosette and Pierre followed her. Felicity ran in the opposite direction. *Drat.*

Abandoning her plan to let them play outside, Mae put the three puppies inside her studio and closed the bottom half of the Dutch door to contain them, then ran outside yelling for their errant sibling. A frantic five minutes elapsed before she spotted the small gray shape halfway down the field in front of her house. Cursing her high-heeled boots, she took off running and finally caught the little urchin just before she reached the street.

"I'm not sure I gave you the right name," she told the wiggly little thing as she carried her up the driveway. "Felicity means happiness. I don't know the French word for trouble, but that might suit you better!"

A black sedan with heavily tinted windows pulled up alongside her. The front window rolled down and a uniformed driver said, "Are you Miss December?"

"I am. And this is Felicity."

The window behind the driver opened. "Would you and Felicity like a ride the rest of the way up?" Governor Featherstone asked with a smile. "This is a steep driveway you have."

"Yes, please." Mae felt her cheeks grow hot. This was *not* how she had intended to greet the Governor of Tennessee. "If it's not any trouble."

The elegant blonde woman reached out for Felicity with both hands. "It's no trouble at all. Give me the puppy and hop in the front seat."

The driver swiftly exited the car. Walking around the front, he opened the door for Mae, who climbed in, cheeks still burning. She turned and looked back. "I'm Mae December. It's an honor to meet you both."

"I'm the First Man—you can call me Richard," the dark-haired man with glasses said with a smile. "This is my bride, Angela. Looks like she already made her choice, but we'd still like to see the other puppies…and their parents, if possible."

It did indeed seem that the governor had decided on her puppy. Felicity had both front feet planted on her blouse and was mouthing the double strand of pearls around Angela Featherstone's slender throat.

The driver stopped at Mae's front steps and opened the governor's door. Richard Featherstone got out and held the door for Mae. She led the way up the steps to the front hall, where Erzulie was standing. "This is Erzulie, Felicity's dam. I have pictures of her sire, but he's not here."

The Featherstones greeted the big dog. Mae was relieved by her dignified behavior—no barking or jumping, thank goodness.

"She's a beauty," the governor said. "And she has lovely manners. How long have you had Erzulie? Such an unusual name."

Mae explained Erzulie's situation, the reason she was living at the farmhouse, and the origin of her name to the fascinated couple while she led them back to the studio. "And here's the rest of the litter: Jacques, Cosette, and Pierre. You're welcome to spend as much time playing with them and observing them as you like. I'll be in the kitchen. Just let me know when you're done." She opened the lower half of the door and closed it behind them.

"Are any of them spoken for?" Richard Featherstone asked, watching his wife reluctantly put Felicity down on the floor.

"I have deposits on one male and one female, but no one has chosen their puppy yet. You can have the one you want...don't worry. And I'll get their papers and the picture of Wolfgang out for you."

"The father dog is named Wolfgang?"

"I know—the names Erzulie and Wolfgang don't go well together. They made some beautiful puppies, though." Mae smiled and left them to it.

TWENTY MINUTES LATER they were saying goodbye, after giving Mae a deposit for Felicity.

"So we can come get her in two weeks?"

"At the earliest, Governor Featherstone."

"Please, call me Angela." She wasn't young, probably in her early sixties, but she was still quite lovely, especially when she smiled.

"I'll try," Mae said. "Is there anything else I can tell you about Felicity or her lineage before you go?"

"No, I don't think so." Richard looked at his wife, then at Mae. "I hope you don't mind me asking, does the artist live with you—Malone?"

Mae laughed. "I live with my fiancé, Ben Bradley—he's the Rose County Sheriff—but the artist lives here too...." She paused. "My given name is actually Maeve Malone December—it got changed to Mae because my sister couldn't pronounce Maeve."

"So you're the artist?" The governor looked at the large oil hanging in the entryway, a winter landscape she had painted for Ben's birthday last year. "You're very talented. We both love the paintings in the studio. Are they of the Voodoo Village?"

"They are. It's a unique place and I'm really enjoying the process of painting them. I gave one to Mira

Canja, Zoé's grandmother. It showed Zoé walking into her house."

"And Zoé is the girl you told us about—Erzulie's owner?" Richard asked.

"Yes, she was." Mae looked down at the floor briefly. "Anyway, I started on the one in the left corner of the studio, then I painted the picture of Zoé by itself. The rest I've been doing as a group."

"Would you consider selling them that way—as a group, I mean?"

"Yes, um, Angela, I would. Once they're finished."

The governor's blue eyes sparkled in the clear November light as she stepped out onto Mae's front porch. "Well, good. Hope to see the completed versions in two weeks then. Thank you, Mae."

Richard gave Mae a nod, took his wife's arm, and they walked down the steps to the waiting car.

THIRTY-THREE

Chief Detective Wayne Nichols

AFTER LEARNING THE identity of Zoé's father last night Wayne planned to track down the Voodoo priest and bring him in for questioning. On his way out to the village, he had decided to consult Jean Paul, his CI in Richland. He caught up with Dory in the hallway as she was headed toward the front door.

"Dory, hold up a minute. I know that Mrs. Coffin is in charge of petty cash now, but she and I are not what could be called *simpatico*. I'm short on cash and I'm going to Richfield. I need some money for a CI named Jean Paul. Can you help?"

Dory rolled her eyes but started toward the reception desk. "How much do you need?" she asked him over her shoulder.

"Seventy should do it," Wayne said.

Dory conversed with Sophie Coffin for a few minutes and then returned to hand him seventy dollars. "The new office policy is that you have to turn in a formal justification for the money you request for CIs, together with a report of what you learned. This is the last time you can get this without doing the paperwork first. Sorry." Dory patted his upper arm. Adjusting her brightly patterned scarf on her shoulder, she called out "Ciao!" on her way out the door.

Wayne cast a quick look at Mrs. Coffin, who didn't look pleased, before walking out to commandeer a patrol car. He had just started the vehicle when he got a text from Ben. It read, "Suspect in custody, on our way back. Won't question him until you get here." Wayne smiled inwardly, thinking that with Perdue in custody he could question his newest CI, Jean Paul, at Randall's Tavern without worrying that Perdue would be hanging around and overhearing the conversation.

DRIVING TOWARD RICHFIELD, Wayne recalled the previous encounter with Jean Paul in Randall's Tavern when his CI reported hearing three businessmen talking about buying the Voodoo Village. He said Zoé had been listening to the conversation, too. Although both he and Ben had suspected the million-dollar offer for the property was at the root of the motive for Zoé's murder, so far they had no solid evidence. The Mambo was no longer a suspect. Once the Voodoo priest had been interrogated, they would know more.

Randall Perdue was also a prime suspect. Carlos Rivera, the cook at the tavern, had said Randall's harassment of Zoé had escalated since his divorce. Wayne hoped Jean Paul would know a little bit more about Randall's obsession with the young woman and had seen or heard something that he could use in his interrogation.

It was likely that Zoé's death had been a crime of passion, but other than the verbally expressed suspicions of Mira Canja, Darnell the bartender, the waitresses, and Zoé's friend Ginny, they had nothing. Randall's fingerprints were not found in Zoé's house, and the red scarf that was the murder weapon had been washed clean by the rain before they discovered her body. Having finally gotten into Zoé's cellphone, they knew that the last call she received at eleven forty-five the night she was killed was from Randall. But any decent defense attorney would be able to explain that away by saying Randall was her boss and just wanted to know when she was coming back to work.

PARKING HIS CAR in front of Randall's Tavern, Wayne wished he had done a more thorough job of vetting Randall's past. Leopards didn't change their spots. If Randall had killed Zoé, he had to have come close to murder before. He wanted to know more about Randall's divorce. If spousal abuse had been involved, why were no assault charges on his record? If Jean Paul could tell him anything about Randall's marriage or where the ex was living now, it would really help. The most important interview with a killer, or a would-be killer, was always with the victim who got away. If Mrs. Perdue had divorced Randall to escape an abusive relationship, she might be persuaded to testify against him. And she might give Wayne a lot more information than he had currently.

Jean Paul was sitting on his usual stool at the bar. Darnell was polishing glassware. Wayne nodded at him. When Jean Paul saw Wayne, his face lit up.

"Hello, my friend," he said, raising a glass.

"Let's sit over there," Wayne said, gesturing to a corner booth. "I'm buying his drinks," he told Darnell.

"That's good," Darnell said with a smile. "His tab's up to fifty bucks."

"Let me talk to him and then I'll settle up." Wayne walked to the corner booth and sat down. "I have some questions for you, Jean Paul. If I get the information I need, I'll settle your bar tab."

"Thank you," John Paul said gratefully as he slurped his beer. "I could use a little food money, too."

"Depends on what you've got for me. I want to know something about Mrs. Randall Perdue. What do you know?"

"Her name's Helene. She moved to Rosedale."

"Did she keep her married name?"

"Think so," Jean Paul said.

"I want to know the reason for their divorce. Did you ever hear what it was?"

"Randall was always after other women and she was tired of it. But the straw that broke the camel's back was when Randall started chasing Zoé. Helene and Randall separated over it. After Randall promised to leave Zoé alone, Helene came back. But she got suspicious that Randall was still stalking Zoé and followed him one night to the Voodoo Village after work. He banged and banged on Zoé's door. Zoé wouldn't let him in, but for Mrs. Perdue, that was it. She filed the papers the next day."

"Anything else, Jean Paul? Did you ever suspect Randall hit her—his wife?"

Jean Paul looked down at the none-too-clean floor of the bar, littered with broken peanut shells and old candy wrappers. He sighed and then said, "I don't hold with it myself. A man should have more pride than to knock his woman around. Randall and Helene used to live in the apartment above the bar here, and there were nights when I heard the sounds of them fighting and her crying. He gave her a black eye a couple of times. She tried to cover it with makeup." He shrugged. "It still showed. When she waitressed here, I often saw bruises on her arms. Asked her once why she put up with it, and she said a funny thing." Jean Paul looked at him with a frown.

Wayne waited. Waiting patiently for information almost always worked.

"She said you couldn't use *rape* as a justification for divorce. A married man had a right to his wife's body."

Wayne nodded. "Thank you, Jean Paul, that's very helpful. I wonder if you remember anything else about the night Zoé Canja disappeared. We know that Randall left the bar around eleven thirty. Did he come back that night?"

Jean Paul looked thoughtful. "Let me think a minute. Yes, I remember now. He did. Must have been about closing time."

"How did he seem to you then? Did he look upset, or disheveled?"

"He did something I hadn't seen him do before. He sat at the bar beside me and he was breathing hard. I asked him what was wrong. He said he'd had some trouble... trouble with a woman."

Wayne felt like all the air had been sucked from the room. He made eye contact with Jean Paul, saying, "Thanks. I'll settle up your bar tab and here's a twenty for your pocket. Use it on food. One last thing: I might need you to testify to what you saw in court—Mrs. Perdue's bruises and the black eyes."

"Any money in it if I do?" John Paul asked, raising his eyebrows hopefully.

Wayne nodded. The sheriff's office was absolutely never allowed to pay a witness to testify, but he would cover Jean Paul somehow, out of his own pocket. The old guy needed it.

"Appreciate it." Jean Paul took a long, shaky swallow.

Wayne settled Jean Paul's tab with Darnell and walked outside. Thanks to his CI, he knew that Randall Perdue had abused his wife when she didn't give him what he wanted. He had the hammer he needed to break Randall in the interrogation. He called Dory on her cellphone.

"Hey, big guy, what d'you need?"

"An address and phone number for Helene Perdue. She lives in Rosedale. I need to speak with her as soon as possible."

"On it," Dory said. She called him back before he reached Rosedale with the address and phone number. Wayne turned on his GPS, entered the address, and headed for the home of Helene Perdue, hoping she would be willing to tell him all about her marriage to Randall and his apparent fixation with Zoé Canja.

WAYNE FOUND HER street address easily. She lived in a two-story townhouse complex in downtown Rosedale. He rang the bell and she came to the door.

"Ms. Helene Perdue?" Wayne asked at the barely cracked door. He heard several chains being unhooked before the door opened a few inches wider.

"Yes, I'm Helene," the woman responded. She was nicely dressed in blue jeans and a paler blue blouse. Her long hair was streaked with white and gathered into a low ponytail.

"My name's Wayne Nichols. I'm a detective with the sheriff's office for Rose County." Wayne pulled out his shield. "I'd like to ask you some questions. Could I come in?"

"Come in then." She looked closely at his badge before opening the door all the way. She scanned the parking lot apprehensively before closing and triple-locking the door. "Have a seat anywhere, Detective. Could I get you some coffee or lemonade?"

"Lemonade would be nice, thank you," Wayne said, taking a seat on her couch. The apartment was small, with the kitchen open to the living room. It was the older style, though, with no island or peninsula separating the kitchen from the living space. She had decorated the room nicely with a navy couch and blue-and-white striped chairs.

Handing Wayne a glass of lemonade, Helene Perdue sat in the chair across the low coffee table from him. "How can I help you, Detective?"

"We're investigating a suspicious death out in the Voodoo Village." He paused, watching her closely.

"Zoé Canja," she said, sighing. "I saw her picture in the local paper. And I read Suzanne December's article about the village."

"Yes, that's right. I wonder if you would mind telling me why you and Mr. Perdue ended your marriage. I understand you've been divorced for about three years now, right?" He kept his tone carefully controlled. When she didn't answer, Wayne looked at her through narrowed eyes. Although he normally waited for quite some time before interjecting more questions, he had come upon domestic assault many times. Usually the women wouldn't admit to the abuse, feeling disgraced. Mrs. Perdue was looking down, but Wayne could see a blush of shame spread across her face.

"I know about the assaults you endured, Mrs. Perdue," Wayne finally said. "Domestic abuse is a pattern of behavior used to establish power and control over another person through fear and intimidation." He glanced at Helene. She still could not meet his eyes. "Was it the beatings that made you leave the marriage?"

She took a deep, shuddering breath before she spoke. "No. The bastard just wouldn't leave Zoé Canja alone.

She was young enough to be his daughter. We had only one child. Our daughter Renee died of childhood leukemia when she was eleven. If Renee had lived, she would be twenty-five." She exhaled shakily.

"Did Randall's attacks ever put you in the hospital?" Wayne asked.

"Rosedale General. Broken arms, bruises...once he broke my cheekbone. It was getting worse. Finally, a woman doctor at the ER told me if I didn't get out, he was going to kill me. I think she saved my life."

I bet it was Lucy. A stab of pride in his woman almost brought tears to his eyes.

"I'm glad you're safe now. Thank you for seeing me and for the lemonade. You're a brave woman, Helene. It takes courage to leave an abusive relationship, and if the woman doesn't leave, it can escalate to murder. I've seen it happen. Keep your doors locked. And you might consider getting a dog."

"I will," she said and shook his hand.

THIRTY-FOUR

Sheriff Ben Bradley

WAYNE APPEARED IN the doorway of Ben's office.

"Good, you're back. Are you ready for the interrogation?"

"Yes, but I'm confused, I thought you picked up Randall Perdue. I just looked in the interrogation room on my way in, and that's not him. Who's in the box?"

Wayne put his mug of coffee back on his desk, still cradling it for warmth. Despite the onset of colder weather, no one had thought to crank up the heat. Or maybe it was just Sophie Coffin, trying to save money.

"Rob and I had a change of plans. We went out to get Perdue, but he was nowhere to be found. So then we went out to the village to get the Houngan. He wasn't there." Ben shrugged. "I thought we'd struck out, but then I remembered what Mae learned from Zoé's friend, Ginny. She said the Offer to Purchase the Voodoo Village came from a group called Valhalla Development, which has an office on Main Street in Rosedale. Rob and I went in and the receptionist said that a Mr. Ti-Jean Flambeau was meeting with the partners. Knowing that the Mambo's name is Ardra Flambeau, we figured that it was her husband, the Voodoo priest, in that meeting. We sat in the car for an hour, and when he came out, we informed him, rather forcefully, that he had to come down to the station. He wasn't happy, but he got in the back of the car." Ben sat back in his chair and clasped his hands behind his head, smiling in satisfaction.

"Nice work, man." Wayne gave him a thumbs up. "Just let me review my notes on the Mambo interrogation then we'll go at him." He was about to leave when he turned back to ask, "Where is she, by the way?"

"The Mambo was released this morning. My aunt must have been in a good mood. I guess London softened her up. Ardra posted bail and will have her hearing in a week or so."

Wayne paused, thinking. "Did Mr. Ti-Jean Flambeau have anything to say on the ride in to the office?"

"Not a word. He was cautioned and declined representation. Very controlled guy, I'd say."

Wayne raised his eyebrows. "Give me fifteen minutes and we'll go in," he said.

ROB WAS ALREADY in the corner of the room, checking out the audio capture equipment. He left when Ben walked in with Wayne.

"This is the detective we've been waiting for." Ben took his seat across from the Voodoo priest.

"Detective Nichols." Wayne sat next to Ben. "Your name is Ti-Jean Flambeau, is that correct?"

Ti-Jean nodded. He was preternaturally calm, as if willing himself into relaxed state. His hands were folded loosely on the table before him.

Ben went on, "You were cautioned earlier, but I need to say again that you have the right to remain silent and to have an attorney present during questioning. You declined an attorney before; is that still your preference?"

Ti-Jean grimaced, but otherwise did not shift his position. "Just want to get this over with. Don't need a lawyer."

"As I mentioned, we're investigating the death of Zoé Canja on the night of October twenty-third. We've already questioned your wife. Now we'd like to hear your account of that night."

Taking a deep breath, Ti-Jean lifted his hands off the table and straightened his shoulders. "I was asleep, and it was late, well after midnight, when I heard a car pull out across the street. The window was open and the sound of the engine woke me. I got up and saw a van driving fast down the road, away from the village. It was an old Chevy panel van, white."

"Did you see the license plate?" Wayne asked.

"No, it was going too fast. I watched the house for a while and then I woke up my wife and told her about the car. She said Zoé had been over earlier and asked for some belladonna to help her sleep. She gave her some and then walked her home. She said Zoé was sleeping on the couch when she left. I told her we ought to go over and check on her. She got dressed and we walked over."

"When you got there, what did you see?"

Ti-Jean was sweating. He swiped his hand across his brow and looked away, avoiding Ben's eyes. "The girl was already dead when we got there, Sheriff. We didn't kill her."

"That's not what your wife told us," Wayne said calmly. "She said you strangled the girl."

He's using the 'Prisoner's Dilemma' to get him to confess. Ben didn't approve of lying, but he had seen Wayne use this interrogation technique to good effect in the past. He let it slide.

Ti-Jean's eyes widened, and he was breathing hard by then. "I don't believe it. She couldn't have said that. It isn't true."

"That is how she saved herself. Now you'll be the person going to prison for the murder."

"I don't believe you. Tell me exactly what she said." The subtle Haitian rhythms of Ti-Jean's speech were intensifying with his stress. Ben glanced at Wayne, who was leaning forward with narrowed eyes.

"She said Zoé was in a deep, drug-induced sleep. You slipped a red scarf around her neck and tightened it. Zoé was dead in seconds. Then you carried her out back and buried her. Your wife admitted to kneeling down and closing Zoé's eyes."

"I'm telling you Zoé was dead when we got there." Ti-Jean looked directly at them and then his whole face crumpled. "Seeing her with that red scarf around her neck just broke me in two. I would never have killed Zoé. She was my daughter; I loved that child." He slumped forward on the table, racked with sobs.

"Excuse us a moment, Mr. Flambeau." Ben got up, and Wayne followed him out of the room.

George, Cam, and Dory were standing expectantly in the hallway.

"I hate to say this, but I believe the man," Ben rolled his shoulders and cracked his stiff neck. "So we still don't know who killed Zoé."

Wayne nodded. "I'm in agreement, but while we have him in the box and he's in a confessional mood, let's push a little on what happened to Laure Canja."

"Let's leave him with his thoughts for a few minutes. Cam, would you take him some coffee, please?"

TEN MINUTES LATER the sheriff and Detective Nichols were back in the room. Ti-Jean was drinking the coffee Cam had brought him and seemed calmer.

"We have some more questions," Wayne said. "First off, did you see anything that could help us identify the white van?"

"I wish I had, but it was way too dark. I've been looking for that van everywhere since Zoé died. Whoever owns it ended my girl's life." His put the cup down and took a shaky breath.

"We'll find it," Ben assured him.

"So you and Laure Canja had a relationship years ago, resulting in Zoé's birth. Laure hasn't been seen in the village for twenty years now. Your wife told us you're responsible for her disappearance."

Wayne was using the same technique again. The Mambo had told them nothing of the sort. Ben stared at the silent Ti-Jean, whose breathing grew louder and more ragged.

"I've found in my line of work that people who've committed and then concealed crimes carry around a terrible burden," Ben said gently. "Get it off your chest, man. Tell us what happened to Zoé's mother."

Ti-Jean straightened his shoulders and said, "You have to understand, Sheriff. I never meant to kill her. It was an accident. It was before Ardra, the Mambo, and I were married."

The two lawmen looked at each other. The whole story would come out now, like water breaking a dam.

"Go on," Ben said.

Ti-Jean spoke quickly, his words punctuated by sobs. "I went to Laure's hair salon, where she worked. It was the middle of the afternoon. She came out behind the building to talk to me, and I told her I was tired of waiting for her. We had Zoé by then, and I asked her once more to marry me. I said it wasn't right that we weren't together."

He sniffed loudly. Ben handed him the box of tissues, and he blew his nose. "She just turned around to go back inside. I yelled at her that I was going to marry Ardra if she wouldn't have me. I thought maybe she would relent. All she said was that she didn't care, and except for Zoé, she wished she'd never slept with me."

"Did you kill her then?" Ben asked.

He wiped his eyes and blew his nose again. "No, but Laure's words, her saying she wished she'd never slept with me, were like acid burning my heart. I kept drinking, shot after shot. The salon was open late that night. She was the only one there. I could see her in the lighted building, laughing and talking with the women. Then a man came in. He was her last client and she washed his hair. Her breasts were so close to his face as she shampooed him...." He was dry-eyed now, and his jaw was tense. "He reached out to touch her and she slapped him, playfully. She was laughing."

As Ben listened to the long-buried confession, he saw again in his mind Zoé's beautiful face in the photograph lying among the golden leaves of late autumn. He and Wayne waited. The tension rose in the room like steam. Neither of them spoke.

"When she turned off the lights, locked the door, and came back out to her car, I was waiting. I accused her of sleeping with the guy. She laughed at me. She said it was none of my business. Something in me cracked wide open, and I grabbed her shoulders and shook her. I pushed her back and she hit her head against the metal edge of the big trash container." Ti-Jean stopped, a sick expression on his face. "She just crumpled." His face was a mask of pain.

"You're going to show us where you buried her,"

Wayne said, his expression implacable. "Now." He took Ti-Jean firmly by the upper arm, and all three of them went out to the patrol car.

At least we know what happened to Laure, but we still have to find Zoé Canja's killer. And time is running out.

THIRTY-FIVE

Chief Detective Wayne Nichols

RANDALL PERDUE HADN'T shown up at work or his house for days. Despite numerous calls and texts asking him to come to the sheriff's office, he was still in the wind. Sheriff Bradley had put Rob and Cam on a stakeout at his residence, and prevailed upon his aunt to issue an arrest warrant. Wayne had instructed Jean Paul and the entire staff of Randall's Tavern to let him know if and when Perdue appeared.

Wayne's cellphone had rung just before midnight on Thursday. Lucy was at work, and he'd gone to bed early. The ringtone jolted him from a sound sleep and he fumbled for the phone in the dark.

"Nichols here."

"Wayne, it's Ben. Rob just called me. He and Cam caught Randall sneaking into his house. I told them to take him in and put him in a cell."

"Do you want to meet me there?" Wayne asked, wide awake now.

"No, just wanted to let you know. See you in the morning."

WAYNE ARRIVED AT the office at eight thirty the morning after Perdue was brought in, just as Mrs. Coffin was making a call. She beckoned to Wayne to come over to her desk.

"Good morning. This is the Rosedale County Sheriff's Office calling for Mr. Ramsey Tremaine. Is he available?"

There was a long pause before she said, "No, there's absolutely no hurry. Just have him call the office when he arrives." She hung up with a satisfied smirk. "Mr. Tremaine isn't expected until shortly before noon. He's in court this morning, no doubt defending some slime bag." Wayne grinned at her feistiness. Sophie Coffin was starting to grow on him. He walked down the hall to Ben's office.

"Morning, boss," he said.

Ben raised his eyebrows. "What have I done to deserve that?" he asked. "You don't usually call me 'boss.'"

"We have our prime suspect in a cell," Wayne said. "I think that calls for recognition of your efforts to keep Rob and Cam on his tail until he got caught," He pointed toward the reception desk. "Mrs. Coffin just called Tremaine and company. He's in court this morning and isn't available until afternoon. I suppose we *could* wait until he arrives, or give it a shot that our prime suspect will talk."

Ben gave a rueful grin. "Can you believe Ramsey Tremaine is Perdue's lawyer? Thought I was done dealing with him for a while. Anyway, before Tremaine shows up, I think I will let you loose on Randall Perdue's sorry butt. And you should take Rob in with you—it's high time he was a principal in a serious interrogation. I'm not even going to watch. You two can handle it."

"Excellent. I can't wait." Wayne grinned in a manner Lucy classified as devilish.

"Holler if you need any help," Ben said.

"Oh, if you hear hollering, it won't be me."

"Well, you can scare him a little, but don't hurt him. Do you think you can break his alibi? You said that the dishwasher wasn't clear on when Randall left the kitchen."

"True. But I'm about to stick a pin in that alibi of his." Wayne winked. "This case is all about Voodoo, you know."

HALF AN HOUR LATER, Rob brought Randall from the cell to the box and offered him coffee. Perdue declined, saying that as soon as Ramsey Tremaine arrived he would be leaving. The whole staff, minus Mrs. Coffin and Ben, were standing in the hall ready to observe the interrogation when Wayne entered the box. Wayne jutted his chin at Rob, a nonverbal signal for him to begin. When Perdue looked at Rob, Wayne touched the thermostat in the room, upping it about ten degrees.

"You are Mr. Randall Perdue of 1244 East Street in Richfield, correct?" Rob asked. Randall nodded. "I need a verbal answer, Mr. Perdue."

"Yes."

"And you are aware that you're under suspicion for the murder of Zoé Canja?"

"Yeah, I am." Perdue's voice was sullen.

"You were cautioned last night, but I need to say again that you have the right to remain silent and to have an attorney present during questioning. Mr. Tremaine has been called. He will be here soon." Rob cast a glance at Wayne, who was leaning nonchalantly against the wall in the corner of the room, his arms crossed in front of his chest.

"I'm asserting my right to remain silent," Perdue said and looked defiantly at Wayne. Wayne sat down at the table and yawned. Then he yawned again. Rob put his hand over his mouth, stifling a yawn. Perdue sat, jaw clenched, unmoving. Wayne could envision the confused glances between members of the staff. Dory was probably asking Cam what the hell she thought Wayne was doing. Wayne yawned again. Rob struggled manfully against a responsive yawn.

"I went to see your ex-wife, Helene, a few days ago," Wayne said, patting his mouth as if trying not to yawn again. "She gave me the lowdown on you, Perdue. Then I went over to the hospital this morning. Your wife gave me permission to get her medical records."

Perdue started to wiggle restively in his seat. "Helene is clumsy. She falls a lot," he said.

Wayne looked away, yawning and looking bored. Rob seemed totally bewildered.

"She might not remember things very well, Randall, because you smacked her around so much. Probably has some brain damage. You gave her a concussion once."

"She fell off—"

"Shut up!" Wayne smacked the table. "Real tough guy, beating a woman when she wouldn't open her legs for you."

Rob's eyes opened wide. He looked horrified.

"A man has a right to have sex with his wife." Randall clearly had no guilt about what he had put his wife through, and Wayne was growing more enraged by the minute.

"I told you to shut up," Wayne warned him in a low, threatening voice. "Your wife told me she finally left you because you were obsessed with Zoé Canja. Young, beautiful girl like that didn't want a dirty old man touching her, did she? She found you repulsive." Wayne sneered.

Randall glanced sideways. He paled, and a sheen of perspiration covered his forehead.

"It's getting hot in here. You're starting to sweat, Randall. Is that because you just remembered that Tennessee's a death penalty state? We're going for the needle on Zoé's murder. Your wife will testify to your fixation with Zoé, and just for fun she's going to tell the jury about all the times you beat her up. Having met Helene, I know she's going to make an excellent impression on a jury. Once she takes the stand, it's over for you. And Helene will inherit the bar and sell it out from under you."

"I'll talk Helene out of taking the stand," Randall said confidently. "And if she doesn't testify, your case will get blown to bits. I don't even have a record."

"Only because your wife was too scared to file a complaint against you. You stalked Zoé. In case you don't know it, stalking is a crime taken seriously around here."

"I didn't even know where Zoé lived," Randall said.

"Quit lying to me." Wayne smacked Randall on the back of his head. "Listen, dumbass, we know you're aware of the location of Zoé's house. You were there before—your wife will attest to that. You drove out there one night and banged and banged on her door. You drive a white panel van, right?"

"Yeah, so what. I need it to pick up supplies for the tavern." He was trying to sound bored with it all, but Wayne could smell his fear.

"But on the night of October twenty-third at midnight you weren't picking up supplies, were you? You were tracking Zoé Canja out to her house."

"I was in the kitchen all night," Randall said. "The dishwasher can tell you."

"Quit lying." Wayne struck the back of Randall's head again.

"You can't do this," Randall said. "I have rights."

"Murderers don't have rights," Wayne said. "Your van was seen parked outside Zoé's house at the time of the murder."

Randall didn't respond.

"Good thing you aren't denying it," Rob chimed in. "We have a witness."

"I just followed the little tease out to her house. We were shorthanded that night and she ditched her shift!" Randall shouted. "I went out there to find out when the hell she was coming back to work."

Intently focused on Randall's every move, Wayne continued to bore into the man. "You were obsessed with Zoé. From your perspective, she had been leading you on for years. Then the girl cuts her shift short on a busy night when you're already short-staffed. The cook was out. I think you decided to teach Zoé a lesson."

"Little slut was sleeping with Darnell."

"Wouldn't give you any, though, would she?" Wayne said. "Sleeps with the help and won't let the boss touch her. That had to piss you off. I gotta tell you; it would have pissed me off." Wayne had often found that commiserating with the suspect made them relax and give you more information. "You gave Zoé the job. You promoted her several times. She *owed* you. Big handsome stud like Darnell—you must have imagined them in bed naked a hundred times. I bet they even got it on at work."

Randall clenched his jaw. He didn't say anything, but he flushed.

"Here's what we have on you, Randall. You had a motive—you were angry that the girl wouldn't sleep with you. You had the opportunity—we have a witness who saw your van parked in front of her house at the time she was killed." Wayne glanced at the table, noting Randall's clenched fists. "As far as the means goes, Zoé was strangled and you look plenty strong enough to wind a red scarf around her neck and tighten it up."

Randall opened his fists and sat back in the chair. "I'm not saying another thing until Tremaine gets here."

"That's your prerogative." Rob Fuller was the voice of reason in the overheated room.

"That night you sexually assaulted the girl and then strangled her with her red scarf so she couldn't identify you," Wayne went on.

"What? No, I didn't. I hardly touched her that night. I think she was drugged or something. She didn't even wake up when I—"

"When you what, Randall? You touched the girl and she slept right through it? No wonder you strangled her. Successful guy like you, own your own business, and she doesn't even wake up when you do it to her." Wayne shook his head.

"I'm telling you, I didn't rape her. Didn't even get her clothes off. Would have been easy, too. She was drugged, I tell you."

"Didn't rape her, just wrapped that red scarf around her throat and tightened it up."

Randall shook his head. "Wasn't me. You got the wrong guy."

"Remember that witness I mentioned…the one who saw your car?" Wayne said. "Turns out he was watching through the window. He saw you strangle her. Happy to testify."

"You're joking. There was no witness," Randall said, but he was falling apart now. Hot sweaty, scared.

"If I was joking, somebody would be laughing, Randall. We have you dead to rights. Tell me everything that happened, and I'll try to help you. I'll talk to the DA, try to get you a shorter sentence. You might even be able to keep the bar. Tell me!" Wayne smacked the table and Randall jumped.

"You drove out to the village. Zoé's front door was open, unlocked. You went in and found her half asleep on the couch. What happened? Did you intend to kill her? Was it premeditated?" Wayne kept firing questions at Perdue.

"Premeditated! No way."

"Was it an accident? Accidental deaths don't get the death penalty."

"I just sat on the couch and watched her sleep. She was so beautiful," Randall's voice was slow and heavy. He licked his lips. "Then I ran my hands over her tits. She never moved. I knew she was drugged, but I'd heard some women get turned on if they're choked a little bit. So I saw this red scarf and put it around her neck. I only tightened it a little, just kept waiting for her to start moaning or something. She never made a sound. I didn't think it would kill her," He shook his head but exhibited no sign of remorse.

A brisk knock on the door startled all three men. Dory stuck her head in and said, "Mr. Tremaine would like a word with his client."

Ramsey Tremaine, dressed in his usual high-dollar suit, barged in.

"Don't say anything, Randall. Not a word. I'm taking my client out of here." Ramsey glared at Wayne.

"Your client just confessed to felony murder," Wayne said. "Stand up, Perdue. You're going back to your cell. Got here a little too late, Tremaine."

Throwing his hands up in the air, Tremaine told Perdue he'd talk with him before his arraignment and left in a huff.

AFTER WAYNE ASKED George to escort Randall Perdue back to his cell, he and Rob were in the hallway with the rest of the staff, clustered around, applauding. At the commotion, Ben came out of his office.

"He confessed." Rob sounded triumphant. "That idiot confessed."

"So what was with all that yawning, Wayne?" Dory asked. "Were you just trying to look bored?"

"No, it's something I learned from Lucy. A yawn is an empathy marker. Once someone yawns in the room, people who observe the yawn can't stop themselves from yawning in response. When she did her psych rotation they used it as a quick mental test during intake. Lack of a responsive yawn is the mark of a sociopath. Randall Perdue doesn't feel other people's pain or fear. He's devoid of empathy."

"Guy's a lunatic. Didn't feel a damn thing when he was strangling Zoé." Rob shook his head. "And what was all that about a witness who saw the murder?"

Wayne shrugged. "I figured we didn't have much time before Tremaine arrived. Just pulled out all the stops."

"Yeah, you pulled out all the stops, all right."

"Okay," Ben said, "back to work, everybody. Detectives, my office. Now."

Wayne looked at Rob, who ducked his head and

walked into Ben's office. He followed with a sigh. Ben sat at his desk, regarding both of them with a cold stare.

"Close the door, Wayne. You two take a seat." The sheriff pinned Rob with his intense blue gaze. "What did you mean by saying 'You pulled out all the stops, all right'? Did Detective Nichols strike the suspect?"

"I take the fifth." Rob gave a queasy little grin.

"Couple of light taps to the back of his head is all I gave him." Wayne was unrepentant.

"Leave us, Detective Fuller." Ben said quietly. When the door closed behind Rob, the sheriff surged to his feet. "What the hell is wrong with you? Now Tremaine will be able to get his confession thrown out."

"No way. The audio will be loud and clear, but there's no video of that interview." Wayne shrugged. "And Perdue didn't say a thing about me smacking the back of his head."

Ben slumped into his chair with a sigh. "You coerced that confession. Randall Perdue will tell Ramsey everything about the interrogation, including the slaps to the back of his head. Because you used excessive force, Randall Perdue might walk." His face was gray.

Wayne felt the heat rise in his cheeks. "I don't think so, Ben. Here's why. Once Randall is indicted and the judge remands him, I'll talk to him again. He really doesn't want his wife to take the stand. If she does, he's likely to get life or even the death penalty. I think the confession will stand because Perdue would rather go to prison than be exposed as the vicious wife-beater he is."

Ben nodded. "I hope to hell you're right. But I have half a mind to put you on administrative leave."

Wayne froze in his chair. "If that's what you need to do…" he finally said, breaking the awkward silence.

"You're a great detective, Wayne. Your methods can be unorthodox and you're certainly a boundary pusher, but this was way over the line…and a terrible example to Rob. He looks up to you. Can you help me understand what was going through your head?"

Wayne swallowed. He hated talking about his past, but the sheriff was a good friend as well as his boss. He knew he had let him down today. "I think learning about his abuse of Helene really brought up some issues from my childhood—my time in foster care. My foster mother's husband used to get drunk and come home and beat her. My foster brother and I couldn't do anything about it, and I felt so powerless."

"You're not powerless anymore," Ben said quietly.

"No, but Ben, that animal raped his own wife! And has no remorse about that…or about killing Zoé."

"He's a sociopath. But you're not. We can't enforce the law and punish those who use force to take what they want by using force to get what we want. We have to be better than that."

Wayne was suddenly flooded with shame. "You're right. I'm sorry. It won't happen again. Would you like me to talk to Rob, explain what I did wrong?"

"That would be a start. You're also going to go see the police psychiatrist and get some counseling to help you resolve these issues so that it *never* happens again. Do I make myself clear?"

Wayne took a deep breath and got out of his chair. "Crystal clear. I'll go talk to Rob right now."

Ben smiled. "Good. And we did solve the case. Fingers crossed that Randall keeps his mouth shut about the interrogation."

THIRTY-SIX

Evangeline Bon Temps

THE PHONE RANG early that Saturday morning. Evangeline had just put some blueberry muffins into the oven to bake. She looked out the window, wondering if it was warm enough for her and Jason to have coffee and muffins on their sheltered back deck.

"Good morning," she answered the phone.

"Good morning, Evangeline." It was Mae's voice. "Hope I didn't wake you."

"No, I've been up for some time."

"I'm calling about Erzulie. I'm sure you remember her."

"Of course I do. Beautiful dog."

"Yes. She's in my kitchen looking beautiful right now, been here all week."

"But we just took her back to Mira on Monday. Why do you have her again?"

"She was miserable there and making everyone else miserable too. Howling and crying. Ben said he thought Mira was going to have a breakdown, so he brought her back to me. And I'd be happy to keep her, but he thinks four dogs is plenty."

"Hmmm. So you're looking for a new home for Erzulie? I'll start thinking about who I know that might take her," Evangeline said. She opened the oven door a crack to peek at the muffins. They were turning from white to tan, and the scent was starting to permeate the air in her kitchen.

"Well, actually, I was thinking about you," Mae said.

"Me? I haven't had a dog since I got married, and Jason isn't much of a dog person. He doesn't have the animal thing."

"Does Jason hunt?"

"He does, but usually with his friend Wally, and they use Wally's dog."

"The Weimaraner was originally bred as a gun dog. Decades ago they hunted big game like deer or bear, but they're also good with pheasant and even rabbit."

"I guess I could ask Jason about it," Evangeline said cautiously. "He was saying Wally's spaniel is getting too old to hunt anymore. Her muzzle is all silvery. As a hunting dog, Erzulie would live in a kennel, I assume?"

"I was also thinking that Erzulie might be good for you, Evangeline, as a house pet."

"Why do you think that?"

"Ben told me you seemed to miss the sense of community in the Voodoo Village, and dogs are good company."

"She *is* appealing." Evangeline could feel herself weakening.

"Part of her appeal lies in her sleek silver-gray coat and light amber eyes. But there's far more to Erzulie than her distinctive appearance. A Weimaraner's first desire is to be with her people, preferably within touching range. Many Weimaraner owners name their dogs 'Shadow.' They'll lie at your feet or follow you through the house." Mae's voice was sweet...and persuasive.

"I would have to talk to Jason, of course, but we might give it a try."

"I'll be over in about twenty minutes," Mae said.

"What," Evangeline was startled, "you're coming now?"

"I learned a long time ago that when someone was hesitating about taking on a puppy, all I had to do was get the merchandise in the customer's hands." Mae giggled and said goodbye.

"Jason," Evangeline called out, "are you about ready for breakfast? We're getting some company. And one of them is apparently moving in."

A startled exclamation was heard from the bedroom.

TEN DAYS LATER, despite Jason's initial insistence that Erzulie be kept in a kennel, she was happily ensconced as a house pet. Evangeline had taken her to the office several times, since the dog seemed reluctant to be parted from her. Erzulie often sat beside her while she drafted legal briefs. Whenever she was struggling with a legal point she was trying to make, Evangeline stroked her smooth silver head and it seemed to clarify her thoughts.

Sitting in her office on this cold morning in November, Evangeline was glad to have her dog beside her. She was thinking about everything that had happened in the last month, and all the memories and feelings that her experiences in the Voodoo Village had awakened. It would soon be Thanksgiving, and Evangeline was grateful that the case had been solved. *And I'm so thankful that I could be of help.*

She glanced down into Erzulie's amber eyes and smiled. "When Jason asks me what I'm giving thanks for this year, I'm going to tell him it's you."

The big dog's tail thumped on the floor and Evangeline gave her a treat out of the stash she kept in her desk

drawer. "Good girl, Erzulie. Good girl." Leaning back in
her chair, Evangeline returned to her thoughts.

Ti-Jean had admitted to grabbing Laure during an argument. In her struggle to get away, she fell and hit her
head. He showed the police where he'd buried her and the
coroner's findings confirmed Mr. Flambeau's account.
Mira and Marie both requested that Laure's final resting place be in the Voodoo Village cemetery. The Canja
sisters wanted a ceremony to be held for her. Laure's
remains had been taken to the local funeral home and
cremated. Evangeline had provided them with a white
ceramic urn to hold Laure's ashes and was picking them
up later today.

With the Voodoo priest in jail, Evangeline had wondered who should do the ceremony. There was a pastor
in Nashville that conducted services for the so-called
"outcast dead"—those John and Jane Does whose bodies
could not be identified. Evangeline had attended one of
the ceremonies years ago, a brief ecumenical service, and
found it moving. But although Laure had been an "outcast" for twenty years, she was now coming home. They
needed someone with a knowledge of Voodoo ceremony.

She talked to Mira, who to Evangeline's surprise said
they would ask the Mambo. Given the Mambo's role in
covering up Zoé's murder and writing the postcards that
were supposedly from Zoé's mother Laure, Evangeline
didn't think Mira would want the Mambo to do the ceremony. But bygones were apparently bygones in the Voodoo Village. Ti-Jean had come up with the plan to send
the postcards and pressured his wife into doing it. She
had suspected the truth, but hadn't known for sure about
Ti-Jean accidentally killing Laure until after his arrest.
And she sincerely regretted her role in helping conceal

Zoé's body. Her legal case was still in limbo. She had paid
a fine, but didn't know yet if she would be serving time.

THE SUN WAS going down when Evangeline and Jason—Erzulie sitting in the backseat next to the urn holding Laure's
remains—set out for the Voodoo Village. The sheriff and
his entire staff followed them in patrol cars. Mae rode
with her parents in their car at the end of the cavalcade.

"Do you think you're at any risk tonight, Evangeline?"
Jason asked as they mounted the hill and began their de-
scent into the Voodoo Village.

Evangeline felt her spirits rise as they drove down into
the darkened village. No electric lights were on in the
houses, but they could see the flickering of candlelight.
"No, it's all over. According to Mira, the Voodoo Court
has passed sentence on Ti-Jean and the Mambo. They
are no longer interested in me, and in fact their judg-
ment mirrored pretty closely the decisions of the judges
in the case. I'll be fine now, Jason." She smiled at him.

They parked in the field as they had for Zoé's funeral
service. A number of cars were already there. The sheriff's staff exited their vehicles and followed Evangeline
and her husband. The Voodoo singers' voices floated in
the cold night air. Evangeline recognized the tune. It was
the French song from *South Pacific* Laure had taught
Zoé as a little child.

Humming along with the singer, Evangeline swallowed, moved to tears by the sad end to both Laure's and
Zoé's lives. The *fête mori* was beginning. Four white-
clad junior priestesses carried lighted votive candles. Two
of them stood beside the Mambo, holding a white tray
between them. When Evangeline and Jason walked up

with Erzulie, the Mambo came toward them, lifted the urn containing Laure's ashes, and placed it on the tray.

Noting Evangeline's all-white apparel, the Mambo said, "After the service, you may follow the pall bearers with the dog. The rest of you will remain here." She waved the sheriff, his staff, Mae, her parents, and Jason away. Jason moved to the edge of the crowd, still keeping Evangeline in view. Evangeline nodded at her husband, feeling a sense of emotional release. It was over. The crime had been solved and Laure Canja had come home. This was the last step before she could put it all behind her.

A young man came forward and lit a small fire of charcoal bricks at the base of the *poto mitan*. They had wrapped the pole in white veiling for this celebration. The feeling tonight was not like the night Zoé had been buried. This was a homecoming. A woman brought a container of water and poured small amounts of the liquid at the north, south, east, and west points of the space, creating the axes along which the Loa would be called to enter the Hounfour. The drums beat louder and the tempo of the singers' song increased. Simultaneously both the singer and the drummers came to an abrupt stop. The singers then began a low plaintive hymn and the Mambo emerged to stand before the crowd. She was dressed in white with a white gele turban around her hair.

"We ask this night for the sacred Loa to bestow their blessings on our sister Laure, who has returned from the dead," Mambo said in a resonant voice.

In unison, the Voodooists said, "We will remember her."

The Mambo raised her arms into the sky, saying "Precious Loa, we know this woman has been known by you and loved by you even when she was buried in unconsecrated ground."

"We will remember her," the people echoed. Evangeline began repeating the words with the others, knowing that as long as she lived, she would never forget Zoé or Laure. The night wind rose and the trees tussled in the dark sky. A pale crescent moon emerged from behind layers of clouds that raced across the moon.

"We will remember her."

"We will remember her."

"We will remember her."

The people said the words faster and faster in time to the beating of a drum. A rush of wind swirled through the space, disturbing late autumn leaves and moving the limbs of the Mapou trees.

"The Loa have arrived," Evangeline whispered to herself. She was shuddering, trembling all over.

She raised her arms in the air, readying herself for the Loa to mount her, and then caught Jason's eye. He looked afraid for her and suddenly she was afraid too. "No," she whispered and recited a brief prayer that the sacred Loa would find someone else to honor with their guidance this night.

The wind swirled away. She had made her final choice. She would remain with her life in Rosedale, with her loving husband, and with the Catholic Church, but she would never forget the Voodoo religion or the Canja family.

Using the language of the Christians, she whispered to the dead, "May God bless and keep you in his care forever, Zoé and Laure."

The Loa selected others in the assembly, who began to dance, a frenzied twirling. The Mambo was seized by the Loa and moaned as the spirit possessed her body and Laure Canja was officially welcomed home.

THIRTY-SEVEN

Mae December

MAE WAS RIDING in the backseat of Evangeline's car on the way to the Voodoo Village, listening to Dory and Evangeline chat up front. She had much to be thankful for on this cold Monday morning in December. Ben's job as Rose County Sheriff was safe for the next four years. The investigation into Zoé's death was closed, and the questions surrounding her mother's disappearance had been answered as well. At least Mira and her sister had closure; Zoé and her mother had been laid to rest and Ti-Jean Flambeau and Randall Perdue were both in jail for their crimes. *I also found good homes for Erzulie and her puppies and sold four paintings to the governor and her husband.*

"You're awfully quiet back there." Dory turned her head to look back at Mae. "You aren't carsick, are you?"

"Not at all. Just thinking about everything that's happened in the last six weeks."

"There's definitely been a lot to process." Evangeline winked at Mae in the rearview mirror before asking, "Dory, are you missing being snuggled up with Al every night?"

"No, I am *not*," she answered emphatically. "I like living alone and visiting Al, or going on trips with him. That and the occasional sleepover is all I need. Plus, I had to get my dog out of his clutches before she was completely spoiled."

Evangeline laughed. "I know what you mean—Jason lets Erzulie sit in his lap to watch TV. If he's not around, she tries to be my lapdog, and she's way too big. She's a good dog, though. And having her encourages me to take more walks…keeps my backside within bounds."

Mae and Dory exclaimed over the diminutive size and perfection of Evangeline's rear end as compared to theirs until she made them stop. "All right, I won't say any more about your booty," Dory said. "But mine almost doubled in the time I stayed with Al. That man loves to eat and he's always bringing me treats." Once more, she looked back at Mae. "If I have to buy new pants, I'm sending the bill to your fiancé for making me stay there so long."

"Go ahead," Mae laughed. "I said something to him about that—asked him if he regretted keeping you out of the case, since it turned out to be unnecessary. He said not at all. Especially since we still don't know who threatened you."

Evangeline cleared her throat. "Just between us, it was the Mambo. Papa Febron told her husband about us asking questions and he sent Ardra to make the veve in front of your house and leave the rooster in my backyard a few days later. She apologized to me when I met with her about the Land Trust on Friday."

Evangeline's car crested the hill and descended into the Voodoo Village. She parked in front of the house shared by the Canja sisters and turned off the car. The three women all got out.

"Can you tell me how the Land Trust is going to work?" Mae asked.

Evangeline paused in her walk toward the front door.

Looking back, she gave Mae a brilliant smile. "I'm surprised your mother didn't tell you all about it. She called
me yesterday and got all the details. I guess she's writing a follow-up piece about the village in the aftermath
of Zoé's death and the mystery of Laure's disappearance being solved. Think your dad's going to take more
photos too."

The front door swung open to reveal Mira and Marie,
regal and welcoming in their colorful clothing. "Come
in, sisters," Mira said.

"Just explain it to all of us at once." Dory gave Evangeline an impatient tap on the back. "It's freezing out here."

Once they were all settled in the small living room
with mugs of hot, sweet tea, Mae presented Mira with
an envelope of cash.

"It's the money from the sale of the puppies," she said.
"The governor of Tennessee actually bought one of the
females, Felicity."

Mira counted the money and gave Mae a sharp look.
"Thank you, but I thought it would be more."

Mae blushed. "I did too. I had trouble selling Jacques,
the runt of the litter. Nobody seemed to want him, so…."
She took a picture out of her purse and handed it to Mira,
who studied it intently, a smile creeping over her face.

"You gave him to Ginny; that is good." She passed
the photo to Marie, who also smiled.

"Yes, she's home from the hospital and her boyfriend
has been wanting a dog. They were delighted to have
him."

"And Erzulie is happy with Jason and Evangeline,"
Dory chimed in. "So that's all the dog business taken
care of. Now she's going to tell all of us about the Land
Trust that's been set up to protect your village."

All eyes turned to Evangeline. "Well, the Mambo feels terrible about what Ti-Jean did to Laure, and what he was trying to do by selling this land to a developer." Mira and her sister both nodded, faces stiff. "She also feels—very strongly—that the people here would literally not survive if they were forced off this land. Since the village has been on or near this very spot for at least one hundred years, we were able to start the process for it to be placed in a Historic Land Trust. Ti-Jean signed over his power-of-attorney to Ardra last week. Since he's in jail for the foreseeable future and couldn't use the funds from the sale anyway, she was able to persuade him."

"How'd she do that?" said Dory, curious as ever.

"She said that was the only way he could make amends to the people of the village—especially Mira and Marie. She also told him that he might get a conjugal visit or two if he agreed; otherwise she'd divorce him and marry someone else while he's in prison."

"The Mambo is very wise," Marie said, a twinkle in her eye.

"So what protections does a Historic Trust provide?" Mae asked.

"No further development can occur without agreement amongst the members of the trust, even if the land itself is sold, and the buildings here cannot be changed—only repaired and maintained. There are also tax advantages and some other benefits to the owners, but Ardra intends that the land be owned collectively by the people, so one person would never have the power to destroy their way of life again. It's going to take some time to work out all the details, but the process has been started."

"But then no new houses could be built."

Evangeline touched her arm lightly. "That's true, Mae.

If the people need more homes or stores, there are several vacant buildings which could be restored. And according to the Mambo, the number of villagers has gone down fairly steadily for many years. If the population of the village increases significantly, they could also rebuild on existing foundations from the original location of the Voodoo Village—before the fire."

The investigator in their midst could no longer stay silent. "What I don't understand is why the developers were so interested in this land," Dory said. "Besides the village, which they wanted to bulldoze, what's so special about acreage in the middle of nowhere?"

The Canja sisters glanced at each other. "We can trust them," Marie said quietly.

Mira explained, "There are natural springs all over this land. Plants grow here that you won't see anywhere else. It's a very special and sacred place to us. I'm sure the developers wanted to exploit that in some way."

"According to the Mambo," Evangeline added, her mouth turned down in a grim line, "their plan was to build a large spa-hotel complex. Some of the buildings would actually be built on top of the springs. They wanted to bring eco-tourism to Rose County and evict all of you from your homes."

"But you and the Mambo are making sure that can never happen, right?"

"Right."

Mae finished her tea and sat up straighter in her chair. "I think you can count on Governor Featherstone and her husband for some protection as well. They bought the other four paintings in my Voodoo Village series and are very interested in this place. She would like to pay you a visit and offer any help you might need."

"We don't want any more attention from the outside world," Marie said with an emphatic gesture. "You've helped us, but most outsiders are more trouble than they're worth."

"She said to tell you it would be a private visit, and she'll only come if it's all right with you, when you're ready. She and her husband are kind people. And they lost their only grandchild in a tragic accident, so they're sensitive to what you've been through. I think you would like them, Mira." Mae reached out and squeezed her hand.

"I will think about it."

BACK AT HER farmhouse on Little Chapel Road that evening, Mae sat with Ben on the living room sofa. "I'm glad Randall didn't tell Tremaine about what happened in the interrogation room," she said. "And it sounds like the Voodoo Village is safe from development, or it will be when Evangeline is done."

Ben put his arm around her. "Did she tell you she's doing all the legal work for free?"

"She didn't mention that. Evangeline is wonderful, though. I'm not surprised."

"Yes, she is." Ben leaned in a little closer. "Thanks to her, we're back down to a somewhat reasonable number of dogs around here."

Mae gave him a soft kiss on the mouth. "Yes, we are," she whispered, "until we get Tatie bred in January. We'll have a houseful of puppies by early March."

A line appeared between Ben's eyebrows. "You do realize we're getting married in March, don't you?"

Mae leaned back against the sofa pillows and gave him a mischievous grin. "Oh, don't worry, it'll all work out. It has to. I invited the Featherstones."

"Very funny." The Rose County Sheriff gave her a look of mingled irritation and amusement. "You did not invite the governor and her husband to the wedding."

"That's what Tammy said." Mae was still smiling. "And I told her the same thing I'm going to tell you. I'm not kidding. I invited them to our wedding and they said yes. Exciting, isn't it?"

Ben rubbed his forehead and grinned. "You're a hard woman to keep up with, Mae December. But you definitely keep life exciting."

* * * * *

ABOUT THE AUTHOR

Lia Farrell is actually two people: the mother and daughter writing team of Lyn Farquhar and Lisa Fitzsimmons.

Lyn Farquhar taught herself to read when she was four years old and honed her storytelling abilities by reading to her little sister. Ultimately, her mother ended the reading sessions because her sister decided she preferred being read to rather than learning to read herself.

Lyn fell in love with library books when a Bookmobile came to her one-room rural school when she was in kindergarten. The day the Bookmobile came, Lyn decided she would rather live in the bookmobile than at home and was only ousted following sustained efforts by her teacher and the bookmobile driver.

She earned her undergraduate and graduate degrees from Michigan State University. She has a master's degree in English literature and a PhD in Education, but has always maintained that she remained a student for such a long time only because it gave her an excuse to read. Lyn holds the rank of Professor Emerita of Medical Education at Michigan State University and has authored numerous journal articles, abstracts, and research grants.

Since her retirement from MSU to become a full-time writer, she has completed a young-adult fantasy series called Tales of the Skygrass Kingdom. The books are titled *Journey to Maidenstone*, *The Songs of Skygrass*, *Skygrass Reunion: Sabra's Story* and *Skygrass Reunion: Ruby's Story*.

Lyn has two daughters and six step children, nine granddaughters and three grandsons. She also has one extremely spoiled Welsh corgi. Her hobby is interior design and she claims she has the equivalent of a master's degree in Interior Design from watching way too many decorating shows.

She is proudest of the books she has written with her daughter, Lisa, under the penname Lia Farrell.

Lisa Fitzsimmons grew up in Michigan and was always encouraged to read, write, and express herself artistically. She was read to frequently. Throughout her childhood and teenage years, she was seldom seen without a book in hand. After becoming a mom at a young age, she attended Michigan State University in a tri-emphasis program with concentrations in fine art, art history and interior design.

Lisa, with her husband and their two children, moved to North Carolina for three exciting years and then on to Tennessee, which she now calls home. She has enjoyed an eighteen-year career as a muralist and interior designer in middle Tennessee, but has always been interested in writing. In January of 2009, Lisa and her mom, Lyn, began working on a writing project inspired by local events. The Mae December Mystery series was born.

Lisa, her husband and Rocky, their Siberian husky, currently divide their time between beautiful Northern

Michigan in the summertime and fabulous middle Tennessee the rest of the year. She and her husband feel blessed that their "empty nest" in Tennessee is just a short distance from their oldest, who has a beautiful family of her own. Their youngest child lives in California. Life is good.

Five Dog Voodoo is the fifth book in the Mae December Mystery Series, which began with *One Dog Too Many*.

You can find Lyn and Lisa online at www.liafarrell.net.

Get 4 FREE REWARDS!

We'll send you 2 FREE Books plus 2 FREE Mystery Gifts.

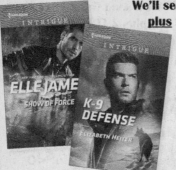

Harlequin Intrigue® books feature heroes and heroines that confront and survive danger while finding themselves irresistibly drawn to one another.

FREE
Value Over
$20

Get 4 FREE REWARDS!

We'll send you 2 FREE Books plus <u>2</u> FREE Mystery Gifts.

Love Inspired® Suspense
books feature Christian
characters facing
challenges to their faith...
and lives.

FREE
Value Over
$20